# ANNA OF THE FIVE TOWNS

The Collected Works of Arnold Bennett

# ANNA OF THE FIVE TOWNS

## *A NOVEL*

BY
## ARNOLD BENNETT

**BOOKS FOR LIBRARIES PRESS**
PLAINVIEW, NEW YORK

**Library of Congress Cataloging in Publication Data**

Bennett, Arnold, 1867-1931.
    Anna of the five towns; a novel.

    (The collected works of Arnold Bennett)
    Reprint of the ed. published by G. H. Doran, New York
    I.  Title.
PZ3.B438An15    [PR6003.E6]        823'.9'12        74-5320
ISBN 0-518-19082-X

"Therefore, although it be a history
Homely and rude, I will relate the same
For the delight of a few natural hearts."

# CONTENTS

ANNA OF THE FIVE TOWNS

# I: THE KINDLING OF LOVE

THE yard was all silent and empty under the burning afternoon heat, which had made its asphalt springy like turf, when suddenly the children threw themselves out of the great doors at either end of the Sunday-school—boys from the right, girls from the left—in two howling, impetuous streams, that widened, eddied, intermingled, and formed backwaters until the whole quadrangle was full of clamour and movement. Many of the scholars carried prize-books bound in vivid tints, and proudly exhibited these volumes to their companions and to the teachers, who, tall, languid, and condescending, soon began to appear amid the restless throng. Near the left-hand door a little girl of twelve years, dressed in a cream-coloured frock, with a wide and heavy straw hat, stood quietly kicking her foal-like legs against the wall. She was one of those who had won a prize, and once or twice she took the treasure from under her arm to glance at its frontispiece with a vague smile of satisfaction. For a time her bright eyes were fixed expectantly on the doorway; then they would wander, and she started to count the windows of the various Connexional buildings which on three sides enclosed the yard—chapel, school, lecture-hall, and chapel-keeper's house. Most of the children had already squeezed through the narrow iron gate into the street beyond, where a steam-car was rumbling and clattering up Duck Bank, attended

by its immense shadow. The teachers remained a little behind. Gradually dropping the pedagogic pose, and happy
in the virtuous sensation of duty accomplished, they forgot
the frets and fatigues of the day, and grew amiably vivacious among themselves. With an instinctive mutual complacency the two sexes mixed again after separation.
Greetings and pleasantries were exchanged, and intimate
conversations begun; and then, dividing into small familiar
groups, the young men and women slowly followed their
pupils out of the gate. The chapel-keeper, who always
had an injured expression, left the white step of his resi-
dence, and, walking with official dignity across the yard,
drew down the side-windows of the chapel one after another.
As he approached the little solitary girl in his course he
gave her a reluctant acid recognition; then he returned to
his hearth. Agnes was alone.

"Well, young lady?"

She looked round with a jump, and blushed, smiling and
screwing up her little shoulders, when she recognised the
two men who were coming towards her from the door of
the lecture-hall. The one who had called out was Henry
Mynors, morning superintendent of the Sunday-school and
conductor of the men's Bible-class held in the lecture-hall
on Sunday afternoons. The other was William Price,
usually styled Willie Price, secretary of the same Bible-
class, and son of Titus Price, the afternoon superintendent.

"I'm sure you don't deserve that prize. Let me see if
it isn't too good for you." Mynors smiled playfully down
upon Agnes Tellwright as he idly turned the leaves of the

book which she handed to him. " Now, do you deserve it? Tell me honestly."

She scrutinised those sparkling and vehement black eyes with the fearless calm of infancy. " Yes, I do," she answered in her high, thin voice, having at length decided within herself that Mr. Mynors was joking.

" Then I suppose you must have it," he admitted, with a fine air of giving way.

As Agnes took the volume from him she thought how perfect a man Mr. Mynors was. His eyes, so kind and sincere, and that mysterious, delicious, inexpressible something which dwelt behind his eyes ; these constituted an ideal for her.

Willie Price stood somewhat apart, grinning, and pulling a thin honey-coloured moustache. He was at the uncouth, disjointed age, twenty-one, and nine years younger than Henry Mynors. Despite a continual effort after ease of manner, he was often sheepish and self-conscious, even, as now, when he could discover no reason for such a condition of mind. But Agnes liked him too. His simple, pale blue eyes had a wistfulness which made her feel towards him as she felt towards her doll when she happened to find it lying neglected on the floor.

" Your big sister isn't out of school yet? " Mynors remarked.

Agnes shook her head. " I've been waiting ever so long," she said plaintively.

At that moment a grey-haired woman, with a benevolent but rather pinched face, emerged with much briskness from the girls' door. This was Mrs. Sutton, a distant relative of Mynors'—his mother had been her second cousin. The men raised their hats.

" I've just been down to make sure of some of you slippery folks for the sewing-meeting," she said, shaking hands with Mynors, and including both him and Willie Price in an embracing maternal smile. She was short-sighted and did not perceive Agnes, who had fallen back.

" Had a good class this afternoon, Henry? " Mrs. Sutton's breathing was short and quick.

" Oh, yes," he said, " very good indeed."

" You're doing a grand work."

" We had over seventy present," he added.

" Eh! " she said, " I make nothing of numbers, Henry. I meant a *good* class. Doesn't it say—Where *two or three* are gathered together . . . ? But I must be getting on. The horse will be restless. I've to go up to Hillport before tea. Mrs. Clayton Vernon is ill."

Scarcely having stopped in her active course, Mrs. Sutton drew the men along with her down the yard, she and Mynors in rapid talk: Willie Price fell a little to the rear, his big hands halfway into his pockets and his eyes diffidently roving. It appeared as though he could not find courage to take a share in the conversation, yet was anxious to convince himself of his right to do so.

Mynors helped Mrs. Sutton into her carriage, which had been drawn up outside the gate of the school-yard. Only two families of the Bursley Wesleyan Methodists kept a carriage, the Suttons and the Clayton Vernons. The latter, boasting lineage and a large house in the aristocratic suburb of Hillport, gave to the society monetary aid and a gracious condescension. But though indubitably above the operation of any unwritten sumptuary law, even the Clayton Vernons ventured only in wet weather to bring their carriage to chapel. Yet Mrs. Sutton, who was a plain woman, might with impunity use her equipage on Sundays. This license granted by Connexional opinion was due to the fact that she so obviously regarded her carriage, not as a carriage, but as a contrivance on four wheels for enabling an infirm creature to move rapidly from place to place. When she got into it she had exactly the air of a doctor on his rounds. Mrs. Sutton's bodily frame had long ago proved inadequate to the ceaseless demands of a spirit indefatigably altruistic, and her continuance in activity was a notable illustration of the dominion of mind over matter. Her husband, a potter's valuer and commission agent, made money with facility in that lucrative vocation, and his wife's charities were famous, notwithstanding her attempts to hide them. Neither husband or wife had allowed riches to put a factitious gloss upon their primal simplicity. They were as they were, save that Mr. Sutton had joined the Five Towns Field Club and acquired some of the habits of an archæologist. The influence of wealth on manners was to be observed only in their daughter Beatrice, who, while favouring her mother, dressed at considerable expense, and at intervals gave much time to the arts of music and painting.

Agnes watched the carriage drive away, and then turned

to look up the stairs within the school doorway. She sighed, scowled, and sighed again, murmured something to herself, and finally began to read her book.

" Not come out yet? " Mynors was at her side once more, alone this time.

" No, not yet," said Agnes, wearied. " Yes. Here she is. Anna, what ages you've been ! "

Anna Tellwright stood motionless for a second in the shadow of the doorway. She was tall, but not unusually so, and sturdily built up. Her figure, though the bust was a little flat, had the lenient curves of absolute maturity. Anna had been a woman since seventeen, and she was now on the eve of her twenty-first birthday. She wore a plain, home-made light frock checked with brown and edged with brown velvet, thin cotton gloves of cream colour, and a broad straw hat like her sister's. Her grave face, owing to the prominence of the cheek-bones and the width of the jaw, had a slight angularity ; the lips were thin, the brown eyes rather large, the eyebrows level, the nose fine and delicate ; the ears could scarcely be seen for the dark brown hair which was brushed diagonally across the temples, leaving of the forehead only a pale triangle. It seemed a face for the cloister, austere in contour, fervent in expression, the severity of it mollified by that resigned and spiritual melancholy peculiar to women who, through the error of destiny, have been born into a wrong environment.

As if charmed forward by Mynors' compelling eyes, Anna stepped into the sunlight, at the same time putting up her parasol. " How calm and stately she is," he thought, as she gave him her cool hand and murmured a reply to his salutation. But even his aquiline gaze could not surprise the secrets of that concealing breast: this was one of the three great tumultuous moments of her life—she realised for the first time that she was loved.

" You are late this afternoon, Miss Tellwright," Mynors began, with the easy inflections of a man well accustomed to prominence in the society of women. Little Agnes seized Anna's left arm, silently holding up the prize, and Anna nodded appreciation.

" Yes," she said as they walked across the yard, " one of my girls has been doing wrong. She stole a Bible from another girl, so of course I had to mention it to the superintendent. Mr. Price gave her a long lecture, and now she is waiting upstairs till he is ready to go with her to her home and talk to her parents. He says she must be dismissed."

" Dismissed ! "

Anna's look flashed a grateful response to him. By the least possible. emphasis he had expressed a complete disagreement with his senior colleague which etiquette forbade him to utter in words.

" I think it's a very great pity," Anna said firmly. " I rather like the girl," she ventured in haste; " you might speak to Mr. Price about it."

" If he mentions it to me."

" Yes, I meant that. Mr. Price said—if it had been anything else but a *Bible*——"

" Um ! " he murmured, very low, but she caught the significance of his intonation.  They did not glance at each other: it was unnecessary.  Anna felt that comfortable easement of spirit which springs from the recognition of another spirit capable of understanding without explanations and of sympathising without a phrase.  Under that calm mask a strange and sweet satisfaction thrilled through her as her precious instinct of common sense—rarest of good qualities, and pining always for fellowship—found a companion in his own.  She had dreaded the overtures which for a fortnight past she had foreseen were inevitably to come from Mynors: he was a stranger, whom she merely respected.  Now in a sudden disclosure she knew him and liked him.  The dire apprehension of those formal " advances " which she had watched other men make to other women faded away.  It was at once a release and a reassurance.

They were passing through the gate, Agnes skipping round her sister's skirts, when Willie Price reappeared from the direction of the chapel.

" Forgotten something? " Mynors inquired of him blandly.

" Ye-es," he stammered, clumsily raising his hat to Anna. She thought of him exactly as Agnes had done.  He hesitated for a fraction of time, and then went up to the yard towards the lecture-hall.

" Agnes has been showing me her prize," said Mynors, as the three stood together outside the gate.  " I ask her if she thinks she really deserves it, and she says she does. What do you think, Miss Big Sister? "

Anna gave the little girl an affectionate smile of comprehension. " What is it called, dear? "

" ' Janey's Sacrifice or the Spool of Cotton, and other stories for children,' " Agnes read out in a monotone: then she clutched Anna's elbow and aimed a whisper at her ear.

" Very well, dear," Anna answered aloud, " but we must be back by a quarter-past four." And turning to Mynors: " Agnes wants to go up to the Park to hear the band play."

" I'm going up there, too," he said. " Come along, Agnes, take my arm and show me the way." Shyly Agnes left her sister's side and put a pink finger into Mynors' hand.

Moor Road, which climbs over the ridge to the mining village of Moorthorne and passes the new park on its way, was crowded with people going up to criticise and enjoy this latest outcome of municipal enterprise in Bursley: sedate elders of the borough who smiled grimly to see one another on Sunday afternoon in that undignified, idly curious throng; white-skinned potters, and miners with the swarthy pallor of subterranean toil; untidy Sabbath loafers whom neither church nor chapel could entice, and the primly-clad respectable, who had not only clothes, but a separate deportment for the seventh day; housewives whose pale faces, as of prisoners free only for a while, showed a naïve and timorous pleasure in the unusual diversion; young women made glorious by richly-coloured stuffs and carrying themselves with the defiant independence of good wages earned in warehouse or painting-shop; youths oppressed by stiff new clothes bought at Whitsuntide, in which the bright necktie and the nosegay revealed a thousand secret aspirations; young children running and yelling with the marvellous energy of their years; here and there a small well-dressed group, whose studious repudiation of the crowd betrayed a conscious eminence of rank; louts, drunkards, idiots, beggars, waifs, outcasts, and every oddity of the town: all were more or less under the influence of a new excitement, and all, with the same face of pleased expectancy, looked towards the spot where, half-way up the hill, a denser mass of sightseers indicated the grand entrance to the Park.

"What stacks of folks!" Agnes exclaimed. "It's like going to a football match."

"Do you go to football matches, Agnes?" Mynors asked. The child gave a giggle.

Anna was relieved when these two began to chatter. She had at once, by a firm natural impulse, subdued the agitation which seized her when she found Mynors waiting with such an obvious intention at the school door; she had conversed with him in tones of quiet ease; his attitude had even enabled her in a few moments to establish a pleasant familiarity with him. Nevertheless, as they joined the stream of people in Moor Road, she longed to be at home, in her kitchen, in order to examine herself and the new situation thus created by Mynors. And yet also she was glad that she must remain at his side, but it was fluttered joy that his presence gave her, too strange for immediate appreciation. As her eye, without directly looking at him, embraced the suave and admirable male creature within its field of vision, she became aware that he was quite inscrutable to her. What were his inmost thoughts, his ideals, the histories of his heart? Surely it was impossible that she should ever know these secrets! He—and she: they were utterly foreign to each other. So the primary dissonances of sex vibrated within her, and her own feelings puzzled her. Still, there was an instant pleasure, delightful, if disturbing and inexplicable. And also there was a sensation of triumph, which, though she tried to scorn it, she could not banish. That a man and a woman should saunter together on that road was nothing; but the circumstance acquired tremendous importance when the man happened to be Henry Mynors and the woman Anna Tellwright. Mynors—handsome, dark, accomplished, exemplary, and prosperous—had walked for ten years circumspect and unscathed amid the glances of a whole legion of maids. As for Anna, the peculiarity of her position had always marked her for special attention: ever since her father settled in Bursley, she had felt herself to be the object of an interest in which awe and pity were equally mingled. She guessed that the fact of her going to the Park with Mynors that afternoon would pass swiftly from mouth to mouth like the rumour of a decisive event. She had no friends; her innate reserve had been misinterpreted, and she was not popular among the Wesleyan community. Many people would say, and more would think, that it was her money which was drawing Mynors from the narrow path of his celibate discretion. She could imagine all the innuendos, the expressive nods, the pursing of lips, the lifting of shoulders and of eyebrows. " Money 'll do owt ": that was the proverb. But she cared not. She had the just and unshakeable self-esteem which is fundamental in all strong and righteous natures; and she knew beyond the possibility of doubt that, though Mynors might have no incurable aversion to a fortune, she herself, the spirit and body of her, had been the sole awakener of his desire.

By a common instinct, Mynors and Anna made little Agnes the centre of attraction. Mynors continued to tease her, and Agnes, growing courageous, began to retort. She was now walking between them, and the other two smiled to each other at the child's sayings over her head, interchanging thus messages too subtle and delicate for the coarse medium of words.

As they approached the Park the bandstand came into sight over the railway cutting, and they could hear the music of " The Emperor's Hymn." The crude, brazen sounds were tempered in their passage through the warm, still air, and fell gently on the ear in soft waves, quickening every heart to unaccustomed emotions. Children leaped forward, and old people unconsciously assumed a lightsome vigour.

The Park rose in terraces from the railway station to a street of small villas almost on the ridge of the hill. From its gilded gates to its smallest geranium-slips it was brand-new, and most of it was red. The keeper's house, the bandstand, the kiosks, the balustrades, the shelters—all these assailed the eye with a uniform redness of brick and tile which nullified the pallid greens of the turf and the frail trees. The immense crowd, in order to circulate, moved along in tight processions, inspecting, one after another, the various features of which they had read full descriptions in the " Staffordshire Signal "—waterfall, grotto, lake, swans, boat, seats, faïence, statues—and scanning with interest the names of the donors so clearly inscribed on such objects of art and craft as, from divers' motives, had been presented to the town by its citizens. Mynors, as he manœuvred a way for the two girls through the main avenue up to the topmost terrace, gravely judged each thing upon its merits, approving this, condemning that. In deciding that under all the circumstances the Park made a very creditable appearance, he only reflected the best local opinion. The town was proud of its achievement, and it had the right to be; for, though this narrow pleasuance was in itself unlovely, it symbolised the first faint renascence of the longing for beauty in a district long given up to unredeemed ugliness.

At length, Mynors having encountered many acquaintances, they got past the bandstand and stood on the highest terrace, which was almost deserted. Beneath them, in front, stretched a maze of roofs, dominated by the gold angel of the Town Hall spire. Bursley, the ancient home of the potter, has an antiquity of a thousand years. It lies towards the north end of an extensive valley, which must have been one of the fairest spots in Alfred's England, but which is now defaced by the activities of a quarter of a million of people.

Five contiguous towns—Turnhill, Bursley, Hanbridge, Knype, and Longshaw—united by a single winding thoroughfare some eight miles in length, have inundated the valley like a succession of great lakes. Of these five Bursley is the mother, but Hanbridge is the largest. They are mean and forbidding of aspect—sombre, hard-featured, uncouth; and the vaporous poison of their ovens and chimneys has soiled and shrivelled the surrounding country till there is no village lane within a league but what offers a gaunt and ludicrous travesty of rural charms. Nothing could be more prosaic than the huddled, red-brown streets; nothing more seemingly remote from romance. Yet be it said that romance is even here—the romance which, for those who have an eye to perceive it, ever dwells amid the seats of industrial manufacture, softening the coarseness, transfiguring the squalor, of these mighty alchemic operations. Look down into the valley from this terrace-height where love is kindling, embrace the whole smoke-girt amphitheatre in a glance, and it may be that you will suddenly comprehend the secret and superb significance of the vast Doing which goes forward below. Because they seldom think, the townsmen take shame when indicted for having disfigured half a county in order to live. They have not understood that this disfigurement is merely an episode in the unending warfare of man and nature, and calls for no contrition.

Here, indeed, is nature repaid for some of her notorious cruelties. She imperiously bids man sustain and reproduce himself, and this is one of the places where in the very act of obedience he wounds and maltreats her. Out beyond the municipal confines, where the subsidiary industries of coal and iron prosper amid a wreck of verdure, the struggle is grim, appalling, heroic—so ruthless is his havoc .of her, so indomitable her ceaseless recuperation. On the one side is a wresting from nature's own bowels of the means to waste her; on the other, an undismayed, enduring fortitude. The grass grows; though it is not green, it grows. In the very heart of the valley, hedged about with furnaces, a farm still stands, and at harvest-time the sooty sheaves are gathered in.

The band stopped playing. A whole population was idle in the Park, and it seemed, in the fierce calm of the sunlight, that of all the strenuous weekday vitality of the district only a murmurous hush remained. But everywhere on the horizon, and nearer, furnaces cast their heavy smoke across the borders of the sky: the Doing was never suspended.

" Mr. Mynors," said Agnes, still holding his hand, when they had been silent a moment, " when do these furnaces go out?"

" They don't go out," he answered, " unless there is a strike. It costs hundreds and hundreds of pounds to light them again."

" Does it?" she said vaguely. " Father says it's smoke that stops my gilliflowers from growing."

Mynors turned to Anna. " Your father seems the picture of health. I saw him out this morning at a quarter to seven, as brisk as a boy. What a constitution!"

" Yes," Anna replied, " he is always up at six."

" But you aren't, I suppose? "

" Yes, I too."

" And me too," Agnes interjected.

" And how does Bursley compare with Hanbridge? " Mynors continued.   Anna paused before replying.

" I like it better," she said.   " At first—last year—I thought I shouldn't."

" By the way, your father used to preach in Hanbridge circuit——"

" That was years ago," she said quickly.

" But why won't he preach here?   I dare say you know that we are rather short of local preachers—good ones, that is."

" I can't say why father doesn't preach now."   Anna flushed as she spoke.   " You had better ask him that."

" Well, I will do," he laughed.   " I am coming to see him soon—perhaps one night this week."

Anna looked at Henry Mynors as he uttered the astonishing words.   The Tellwrights had been in Bursley a year, but no visitor had crossed their doorsteps except the minister, once, and such poor defaulters as came, full of excuse and obsequious conciliation, to pay rent overdue.

" Business, I suppose? " she said, and prayed that he might not be intending to make a mere call of ceremony.

" Yes, business," he answered lightly.   " But you will be in? "

" I am always in," she said.   She wondered what the business could be, and felt relieved to know that his visit would have at least some assigned pretext; but already her heart beat with apprehensive perturbation at the thought of his presence in their household.

"See!" said Agnes, whose eyes were everywhere. "There's Miss Sutton."

Both Mynors and Anna looked sharply round. Beatrice Sutton was coming towards them along the terrace. Stylishly clad in a dress of pink muslin, with harmonious hat, gloves, and sunshade, she made an agreeable and rather effective picture, despite her plain, round face and stoutish figure. She had the air of being a leader. Grafted on to the original simple honesty of her eyes there was the unconsciously-acquired arrogance of one who had always been accustomed to deference. Socially, Beatrice had no peer among the young women who were active in the Wesleyan Sunday-school. Beatrice had been used to teach in the afternoon school, but she had recently advanced her labours from the afternoon to the morning, in response to a hint that, if she did so, the force of her influence and example might lessen the chronic dearth of morning teachers.

"Good-afternoon, Miss Tellwright," Beatrice said as she came up. "So you have come to look at the Park."

"Yes," said Anna, and then stopped awkwardly. In the tone of each there was an obscure constraint, and something in Mynors" smile of salute to Beatrice showed that he too shared it.

"Seen you be ore," Beatrice said to him familiarly, without taking his hand; then she bent down and kissed Agnes.

"What are you doing here, mademoiselle?" Mynors asked her.

"Father's just down below, near the lake. He caught sight of you, and sent me up to say that you were to be sure to come in to supper to-night. You will, won't you?"

"Yes, thanks. I had meant to."

Anna knew that they were related, and also that Mynors was constantly at the Suttons' house, but the close intimacy between these two came nevertheless like a shock to her. She could not conquer a certain resentment of it, however absurd such a feeling might seem to her intelligence. And this attitude extended not only to the intimacy, but to Beatrice's handsome clothes and facile urbanity, which by contrast emphasised her own poor little frock and tongue-tied manner. The mere existence of Beatrice so near to Mynors was like an affront to her. Yet at heart, and even while admiring this shining daughter of success, she was conscious within herself of a fundamental superiority. The soul of her condescended to the soul of the other one.

They began to discuss the Park.

"Papa says it will send up the value of that land over there enormously," said Beatrice, pointing with her ribboned sunshade to some building plots which lay to the north, high up the hill. "Mr. Tellwright owns most of that, doesn't he?" she added to Anna.

"I dare say he does," said Anna. It was torture to her to refer to her father's possessions.

"Of course it will be covered with streets in a few months. Will he build himself, or will he sell it?"

" I haven't the least idea," Anna answered, with an effort after gaiety of tone, and then turned aside to look at the crowd. There, close against the bandstand, stood her father, a short, stout, ruddy, middle-aged man in a shabby brown suit. He recognised her, stared fixedly, and nodded with his grotesque and ambiguous grin. Then he sidled off towards the entrance of the Park. None of the others had seen him.

" Agnes, dear," she said abruptly, " we must go now, or we shall be late for tea."

As the two women said good-bye their eyes met, and in the brief second of that encounter each tried to wring from the other the true answer to a question which lay unuttered in her heart. Then, having bidden adieu to Mynors, whose parting glance sang its own song to her, Anna took Agnes by the hand and left him and Beatrice together.

## II: THE MISER'S DAUGHTER

ANNA sat in the bay window of the front parlour, her accustomed place on Sunday evenings in summer, and watched Mr. Tellwright and Agnes disappear down the slope of Trafalgar Road on their way to chapel. Trafalgar Road is the long thoroughfare which, under many aliases, runs through the Five Towns from end to end, uniting them as a river might unite them. Ephraim Tellwright could remember the time when this part of it was a country lane, flanked by meadows and market gardens. Now it was a street of houses up to and beyond Bleakridge, where the Tellwrights lived; on the other side of the hill the houses came only in patches until the far-stetching borders of Hanbridge were reached. Within the municipal limits Bleakridge was the pleasantest quarter of Bursley— Hillport, abode of the highest fashion, had its own government and authority—and to reside " at the top of Trafalgar Road " was still the final ambition of many citizens, though the natural growth of the town had robbed Bleakridge of some of that exclusive distinction which it once possessed. Trafalgar Road, in its journey to Bleakridge from the centre of the town, underwent certain changes of character. First came a succession of manufactories and small shops; then, at the beginning of the rise, a quarter of a mile of superior cottages; and lastly, on the brow, occurred the houses of the comfortable-de-

tached, semi-detached, and in terraces, with rentals from
25*l.* to 60*l.* a year.   The Tellrights lived in Manor Terrace
(the name being a last reminder of the great farmstead
which formerly occupied the western hillside): their house,
of light yellow brick, was two-storied, with a long narrow
garden behind, and the rent £30.   Exactly opposite was
an antique red mansion, standing back in its own ground
—home of the Mynors family for two generations, but now
a school, the Mynors family being extinct in the district
save for one member.   Somewhat higher up, still on the
opposite side to Manor Terrace, came an imposing row of
four new houses, said to be the best planned and best built
in the town, each erected separately and occupied by its
owner.   The nearest of these four was Councillor Sutton's,
valued at 60*l.* a year.   Lower down, below Manor Terrace
and on the same side, lived the Wesleyan superintendent
minister, the vicar of St. Luke's Church, an alderman, and
a doctor.

It was nearly six o'clock.   The sun shone, but gentlier;
and the earth lay cooling in the mild, pensive effulgence
of a summer evening.   Even the onrush of the steam-car,
as it swept with a gay load of passengers to Hanbridge,
seemed to be chastened; the bell of the Roman Catholic
chapel sounded like the bell of some village church heard
in the distance; the quick, but sober, tramp of the chapel-
goers fell peacefully on the ear.   The sense of calm increased, and, steeped in this meditative calm, Anna from the
open window gazed idly down the perspective of the road,
which ended a mile away in the dim concave forms of ovens

suffused in a pale mist.  A book from the Free Library lay
on her lap; she could not read it.  She was conscious of
nothing save the quiet enchantment of reverie.  Her mind,
stimulated by the emotions of the afternoon, broke the fetters of habitual self-discipline, and ranged voluptuously
free over the whole field of recollection and anticipation.
To remember, to hope: that was sufficient joy.

In the dissolving views of her own past, from which the
rigour and pain seemed to have mysteriously departed, the
chief figure was always her father—that sinister and formidable individuality, whom her mind hated, but her heart
disobediently loved.  Ephraim Tellwright * was one of the
most extraordinary and most mysterious men in the Five
Towns.  The outer facts of his career were known to all,
for his riches made him notorious; but of the secret and intimate man none knew anything except Anna, and what little
Anna knew had come to her by divination rather than dis-
cernment.  A native of Hanbridge, he had inherited a small
fortune from his father, who was a prominent Wesleyan
Methodist.  At thirty, owing mainly to investments in
property which his calling of potter's valuer had helped him
to choose with advantage, he was worth twenty thousand
pounds, and he lived in lodgings on a total expenditure of
about a hundred a year.  When he was thirty-five he suddenly married, without any perceptible public wooing, the
daughter of a wood merchant at Oldcastle, and shortly after
the marriage his wife inherited from her father a sum of

* *Tellwright*=tile-wright, a name specially characteristic of, and possibly originating in, this clay-manufacturing district.

eighteen thousand pounds. The pair lived narrowly in a small house up at Pireford, between Hanbridge and Old-castle. They visited no one, and were never seen together except on Sundays. She was a rosy-cheeked, very unassuming and simple woman, who smiled easily and talked with difficulty, and for the rest lived apparently a servile life of satisfaction and content. After five years Anna was born, and in another five years Mrs. Tellwright died of erysipelas. The widower engaged a housekeeper; otherwise his existence proceeded without change. No stranger visited the house, the housekeeper never gossiped; but tales will spread, and people fell into the habit of regarding Tellwright's child and his housekeeper with commiseration.

During all this period he was what is termed " a good Wesleyan," preaching and teaching, and spending himself in the various activities of Hanbridge chapel. For many years he had been circuit treasurer. Among Anna's earliest memories was a picture of her father arriving late for supper one Sunday night in autumn after an anniversary service, and pouring out on the white table-cloth the contents of numerous chamois-leather money-bags. She recalled the surprising dexterity with which he counted the coins, the peculiar smell of the bags, and her mother's bland exclamation, " Eh, Ephraim ! " Tellwright belonged by birth to the Old Guard of Methodism; there was in his family a tradition of holy valour for the pure doctrine: his father, a Bursley man, had fought in the fight which preceded the famous Primitive Methodist Secession of 1808 at Bursley, and had also borne a notable part in the Warren affrays of '28, and the disastrous trouble of the Fly-Sheets in '49, when Methodism lost a hundred thousand members. As for Ephraim,, he expounded the mystery of the Atonement in village conventicles and grew garrulous with God at prayer-meetings in the big Bethesda chapel; but he did these things as routine, without skill and without enthusiasm, because they gave him an unassailable position within the central group of the society. He was not, in fact, much smitten with either the doctrinal or the spiritual side of Methodism. His chief interest lay in those fiscal schemes of organisation without whose aid no religious propaganda can possibly succeed. It was in the finance of salvation that he rose supreme—the interminable alternation of debt-raising and new liability which provides a lasting excitement for Nonconformists. In the negotiation of mortgages, the artful arrangement of the incidence of collections, the manufacture of special appeals, the planning of anniversaries and of mighty revivals, he was an undisputed leader. To him the circuit was a " going concern," and he kept it in motion, serving the Lord in committee and over statements of account. The minister by his pleading might bring sinners to the penitent form, but it was Ephraim Tellwright who reduced the cost per head of souls saved, and so widened the frontiers of the Kingdom of Heaven.

Three years after the death of his first wife it was rumoured that he would marry again, and that his choice had fallen on a young orphan girl, thirty years his junior, who " assisted " at the stationer's shop where he bought his daily newspaper. The rumour was well-founded. Anna, then eight years of age, vividly remembered the home-coming of the pale wife, and her own sturdy attempts to explain, excuse, or assuage to this wistful and fragile creature the implacable harshness of her father's temper. Agnes was born within a year, and the pale girl died of puerperal fever. In that year lay a whole tragedy, which could not have been more poignant in its perfection if the year had been a thousand years. Ephraim promptly re-engaged the old housekeeper, a course which filled Anna with secret childish revolt, for Anna was now nine, and accomplished in all domesticity. In another seven years the housekeeper died, a gaunt grey ruin, and Anna at sixteen became mistress of the household, with a small sister to cherish and control. About this time Anna began to perceive that her father was generally regarded as a man of great wealth, having few rivals in the entire region of the Five Towns. Definite knowledge, however, she had none; he never spoke of his affairs; she knew only that he possessed houses and other property in various places, that he always turned first to the money article in the newspaper, and that long envelopes arrived for him by post almost daily. But she had once heard the surmise that he was worth sixty thousand of his own, apart from the fortune of his first wife, Anna's mother. Nevertheless, it did not occur to her to think of her father, in plain terms, as a miser, until one day she happened to read in the " Staffordshire Signal " some particulars of the last will and testament of William Wilbraham, J. P., who had just died. Mr. Wilbraham had been a famous magnate and benefactor of the Five Towns; his revered name was in every mouth; he had a fine seat, Hillport House, at Hillport; and his superb horses were constantly seen, winged and nervous, in the streets of Bursley and Hanbridge. The "Signal" said that the net value of his estate was sworn at fifty-nine thousand pounds. This single fact added a definite and startling significance to figures which had previously conveyed nothing to Anna except an idea of vastness. The crude contrast between the things of Hillport House and the things of the six-roomed abode in Manor Terrace gave food for reflection, silent but profound.

Tellwright had long ago retired from business, and three years after the housekeeper died he retired, practically, from religious work, to the grave detriment of the Hanbridge circuit. In reply to sorrowful and pained questioners, he said merely that he was getting old and needed rest, and that there ought to be plenty of younger men to fill his shoes. He gave up everything except his pew in the chapel. The circuit was astounded by this sudden defection of a class-leader, a local preacher, and an officer. It was an inexplicable fall from grace. Yet the solution of the problem was quite simple. Ephraim had lost interest in his religious avocations; they had ceased to amuse him, the old ardour had cooled. The phenomenon is a common enough experience with men who have passed their fiftieth year— men, too, who began with the true and sacred zeal which Tellwright never felt. The difference in Tellwright's case was that, characteristically, he at once yielded to the new

instinct, caring naught for public opinion. Soon afterwards, having purchased a lot of cottage-property in Bursley, he decided to migrate to the town of his fathers. He
had more than one reason for doing so, but perhaps the chief
was that he found the atmosphere of Hanbridge Wesleyan
chapel rather uncongenial. The exodus from it was his
silent and malicious retort to a silent rebuke.

He appeared now to grow younger, discarding in some
measure a certain morose taciturnity which had hitherto
marked his demeanour. He went amiably about in the manner of a veteran determined to enjoy the brief existence of
life's winter. His stout, stiff, deliberate yet alert figure
became a familiar object to Bursley: that ruddy face, with
its small blue eyes, smooth upper lip, and short grey beard
under the smooth chin, seemed to pervade the streets, offering everywhere the conundrum of its vague smile. Though
no friend ever crossed his doorstep, he had dozens ·of acquaintances of the footpath. He was not, however, a facile
talker, and he seldom gave an opinion; nor were his remarks
often noticeably shrewd. He existed within himself, unre-
vealed. To the crowd, of course, he was a marvellous
legend, and moving always in the glory of that legend he
received their wondering awe—an awe tinged with contempt for his lack of ostentation and public splendour.
Commercial men with whom he had transacted business liked
to discuss his abilities, thus disseminating that solid respect
for him which had sprung from a personal experience of
those abilities, and which not even the shabbiness of his
clothes could weaken.

Anna was disturbed by the arrival at the front door of the milk-girl. Alternately with her father, she stayed at home on Sunday evenings, partly to receive the evening milk and partly to guard the house. The Persian cat with one ear preceded her to the door as soon as he heard the clatter of the can. The stout little milk-girl dispensed one pint of milk into Anna's jug, and spilt an eleemosynary supply on the step for the cat. " He does like it fresh, miss," said the milk-girl, smiling at the greedy cat, and then, with a " Lovely evenin'," departed down the street, one fat red arm stretched horizontally out to balance the weight of the can in the other. Anna leaned idly against the doorpost, waiting while the cat finished, until at length the swaying figure of the milk-girl disappeared in the dip of the road. Suddenly she darted within, shutting the door, and stood on the hall-mat in a startled attitude of dismay. She had caught sight of Henry Mynors in the distance, approaching the house. At that moment the kitchen clock struck seven, and Mynors, according to the rule of a lifetime, should have been in his place in the " orchestra " (or, as some term it, the " singing-seat ") of the chapel, where he was an admired baritone. Anna dared not conjecture what impulse had led him into this extraordinary, incredible deviation. She dared not conjecture, but despite herself she knew, and the knowledge shocked her sensitive and peremptory conscience. Her heart began to beat rapidly; she was in distress. Aware that her father and sister had left her alone, did he mean to call? It was absolutely impossible, yet she feared it, and blushed, all solitary there

in the passage, for shame. Now she heard his sharp, decided footsteps, and through the glazed panels of the door
she could see the outline of his form. He stopped; his hand
was on the gate, and she ceased to breathe. He pushed
the gate open, and then, at the whisper of some blessed
angel, he closed it again and continued his way up the street.
. . . After a few moments Anna carried the milk into
the kitchen, and stood by the dresser, moveless, each muscle
braced in the intensity of profound contemplation. Gradually the tears rose to her eyes and fell; they were the
tincture of a strange and mystic joy, too poignant to be
endured. As it were under compulsion she ran outside, and
down the garden path to the low wall which looked over the
grey fields of the valley up to Hillport. Exactly opposite,
a mile and a half away, on the ridge, was Hillport Church,
dark and clear against the orange sky. To the right, and
nearer, lay the central masses of the town, tier on tier of
richly-coloured ovens and chimneys. Along the field-paths
couples moved slowly. All was quiescent, languorous, beautiful in the glow of the sun's stately declension. Anna
put her arms on the wall. Far more impressively than in
the afternoon she realised that this was the end of one
epoch in her career and the beginning of another. En-
thralled by austere traditions and that stern conscience of
hers, she had never permitted herself to dream of the possibility of an escape from the parental servitude. She had
never looked beyond the horizons of her present world, but
had sought spiritual satisfaction in the ideas of duty and
sacrifice. The worst tyrannies of her father never dulled

the sense of her duty to him; and, without perhaps being aware of it, she had rather despised love and the dalliance of the sexes.   In her attitude towards such things there had been not only a little contempt, but also some disapproval, as though man were destined for higher ends.   Now she saw, in a quick revelation, that it was the lovers, and not she, who had the right to scorn.   She saw how miserably narrow, tepid, and trickling the stream of her life had been, and had threatened to be.   Now it gushed forth warm, impetuous, and full, opening out new and delicious vistas. She lived; and she was finding the sight to see, the courage to enjoy.   Now, as she leaned over the wall, she would not have cared if Henry Mynors indeed had called that night. She perceived something splendid and free in his abandonment of habit and discretion at the bidding of a desire.   To be the magnet which could draw that pattern and exemplar of seemliness from the strict orbit of virtuous custom!   It was she, the miser's shabby daughter, who had caused this amazing phenomenon.   The thought intoxicated her. Without the support of the wall she might have fallen.   In a sort of trance she murmured these words: " He loves me."

This was Anna Tellwright, the ascetic, the prosaic, the impassive.

After an interval which to her was as much like a minute as a century, she went back into the house.   As she entered by the kitchen she heard an impatient knocking at the front door.

" At last," said her father grimly, when she opened the door.   In two words he had resumed his terrible sway over her. Agnes looked timidly from one to the other and slipped past them into the house.

" I was in the garden," Anna explained. " Have you been here long? " She tried to smile apologetically.

" Only about a quarter of an hour," he answered, with a grimness still more portentous.

" He won't speak again to-night," she thought fearfully. But she was mistaken. After he had carefully hung his best hat on the hat-rack, he turned towards her, and said, with a queer smile:

" Ye've been day-dreaming, eh, Sis? "

" Sis " was her pet name, used often by Agnes, but by her father only at the very rarest intervals. She was staggered at this change of front, so unaccountable in this man, who, when she had unwittingly annoyed him, was capable of keeping an awful silence for days together. What did he know? What had those old eyes seen?

" I forgot," she stammered, gathering herself together happily, " I forgot the time." She felt that after all there was a bond between them which nothing could break—the tie of blood. They were father and daughter, united by sympathies obscure, but fundamental. Kissing was not in the Tellwright blood, but she had a fleeting wish to hug the tyrant.

## III: THE BIRTHDAY

THE next morning there was no outward sign that anything unusual had occurred. As the clock in the kitchen struck eight Anna carried to the back parlour a tray on which were a dish of bacon and a coffee-pot. Breakfast was already laid for three. She threw a house-keeper's glance over the table, and called: " Father! " Mr. Tellwright was resetting some encaustic tiles in the lobby. He came in, coatless, and, dropping a trowel on the hearth, sat down at the end of the table nearest the fireplace. Anna sat opposite to him, and poured out the coffee.

On the dish were six pieces of bacon. He put one piece on a plate, and set it carefully in front of Agnes's vacant chair, two he passed to Anna, three he kept for himself.

" Where's Agnes? " he enquired.

" Coming—she's finishing her arithmetic."

In the middle of the table was an unaccustomed small jug containing gilliflowers. Mr. Tellwright noticed it instantly.

" What an we gotten here? " he said, indicating the jug.

" Agnes gave me them first thing when she got up. She's grown them herself, you know," Anna said, and then added: " It's my birthday."

" Ay! " he exclaimed, with a trace of satire in his voice. " Thou'rt a woman now, lass."

No further remark on that matter was made during the meal.

Agnes ran in, all pinafore and legs. With a toss backwards of her light golden hair she slipped silently into her seat, cautiously glancing at the master of the house. Then she began to stir her coffee.

" Now, young woman," Tellwright said curtly.

She looked a startled interrogative.

" Were waiting," he explained.

" Oh!" said Agnes, confused. " I thought you'd said it. ' God sanctify this food to our use and us to His service for Christ's sake, Amen.' "

The breakfast proceeded in silence. Breakfast at eight, dinner at noon, tea at four, supper at eight: all the meals in this house occurred with absolute precision and sameness. Mr. Tellwright seldom spoke, and his example imposed silence on the girls, who felt as nuns feel when assisting at some grave, but monotonous and perfunctory rite. The room was not a cheerful one in the morning, since the window was small and the aspect westerly. Besides the table and three horse-hair chairs, the furniture consisted of an arm-chair, a bent-wood rocking chair, and a sewing-machine. A fatigued Brussels carpet covered the floor. Over the mantelpiece was an engraving of " The Light of the World," in a frame of polished brown wood. On the other walls were some family photographs in black frames. A two-light chandelier hung from the ceiling, weighed down on one side by a patent gas-saving mantle and a glass shade; over this the ceiling was deeply discoloured. On either side of the chimney-breast were cupboards about three feet high; some cardboard boxes, a work-basket, and Agnes's school books lay on the tops of these cupboards. On the window-sill was a pot of mignonette in a saucer. The window was wide open, and flies buzzed to and fro, constantly rebounding from the window panes with terrible thuds. In the blue-paved yard beyond the cat was licking himself in the sunlight with an air of being wholly absorbed in his task.

Mr. Tellwright demanded a second and last cup of coffee, and having drunk it pushed away his plate as a sign that he had finished. Then he took from the mantelpiece at his right hand a bundle of letters and opened them methodically. When he had arranged the correspondence in a flattened pile, he put on his steel-rimmed spectacles and began to read.

" Can I return thanks, father? " Agnes asked, and he nodded, looking at her fixedly over his spectacles.

" Thank God for our good breakfast, Amen."

In two minutes the table was cleared, and Mr. Tellwright was alone. As he read laboriously through communications from solicitors, secretaries of companies, and tenants, he could hear his daughters talking together in the kitchen. Anna was washing the breakfast things while Agnes wiped. Then there were flying steps across the yard: Agnes had gone to school.

After he had mastered his correspondence, Mr. Tellwright took up the trowel again and finished the tile-setting in the lobby. Then he resumed his coat, and, gathering together the letters from the table in the back parlour, went into the front parlour and shut the door. This room was his office. The principal things in it were an old oak bureau and an oak desk-chair which had come to him from his first wife's father; on the walls were some sombre landscapes in oil, received from the same source; there was no carpet on the floor, and only one other chair. A safe stood in the corner opposite the door. On the mantelpiece were some books—Woodfall's· " Landlord and Tenant," Jordan's " Guide to Company Law," Whitaker's Almanac, and a Gazetteer of the Five Towns. Several wire files, loaded with papers, hung from the mantelpiece. With the exception of a mahogany what-not with a Bible on it, which stood in front of the window, there was nothing else whatever in the room. He sat down to the bureau and opened it, and took from one of the pigeonholes a packet of various documents: these he examined one by one, from time to time referring to a list. Then he unlocked the safe and extracted from it another bundle of documents which had evidently been placed ready. With these in his hand, he opened the door, and called out:

" Anna."

" Yes, father "; her voice came from the kitchen.

" I want ye."

" In a minute. I'm peeling potatoes."

When she came in, she found him seated at the bureau as usual. He did not look round.

" Yes, father."

She stood there in her print dress and white apron, full in the eye of the sun, waiting for him. She could not guess what she had been summoned for. As a rule, she never saw her father between breakfast and dinner. At length he turned.

" Anna," he said in his harsh, abrupt tones, and then stopped for a moment before continuing. His thick, short fingers held the list which he had previously been consulting. She waited in bewilderment. " It's your birthday, ye told me. I hadna' forgotten. Ye're of age to-day, and there's summat for ye. Your mother had a fortune of her own, and under your grandfeyther's will it comes to you when you're twenty-one. I'm th' trustee. Your mother had eighteen thousand pounds i' Government stock." He laid a slight sneering emphasis on the last two words. " That was near twenty-five year ago. I've nigh on trebled it for ye, what wi' good investments and interest accumulating. Thou'rt worth "—here he changed to the second personal singular, a habit with him—" thou'rt worth this day as near fifty thousand as makes no matter, Anna. And that's a tidy bit."

" Fifty thousand—*pounds!* " she exclaimed, aghast.

" Ay, lass."

She tried to speak calmly. " Do you mean it's mine, father? "

" It's thine, under thy grandfeyther's will—haven't I told thee? I'm bound by law for to give it to thee this day, and thou mun give me a receipt in due form for the securities. Here they are, and here's the list. Tak' the list, Anna, and read it to me while I check off."

She mechanically took the blue paper and read:

" Toft End Colliery and Brickworks Limited, five hundred shares of ten pounds."

" They paid ten per cent. last year," he said, " and with coal up as it is they'll pay fiftane this. Let's see what thy arithmetic is worth, lass. How much is fiftane per cent. on five thousand pun? "

" Seven hundred and fifty pounds," she said, getting the correct answer by a superhuman effort worthy of that occasion.

" Right," said her father, pleased. " Recollect that's more till two pun a day. Go on."

" North Staffordshire Railway Company ordinary stock, ten thousand and two hundred pounds."

" Right. Th' owd North Stafford's getting up i' the world. It 'll be a five per cent. line yet. Then thou mun sell out."

She had only a vague idea of his meaning, and continued: " Five Towns Waterworks Company Limited consolidated stock, eight thousand five hundred pounds."

" That's a tit-bit, lass," he interjected, looking absently over his spectacles at something outside in the road. " You canna' pick that up on shardrucks."

" Norris's Brewery Limited, six hundred ordinary shares of ten pounds."

" Twenty per cent.," said the old man. " Twenty per cent. regular." He made no attempt to conceal his pride in these investments. And he had the right to be proud of them. They were the finest in the market, the aristocracy of investments, based on commer-

cial enterprises of which every business man in the Five
Towns knew the entire soundness. They conferred distinction on the possessor, like a great picture or a rare
volume. They stifled all questions and insinuations. Put
before any jury of the Five Towns as evidence of character,
they would almost have exculpated a murderer.

Anna continued reading the list, which seemed endless:
long before she had reached the last item her brain was a
menagerie of monstrous figures. The list included, besides
all sorts of shares English and American, sundry properties
in the Five Towns, and among these was the earthenware
manufactory in Edward Street occupied by Titus Price, the
Sunday-school superintendent. Anna was a little alarmed
to find herself the owner of this works; she knew that her
father had had some difficult moments with Titus Price,
and that the property was not without grave disadvantages.

" That's all? " Tellwright asked, at length.

" That's all."

" Total face value," he went on, " as I value it, forty-
eight thousand and fifty pounds, producing a net annual
income of three thousand two hundred and ninety pounds
or thereabouts. There's not many in this district as 'as
gotten that to their names, Anna—no, nor half that—let
'em be who they will."

Anna had sensations such as a child might have who has
received a traction-engine to play with in a back-yard.
" What am I to do with it? " she asked plaintively.

" Do wi' it? " he repeated, and stood up and faced her,
putting his lips together: " Do wi' it, did ye say? "

" Yes."

" Tak' care on it, my girl. Tak' care on it. And re-member it's thine. Thou mun sign this list, and all these transfers and fal-fals, and then thou mun go to th' Bank, and tell Mester Lovatt I've sent thee. There's four hun-dred pound there. He'll give thee a cheque-book. I've told him all about it. Thou'lt have thy own account, and be sure thou keeps it straight."

" I shan't know a bit what to do, father, and so it's no use talking," she said quietly.

" I'll learn ye," he replied. " Here, tak' th' pen, and let's have thy signature."

She signed her name many times and put her finger on many seals. Then Tellwright gathered up everything into a bundle, and gave it to her to hold.

" That's the lot," he said. " Have ye gotten 'em? "

" Yes," she said.

They both smiled self-consciously. As for Tellwright, he was evidently impressed by the grandeur of this superb renunciation on his part. " Shall I keep 'em for ye? "

" Yes, please."

" Then give 'em me."

He took back all the documents.

" When shall I call at the Bank, father?

" Better call this afternoon—afore three, mind ye."

" Very well. But I shan't know what to do."

" You've gotten a tongue i' that noddle of yours, haven't ye? " he said. " Now go and get along wi' them po-tatoes."

Anna returned to the kitchen. She felt no elation or ferment of any kind; she had not begun to realise the significance of what had occurred. Like the soldier whom a bullet has struck, she only knew vaguely that *something* had occurred. She peeled the potatoes with more than her usual thrifty care; the peel was so thin as to be almost transparent. It seemed to her that she could not arrange or examine her emotions until after she had met Henry Mynors again. More than anything else she wished to see him: it was as if out of the mere sight of him something definite might emerge; as if, when her eyes had rested on him, and not before, she might perceive some simple solution of the problems which she obscurely discerned ahead of her.

During dinner a boy brought a note for her father. He read it, snorted, and threw it across the table to Anna.

" Here," he said, " that's your affair."

The letter was from Titus Price: it said that he was sorry to be compelled to break his promise, but it was quite impossible for him to pay twenty pounds on account of rent that day. He would endeavour to pay at least twenty pounds in a week's time.

" You'd better call there, after you've been to th' Bank," said Tellwright, " and get summat out of him, if it's only ten pun."

" Must I go to Edward Street? "

" Yes."

" What am I to say? I've never been there before."

" Well, it's high time as ye began to look after your

own property. You mun see owd Price, and tell him ye cannot accept any excuses."

" How much does he owe."

" He owes ye a hundred and twenty-five pun altogether—he's five quarters in arrear."

" A hundred and——! Well, I never!" Anna was aghast. The sum appeared larger to her than all the thousands and tens of thousands which she had received in the morning. She reflected that the weekly bills of the household amounted to about a sovereign, and that the total of this debt of Price's would therefore keep them in food for two years. The idea of being in debt was abhorrent to her. She could not conceive how a man who was in debt could sleep at nights. " Mr. Price ought to be ashamed of himself," she said warmly. " I'm sure he's quite able to pay." The image of the sleek and stout superintendent of the Sunday-school, arrayed in his rich, almost voluptuous, broadcloth, offended her profoundly. That he, debtor and promise-breaker, should have the effrontery to pray for the souls of children, to chastise their petty furtive crimes, was nearly incredible.

" Oh! Price is all *right*," her father remarked, with an apparent benignity which surprised her. " He'll pay when he can."

" I think it's a shame," she repeated emphatically.

Agnes looked with a mystified air from one to the other, instinctively divining that something very extraordinary had happened during her absence at school.

" Ye mun'na be too hard, Anna," said Tellwright. " Supposing ye sold owd Titus up? When then? D'ye reckon ye'd get a tenant for them ramshackle works? A thousand pound spent would'na 'tice a tenant. That Edward Street property was one o' ye grandfeyther's specs; 'twere none o' mine. You'd best tak' what ye can get."

Anna felt a little ashamed of herself, not because of her bad policy, but because she saw that Mr. Price might have been handicapped by the faults of her property.

That afternoon it was a shy and timid Anna who swung back the heavy polished and glazed portals of the Bursley branch of the Birmingham, Sheffield and District Bank, the opulent and spacious erection which stands commandingly at the top of St. Luke's Square. She looked about her across broad counters, enormous ledgers, and rows of bent heads, and wondered whom she should address. Then a bearded gentleman, who was weighing gold in a balance, caught sight of her: he slid the gold into a drawer, and whisked round the end of the counter with a celerity which was, at any rate, not born of practice, for he, the cashier, had not done such a thing for years.

" Good-afternoon, Miss Tellwright."

" Good-afternoon. I———"

" May I trouble you to step into the manager's room? " and he drew her forward, while every clerk's eye watched. Anna tried not to blush, but she could feel the red mounting even to her temples.

" Delightful weather we're having. But of course we've the right to expect it at this time of year." He opened a door on the glass of which was painted " Manager," and bowed. " Mr. Lovatt—Miss Tellwright."

Mr. Lovatt greeted his new customer with a formal and rather fatigued politeness, and invited her to sit in a large leather armchair in front of a large table; on this table lay a large open book. Anna had once in her life been to the dentist's; this interview reminded her of that experience.

" Your father told me I might expect you to-day," said Mr. Lovatt in his high-pitched, perfunctory tones. Richard Lovatt was probably the most influential man in Bursley. Every Saturday morning he irrigated the whole town with fertilising gold. By a single negative he could have ruined scores of upright merchants and manufacturers. He had only to stop a man in the street and murmur, " By the way, your overdraft——," in order to spread discord and desolation through a refined and pious home. His estimate of human nature was falsified by no common illusions; he had the impassive and frosty gaze of a criminal judge. Many men deemed they had cause to hate him, but no one did hate him: all recognised that he was set far above hatred.

" Kindly sign your full name here," he said, pointing to a spot on the large open page of the book, " and your ordinary signature, which you will attach to cheques, here."

Anna wrote, but in doing so she became aware that she had no ordinary signature; she was obliged to invent one.

" Do you wish to draw anything out now? There is already a credit of four hundred and twenty pounds in your favour," said Mr. Lovatt, after he had handed her a cheque-book, a deposit-book, and a pass-book.

" Oh, no, thank you," Anna answered quickly.  She keenly desired some money, but she well knew that courage would fail her to demand it without her father's consent; moreover, she was in a whirl of uncertainty as to the uses of the three books, though Mr. Lovatt had expounded them severally to her in simple language.

" Good-day, Miss Tellwright."

" Good-day."

" My compliments to your father."

His final glance said half cynically, half in pity: " You are naïve and unspoilt now, but these eyes will see yours harden like the rest.  Wretched victim of gold, you are only one in a procession, after all."

Outside, Anna thought that everyone had been very agreeable to her.  Her complacency increased at a bound. She no longer felt ashamed of her shabby cotton dress. She surmised that people would find it convenient to ignore any difference which might exist between her costume and that of other girls.

She went on to Edward Street, a short steep thorough-fare at the eastern extremity of the town, leading into a rough road across unoccupied land dotted with the mouths of abandoned pits: this road climbed up to Toft End, a mean annex of the town, about half a mile east of Bleakridge. From Toft End, lying on the highest hill in the district, one had a panoramic view of Hanbridge and Bursley, with Hillport to the west, and all the moorland and mining villages to the north and northeast. Titus Price and his son lived in what had once been a farmhouse at Toft End; every morning and evening they traversed the desolate and featureless grey road between their dwelling and the works.

Anna had never been in Edward Street before. It was a miserable quarter—two rows of blackened infinitesimal cottages, and her manufactory at the end—a frontier post of the town. Price's works was small, old-fashioned, and out of repair—one of those properties which are forlorn from the beginning, which bring despair into the hearts of a succession of owners, and which, being ultimately deserted, seem to stand forever in pitiable ruin. The arched entrance for carts into the yard was at the top of the steepest rise of the street, when it might as well have been at the bottom; and this was but one example of the architect's fine disregard for the principle of economy in working— that principle to which, in the scheming of manufactories, everything else is now so strictly subordinated. Ephraim Tellwright used to say (but not to Titus Price) that the situation of that archway cost five pounds a year in horseflesh, and that five pounds was the interest on a hundred. The place was badly located, badly planned, and badly constructed. Its faults defied improvement. Titus Price remained in it only because he was chained there by arrears of rent; Tellwright hesitated to sell it only because the rent was a hundred a year, and the whole freehold would not have fetched eight hundred. He promised repairs in exchange for payment of arrears which he knew would never be paid, and his policy was to squeeze the last penny out of Price without forcing him into bankruptcy. Such was the predicament when Anna assumed ownership. As she surveyed the irregular and huddled frontage from the opposite side of the street, her first feeling was one of depression at the broken and dirty panes of the windows. A man in shirt-sleeves was standing on the weighing platform under the archway; his back was towards her, but she could see the smoke issuing in puffs from his pipe. She crossed the road. Hearing her footfalls, the man turned round: it was Titus Price himself. He was wearing an apron, but no cap; the sleeves of his shirt were rolled up, exposing forearms covered with auburn hair. His puffed, heavy face, and general bigness and untidiness, gave the idea of a vast and torpid male slattern. Anna was astounded by the contrast between the Titus of Sunday and the Titus of Monday: a single glance compelled her to readjust all her notions of the man. She stammered a greeting, and he replied, and then they were both silent for a moment: in the pause Mr. Price thrust his pipe between apron and waistcoat.

" Come inside, Miss Tellwright," he said, with a sickly, conciliatory smile. " Come into the office, will ye? "

She followed him without a word through the archway. To the right was an open door into the packing-house, where a man, surrounded by straw, was packing basins in a crate: with swift, precise movements, twisting straw between basin and basin, he forced piles of ware into a space inconceivably small. Mr. Price lingered to watch him for a few seconds, and passed on. They were in the yard, a small quadrangle paved with black, greasy mud. In one corner a load of coal had been cast; in another lay a heap of broken saggars. Decrepit doorways led to the various "shops" on the ground floor; those on the upper floor were reached by narrow wooden stairs, which seemed to cling insecurely to the exterior walls. Up one of these stairways Mr. Price climbed with heavy, elephantine movements: Anna prudently waited till he had reached the top before beginning to ascend. He pushed open a flimsy door, and with a nod bade her enter. The office was a long, narrow room, the dirtiest that Anna had ever seen. If such was the condition of the master's quarters, she thought, what must the workshops be like? The ceiling, which bulged downwards, was as black as the floor, which sank away in the middle till it was hollow like a saucer. The revolution of an engine somewhere below shook everything with a periodic muffled thud. A greyish light came through one small window. By the window was a large double desk, with chairs facing each other. One of these chairs was occupied by Willie Price. The youth did not observe at first that another person had come in with his father. He was casting up figures in an account book, and murmuring numbers to himself. He wore an office coat, short at the wrists and torn at the elbows, and a battered felt hat was thrust far back over his head, so that the brim rested on his dirty collar. He turned round at length, and, on seeing Anna, blushed brilliant crimson, and rose, scraping the legs of his chair horridly across the floor. Tall, thin, and ungainly in every motion, he had the look of a ninny: it was the fact that at school all the boys by a common instinct had combined to tease him, and that on the works the young paintresses continually made private sport of him. Anna, however, had not the least impulse to mock him in her thoughts. For her there was nothing in his blue eyes but simplicity and good intentions. Beside him she felt old, sagacious, crafty; it seemed to her that someone ought to shield that transparent and confiding soul from his father and the intriguing world.

He spoke to her and lifted his hat, holding it afterwards in his great bony hand.

" Get down to th' entry, Will," said his father, and Willie, with an apologetic sort of cough, slipped silently away through the door.

" Sit down, Miss Tellwright," said old Price, and she took the windsor chair that had been occupied by Willie. Her tenant fell into the seat opposite—a leathern chair from which the stuffing had exuded, and with one of its arms broken. " I hear as ye father is going into partnership with young Mynors—Henry Mynors."

Anna started at this surprising item of news, which was entirely fresh to her. " Father has said nothing to me about it," she replied coldly.

" Oh! Happen I've said too much. If so, you'll excuse me, miss. A smart fellow, Mynors. Now you should see *his* little works: not very much bigger than this, but there's everything you can think of there—all the latest machinery and dodges, and not over-rented, I'm told. The biggest fool i' Bursley couldn't help but make money there. This 'ere works 'ere, Miss Tellwright, wants mendin' with a new 'un."

" It looks very dirty, I must say," said Anna.

" Dirty!" he laughed—a short, acrid laugh—" I suppose you've called about the rent."

" Yes, father asked me to call."

" Let me see, this place belongs to you i' your own right, doesn't it, miss? "

" Yes," said Anna. " It's mine—from my grandfather, you know."

" Ah! Well, I'm sorry for to tell ye as I can't pay anything now—no, not a cent. But I'll pay twenty pounds in a week. Tell ye father I'll pay twenty pounds in a week."

" That's what you said last week," Anna remarked, with more brusqueness than she had intended. At first she was fearful at her own temerity in thus addressing a superintendent of the Sunday-school; then, as nothing happened, she felt reassured, and strong in the justice of her position.

" Yes," he admitted obsequiously. " But I've been disappointed. One of our best customers put us off, to tell ye the truth. Money's tight, very tight. It's got to be give and take in these days, as ye father knows. And I may as well speak plain to ye, Miss Tellwright. We canna' stay here; we shall be compelled to give ye notice. What's amiss with this bank* is that it wants pullin' down."

He went off into a rapid enumeration of ninety and nine

* Bank = manufactory.

alterations and repairs that must be done without the loss of a moment, and concluded: " You tell ye father what I've told ye, and say as I'll send up twenty pounds next week. I can't pay anything now; I've nothing by me at all."

" Father said particularly I was to be sure and get something on account." There was a flinty hardness in her tone which astonished herself perhaps more than Titus Price. A long pause followed, and then Mr. Price drew a breath, seeming to nerve himself to a tremendous sacrificial deed.

" I tell ye what I'll do. I'll give ye ten pounds now, and I'll do what I can next week. I'll do what I can. There! "

" Thank you," said Anna. She was amazed at her success.

He unlocked the desk, and his head disappeared under the lifted lid. Anna gazed through the window. Like many women, and not a few men, in the Five Towns, she was wholly ignorant of the staple manufacture. The interior of a works was almost as strange to her as it would have been to a farm-hand from Sussex. A girl came out of a door on the opposite side of the quadrangle: the creature was clothed in clayey rags, and carried on her right shoulder a board laden with biscuit* cups. She began to mount one of the wooden stairways, and as she did so the board, six feet in length, swayed alarmingly to and fro. Anna expected to see it fall with a destructive crash, but the girl went up in safety, and with a nonchalant jerk of the shoul-

* Biscuit = a term applied to ware which has been fired only once.

der aimed the end of the board through another door and vanished from sight. To Anna it was a thrilling feat, but she noticed that a man who stood in the yard did not even turn his head to watch it. Mr. Price recalled her to the business of her errand.

" Here's two fives," he said, shutting down the desk with the sigh of a crocodile.

" Liar! You said you had nothing!" her unspoken thought ran, and at the same instant the Sunday-school and everything connected with it grievously sank in her estimation; she contrasted this scene with that on the previous day with the peccant schoolgirl: it was an hour of disillusion. Taking the notes, she gave a receipt and rose to go.

" Tell ye father "—it seemed to Anna that this phrase was always on his lips—" tell ye father he must come down and look at the state this place is in," said Mr. Price, enheartened by the heroic payment of ten pounds. Anna said nothing; she thought a fire would do more good than anything else to the foul, squalid buildings: the passing fancy coincided with Mr. Price's secret and most intense desire.

Outside she saw Willie Price superintending the lifting of a crate on to a railway lorry. After twirling in the air, the crate sank safely into the waggon. Young Price was perspiring.

" Warm afternoon, Miss Tellwright," he called to her as she passed, with his pleasant, bashful smile. She gave an affirmative. Then he came to her, still smiling, his face full of an intention to say something, however insignificant.

" I suppose you'll be at the special teachers' meeting to-morrow night," he remarked.

" I hope to be," she said.   That was all: William had achieved his small-talk: they parted.

" So father and Mr. Mynors are going into partnership," she kept saying to herself on the way home.

## IV: A VISIT

THE Special Teachers' Meeting to which Willie Price had referred was one of the final preliminaries to a Revival—that is, a revival of godliness and Christian grace—about to be undertaken by the Wesleyan Methodist Society in Bursley. Its object was to arrange for a personal visitation of the parents of Sunday-school scholars in their homes. Hitherto Anna had felt but little interest in the Revival: it had several times been brought indirectly before her notice, but she had regarded it as a pheomenon which recurred at intervals in the cycle of religious activity, and as not in any way affecting herself. The gradual centring of public interest, however—that mysterious movement which, defying analysis, gathers force as it proceeds, and ends by coercing the most indifferent—had already modified her attitude towards this forthcoming event. It got about that the preacher who had been engaged, a specialist in revivals, was a man of miraculous powers: the number of souls which he had snatched from eternal torment was precisely stated, and it amounted to tens of thousands. He played the cornet to the glory of God, and his cornet was of silver: his more distant past had been ineffably wicked, and the faint rumour of that dead wickedness clung to his name like a piquant odour. As Anna walked up Trafalgar Road from Price's she observed that the hoardings had been billed with great posters announing the Revival and the revivalist, who was to commence his work on Friday night.

During tea Mr. Tellwright interrupted his perusal of the evening " Signal " to give utterance to a rather remarkable speech.

" Bless us! " he said.   " Th' old trumpeter 'll turn the town upside down! "

" Do you mean the revivalist, father? " Anna asked.

" Ay! "

" He's a beautiful man," Agnes exclaimed with enthusiasm.   " Our teacher showed us his portrait after school this afternoon.   I never saw such a beautiful man."

Her father gazed hard at the child for an instant, cup in hand, and then turned to Anna with a slightly sardonic air.

" What are you doing i' this Revival, Anna? "

" Nothing," she said.   " Only there's a teachers' meeting about it to-morrow night, and I have to go to that. Young Mr. Price mentioned it to me specially to-day."

A pause followed.

" Didst get anything out o' Price? " Tellwright asked.

" Yes; he gave me ten pounds.   He wants you to go and look over the works—says they're falling to pieces."

" Cheque, I reckon? "

She corrected the surmise.

" Better give me them notes, Anna," he said after tea. " I'm going to th' Bank i' th' morning, and I'll pay 'em in to your account."

There was no reason why she should not have suggested

the propriety of keeping at least one of the notes for her private use. But she dared not. She had never had any money of her own, not a penny; and the effective possession of five pounds seemed far too audacious a dream. She hesitated to imagine her father's reply to such a request, even to frame the request to herself. The thing, viewed close, was utterly impossible. And when she relinquished the notes she also, without being asked, gave up her cheque-book, deposit-book, and pass-book. She did this while ardently desiring to refrain from doing it, as it were under the compulsion of an invincible instinct. Afterwards she felt more at ease, as though some disturbing question had been settled once and for all.

During the whole of that evening she timorously expected Mynors, saying to herself, however, that he certainly would not call before Thursday. On Tuesday evening she started early for the teachers' meeting. Her intention was to arrive among the first and to choose a seat in obscurity, since she knew well that every eye would be upon her. She was divided between the desire to see Mynors and the desire to avoid the ordeal of being seen by her colleagues in his presence. She trembled lest she should be incapable of commanding her mien so as to appear unconscious of this inspection by curious eyes.

The meeting was held in a large class-room, furnished with wooden seats, a chair, and a small table. On the grey distempered walls hung a few Biblical cartoons depicting scenes in the life of Joseph and his brethren—but without reference to Potiphar's wife. From the whitewashed ceiling depended a T-shaped gas-fitting, one burner of which showed a glimmer, though the sun had not yet set. The evening was oppressively warm, and through the wide-open window came the faint effluvium of populous cottages and the distant, but raucous, cries of children at play. When Anna entered a group of young men were talking eagerly round the table; among these was Willie Price, who greeted her. No others had come: she sat down in a corner by the door, invisible except from within the room. Gradually the place began to fill. Then at last Mynors entered: Anna recognised his authoritative step before she saw him. He walked quickly to the chair in front of the table, and, including all in a friendly and generous smile, said that in the absence of Mr. Titus Price it fell to him to take the chair: he was glad that so many had made a point of being present. Everyone sat down. He gave out a hymn, and led the singing himself, attacking the first note with an assurance born of practice. Then he prayed, and as he prayed Anna gazed at him intently. He was standing up, the ends of his fingers pressed against the top of the table. Very carefully dressed as usual, he wore a brilliant new red necktie, and a gardenia in his button-hole. He seemed happy, wholesome, earnest, and unaffected. He had the elasticity of youth with the firm wisdom of age. And it was as if he had never been younger and would never grow older, remaining always at just thirty and in his prime. Incomparable to the rest, he was clearly born to lead. He fulfilled his functions with tact, grace, and dignity. In such an affair as this present he disclosed the attributes of the skilled workman, whose easy and exact movements are a joy and wonder to the beholder. And behind all was the man, his excellent and strong nature, his kindliness, his sincerity. Yes, to Anna, Mynors was perfect that night; the reality of him exceeded her dreamy meditations. Fearful on the brink of an ecstatic bliss, she could scarcely believe that from the enticements of a thousand women this paragon had been preserved for her. Like most of us, she lacked the high courage to grasp happiness boldly and without apprehension; she had not learnt that nothing is too good to be true.

Mynors' prayer was a cogent appeal for the success of the Revival. He knew what he wanted, and confidently asked for it, approaching God with humility but with self-respect. The prayer was punctuated by Amens from various parts of the room. The atmosphere became suddenly fervent, emotional, and devout. Here was lofty endeavour, idealism, a burning spirituality; and not all the pettinesses unavoidable in such an organisation as a Sunday-school could hide the difference between this impassioned altruism and the ignoble selfishness of the worldly. Anna felt, as she had often felt before, but more acutely now, that she existed only on the fringe of the Methodist society. She had not been converted; technically she was a lost creature: the converted knew it, and in some subtle way their bearing towards her, and others in her case, always showed that they knew it.

Why did she teach? Not from the impulse of religious zeal. Why was she allowed to have charge of a class of immortal souls? The blind could not lead the blind, nor the lost save the lost. These considerations troubled her. Conscience pricked, accusing her of a continual pretence. The *rôle* of professing Christian, through false shame, had seemed distasteful to her: she had said that she could never stand up and say " I am for Christ," without being uncomfortable. But now she was ashamed of her inability to profess Christ. She could conceive herself proud and happy in the very part which formerly she had despised. It was these believers, workers, exhorters, wrestlers with Satan, who had the right to disdain; not she.

At that moment, as if divining her thoughts, Mynors prayed for those among them who were not converted. She blushed, and when the prayer was finished she feared lest every eye might seek hers in enquiry; but no one seemed to notice her.

Mynors sat down, and, seated, began to explain the arrangements for the Revival. He made it plain that prayers without industry would not achieve success. His remarks revealed the fact that underneath the broad religious structure of the enterprise, and supporting it, there was a basis of individual diplomacy and solicitation. The town had been mapped out into districts, and each of these was being importuned, as at an election: by the thoroughness and instancy of this canvass, quite as much as by the intensity of prayerful desire, would Christ conquer. The affair was a campaign before it was a prostration at the Throne of Grace. He spoke of the children, saying that in connection with these they, the teachers, had at once the highest privilege and the most sacred responsibility. He told of a special service for the children, and the need of visiting them in their homes and inviting the parents also to this feast of God. He wished every teacher during to-morrow and the next day and the next day to go through the list of his or her scholars' names, and call, if possible, at every house. There must be no shirking. "Will you ladies do that?" he exclaimed with an appealing, serious smile. "Will you, Miss Dickinson? Will you, Miss Machin? Will you, Mrs. Salt? Will you, Miss Sutton? Will you——" Until at last it came: "Will you, Miss Tellwright?" "I will," she answered, with averted eyes. "Thank you. Thank you all."

Some others spoke, hopefully, enthusiastically, and one or two prayed. Then Mynors rose: "May the blessing of God the Father, the Son, and the Holy Ghost rest upon us now and for ever." "Amen," someone ejaculated. The meeting was over.

Anna passed rapidly out of the door, down the Quadrangle, and into Trafalgar Road. She was the first to leave, daring not to stay in the room a moment. She had seen him; he had not altered since Sunday; there was no disillusion, but a deepening of the original impression. Caught up by the soaring of his spirit, her spirit lifted, and she was conscious of vague, but intense, longing skyward. She could not reason or think in that dizzying hour, but she made resolutions which had no verbal form, yielding eagerly to his influence and his appeal. Not till she had reached the bottom of Duck Bank and was breasting the first rise towards Bleakridge did her pace slacken. Then a voice called to her from behind. She recognised it, and turned sharply beneath the shock. Mynors raised his hat and greeted her.

" I'm coming to see your father," he said.

" Yes? " she said, and gave him her hand.

" It was a very satisfactory meeting to-night," he began, and in a moment they were talking seriously of the Revival. With the most oblique delicacy, the most perfect assumption of equality between them, he allowed her to perceive his genuine and profound anxiety for her spiritual welfare. The atmosphere of the meeting was still round about him, the divine fire still uncooled. " I hope you will come to the first service on Friday night," he pleaded.

" I must," she replied. " Oh, yes! I shall come."

" That is good," he said. " I particularly wanted your promise."

They were at the door of the house. Agnes, obviously expectant and excited, answered the bell. With an effort Anna and Mynors passed into a lighter mood.

" Father said you were coming, Mr. Mynors," said Agnes, and, turning to Anna, " I've set supper all myself."

" Have you? " Mynors laughed. " Capital! You must let me give you a kiss for that." He bent down and kissed her, she holding up her face to his with no reluctance. Anna looked on, smiling.

Mr. Tellwright sat near the window of the back parlour, reading the paper. Twilight was at hand. He lowered his head as Mynors entered with Agnes in train, so as to see over his spectacles, which were half-way down his nose.

" How d'ye do, Mr. Mynors? I was just going to begin my supper. I don't wait, you know," and he glanced at the table.

" Quite right," said Mynors, " so long as you wouldn't eat it all. Would he have eaten it all, Agnes, do you think?" Agnes pressed her head against Mynors' arm and laughed shyly. The old man sardonically chuckled.

Anna, who was still in the passage, wondered what could be on the table. If it was only the usual morsel of cheese she felt that she should expire of mortification. She peeped: the cheese was at one end, and at the other a joint of beef, scarcely touched.

" Nay, nay," said Tellwright, as if he had been engaged some seconds upon the joke, " I'd have saved ye the bone."

Anna went upstairs to take off her hat, and immediately Agnes flew after her. The child was breathless with news.

" Oh, Anna! As soon as you'd gone out father told me that Mr. Mynors was coming for supper. Did you know before? "

" Not till Mr. Mynors told me, dear." It was characteristic of her father to say nothing until the last moment.

" Yes, and he told me to put an extra plate, and I asked him if I had better put the beef on the table, and first he said ' No,' cross—you know—and then he said I could please myself, so I put it on.. Why has Mr. Mynors come, Anna? "

" How should I know? Some business between him and father, I expect."

" It's very *queer*," said Agnes positively, with the child's aptitude for looking a fact squarely in the face.

" Why ' queer '? "

" You know it is, Anna," she frowned, and then breaking into a joyous smile. " But isn't he nice? I think he's lovely."

" Yes," Anna assented coldly.

" But really? " Agnes persisted.

Anna brushed her hair and determined not to put on the apron which she usually wore in the house.

" Am I tidy, Anna? "

" Yes. Run downstairs now. I'm coming directly."

" I want to wait for you," Agnes pouted.

" Very well, dear."

They entered the parlour together, and Henry Mynors jumped up from his chair, and would not sit at table until they were seated. Then Mr. Tellwright carved the beef; giving each of them a very small piece, and taking only cheese for himself. Agnes handed the water-jug and the bread. Mynors talked about nothing in especial, but he talked and laughed the whole time; he even made the old man laugh, by a comical phrase aimed at Agnes's mad passion for gilliflowers. He seemed not to have detected any shortcomings in the table appointments—the coarse cloth and plates, the chipped tumblers, the pewter cruet, and the stumpy knives—which caused anguish in the heart of the housewife. He might have sat at such a table every night of his life.

"May I trouble you for a little more beef?" he asked presently, and Anna fancied a shade of mischief in his tone as he thus forced the old man into a tardy hospitality. "Thanks. *And* a morsel of fat."

She wondered whether he guessed that she was worth fifty thousand pounds, and her father worth perhaps more.

But on the whole Anna enjoyed the meal. She was sorry when they had finished and Agnes had thanked God for the beef. It was not without considerable reluctance that she rose and left the side of the man whose arm she could have touched at any time during the previous twenty minutes. She had felt happy and perturbed in being so near to him, so intimate and free; already she knew his face by heart. The two girls carried the plates and dishes into the kitchen, Agnes making the last journey with the tablecloth, which Mynors had assisted her to fold.

"Shut the door, Agnes," said the old man, getting up to light the gas. It was an order of dismissal to both his daughters. "Let me light that," Mynors exclaimed, and the gas was lighted before Mr. Tellwright had struck a match. Mynors turned on the full force of gas. Then

Mr. Tellwright carefully lowered it. The summer quarter's gas-bill at that house did not exceed five shillings.

Through the open windows of the kitchen and parlour, Anna could hear the voices of the two men in conversation, Mynors' vivacious and changeful, her father's monotonous, curt, and heavy. Once she caught the old man's hard dry chuckle. The washing-up was done, Agnes had accomplished her home-lessons; the grandfather's clock chimed the half-hour after nine.

" You must go to bed, Agnes."

" Mustn't I say good-night to him? "

" No, I will say good-night for you."

" Don't forget to. I shall ask you in the morning."

The regular sound of talk still came from the parlour. A full moon passed along the cloudless sky. By its light and that of a glimmer of gas, Anna sat cleaning silver, or rather nickel, at the kitchen table. The spoons and forks were already clean, but she felt compelled to busy herself with something. At length the talk stopped and she heard the scraping of chair-legs. Should she return to the parlour? Or should she——? Even while she hesitated, the kitchen door opened.

" Excuse me coming in here," said Mynors. " I wanted to say good-night to you."

She sprang up and he took her hand. Could he feel the agitation of that hand?

" Good-night."

" Good-night." He said it again.

" And Agnes wished me to say good-night to you for her."

" Did she? " He smiled; till then his face had been serious. " You won't forget Friday? "

" As if I could! " she murmured after he had gone.

# V: THE REVIVAL

**A**NNA spent the afternoons in visiting two following the houses of her school-children. She had no talent for such work, which demands the vocal rather than the meditative temperament, and the apparent futility of her labours would have disgusted and disheartened her, had she not been sustained and urged forward by the still active influence of Mynors and the teachers' meeting. There were fifteen names in her class-book, and she went to each house, except four whose tenants were impeccable Wesleyan families and would have considered themselves insulted by a quasi-didactic visit from an upstart like Anna. Of the eleven, some parents were rude to her; others begged, and she had nothing to give; others made perfunctory promises; only two seemed to regard her as anything but a somewhat tiresome impertinence. The fault was doubtless her own. Nevertheless she found joy in the uncongenial and ill-performed task—the cold, fierce joy of the nun in her penance. When it was done she said " I have done it," as one who had sworn to do it come what might, yet without quite expecting to succeed.

On the Friday afternoon, during tea, a boy brought up a large foolscap packet addressed to Mr. Tellwright. " From Mr. Mynors," the boy said. Tellwright opened it leisurely after the boy had gone, and took out some sheets covered with figures which he carefully examined. " Anna," he said, as she was clearing away the tea-things, "I understand thou'rt going to the Revival meeting to-night. I shall have a message as thou mun give to Mr. Mynors."

When she went upstairs to dress, she saw the Suttons' landau standing outside their house on the opposite side of the road. Mrs. Sutton came down the front steps and got into her carriage, and was followed by a little restless, nervous, alert man who carried in his hand a black case of peculiar form. "The revivalist!" Anna exclaimed, remembering that he was to stay with the Suttons during the Revival week. Then this was the renowned crusader, and the case held his renowned cornet! The carriage drove off down Trafalgar Road, and Anna could see that the little man was talking vehemently and incessantly to Mrs. Sutton, who listened with evident interest; at the same time the man's eyes were everywhere, absorbing all details of the street and houses with unquenchable curiosity.

"What is the message for Mr. Mynors, father?" she asked in the parlour, putting on her cotton gloves.

"Oh!" he said, and then paused. "Shut th' door, lass."

She shut it, not knowing what this cautiousness foreshadowed. Agnes was in the kitchen.

"It's o' this'n," Tellwright began. "Young Mynors wants a partner wi' a couple o' thousand pounds, and he come to me. Ye understand; 'tis what they call a sleeping partner he's after. He'll give a third share in his concern for two thousand pound now. I've looked into it and there's money in it. He's no fool and he's gotten hold of a good thing. He sent me up his stock-taking and balance sheet to-day, and I've been o'er the place mysen. I'm telling thee this, lass, because I have na' two thousand o' my own idle just now, and I thought as thou might happen like th' investment."

" But, father——"

" Listen. I know as there's only four hundred o' thine in th' Bank now, but next week 'll see the beginning o' July and dividends coming in. I've reckoned as ye'll have nigh on fourteen hundred i' dividends and interests, and I can lend ye a couple o' hundred in case o' necessity. It's a rare chance; thou's best tak' it."

" Of course, if you think it's all right, father, that's enough," she said without animation.

" Am' na I telling thee I think it's all right?" he remarked sharply. " You mun tell Mynors as I say it's satisfactory. Tell him that, see? I say it's satisfactory. I shall want for to see him later on. He told me he couldna' come up any night next week, so ask him to make it the week after. There's no hurry. Dunna' forget."

What surprised Anna most in the affair was that Henry Mynors should have been able to tempt her father into a speculation. Ephraim Tellwright the investor was usually as shy as a well-fed trout, and this capture of him by a youngster only two years established in business might fairly be regarded as a prodigious feat. It was indeed the highest distinction of Mynors' commercial career. Henry was so prominently active in the Wesleyan Society that the members of that society, especially the women, were apt to ignore the other side of his individuality. They knew him supreme as a religious worker; they did not realise the likelihood of his becoming supreme in the staple manufacture. Left an orphan at seventeen, Mynors belonged to a family now otherwise extinct in the Five Towns—one of those families which by virtue of numbers, variety, and personal force seem to permeate a whole district, to be a calculable item of it, an essential part of its identity. The elders of the Mynors blood had once occupied the red house opposite Tellwright's, now used as a school, and had there reared many children: the school building was still known as " Mynors's " by old-fashioned people. Then the parents died in middle age: one daughter married in the North, another in the South; a third went to China as a missionary and died of fever; the eldest son died; the second had vanished into Canada and was reported a scapegrace; the third was a sea-captain. Henry (the youngest) alone was left, and of all the family Henry was the only one to be connected with the earthenware trade. There was no inherited money, and during ten years he had worked for a large firm in Turnhill, as clerk, as traveller, and last as manager, living always quietly in lodgings. In the fulness of time he gave notice to leave, was offered a partnership, and refused it. Taking a newly erected manufactory in Bursley near the canal, he started in business for himself, and it became known that, at the age of twenty-eight, he had saved fifteen hundred pounds. Equally expert in the labyrinths of manufacture and in the niceties of the markets (he was reckoned a peerless traveller), Mynors inevitably flourished. His order-books were filled and flowing over at remunerative prices, and insufficiency of capital was the sole peril to which he was exposed. By the raising of a finger he could have had a dozen working and moneyed partners, but he had no desire for a working partner. What he wanted was a capitalist who had confidence in him, Mynors. In Ephraim Tellwright he found the man. Whether it was by instinct, good luck, or skilful diplomacy that Mynors secured this invaluable prize no one could positively say, and perhaps even he himself could not have catalogued all the obscure motives that had guided him to the shrewd miser of Manor Terrace.

Anna had meant to reach chapel before the commencement of the meeting, but the interview with her father threw her late. As she entered the porch an officer told her that the body of the chapel was quite full and that she should go into the gallery, where a few seats were left near the choir. She obeyed: pew-holders had no rights at that service.

The scene in the auditorium astonished her, effectually putting an end to the worldly preoccupation caused by her father's news. The historic chapel was crowded almost in every part, and the congregation—impressed, excited, eager—sang the opening hymn with unprecedented vigour and sincerity; above the rest could be heard the trained voices of a large choir, and even the choir, usually perfunctory, seemed to share the general fervour. In the vast mahogany pulpit the Reverend Reginald Banks, the superintendent minister, a stout pale-faced man with pendent cheeks and cold grey eyes, stood impassively regard-

ing the assemblage, and by his side was the revivalist, a
mannikin in comparison with his colleague; on the broad
balustrade of the pulpit lay the cornet. The fiery and in-
quisitive eyes of the revivalist probed into the furthest
corners of the chapel; apparently no detail of any single
face or of the florid decoration escaped him, and as Anna
crept into a small empty pew next to the east wall she felt
that she too had been separately observed. Mr. Banks gave
out the last verse of the hymn, and simultaneously with the
leading chord from the organ the revivalist seized his cornet
and joined the melody. Massive, yet exultant, the tones
rose clear over the mighty volume of vocal sound, an in-
citement to victorious effort. The effect was instant: an
ecstatic tremor seemed to pass through the congregation,
like wind through ripe corn, and at the close of the hymn
it was not until the revivalist had put down his cornet that
the people resumed their seats. Amid the *frou-frou* of
dresses and subdued clearing of throats, Mr. Banks retired
softly to the back of the pulpit, and the revivalist, mounting a stool, suddenly dominated the congregation. His
glance swept masterfully across the chapel and round the
gallery. He raised one hand with the stilling action of a
mesmerist, and the people, either kneeling or inclined
against the front of the pews, hid their faces from those
eyes. It was as though the man had in a moment measured
their iniquities and had courageously resolved to intercede for them with God, but was not very sanguine as
to the result. Everyone except the organist, who was
searching his tune-book for the next tune, seemed to feel

humbled, bitterly ashamed, as it were caught in the act of sin. There was a solemn and terrible pause.

Then the revivalist began:

"Behold us, O dread God, suppliants for thy mercy——"

His voice was rich and full, but at the same time sharp and decisive. The burning eyes were shut tight, and Anna, who had a profile view of his face, saw that every muscle of it was drawn tense. The man possessed an extraordinary histrionic gift, and he used it with imagination. He had two audiences, God and the congregation. God was not more distant from him than the congregation, or less real to him, or less a heart to be influenced. Declamatory and full of effects carefully calculated—a work of art, in fact—his appeal showed no error of discretion in its approach to the Eternal. There was no minimising of committed sin, nor yet an insincere and grovelling self-accusation. A tyrant could not have taken offence at its tone, which seemed to pacify God while rendering the human audience still more contrite. The conclusion of the catalogue of wickedness and swift confident turn to Christ's cross was marvellously impressive. The congregation burst out into sighs, groans, blessings, and Amens; and the pillars of distant rural conventicles, who had travelled from the confines of the circuit to its centre in order to partake of this spiritual excitation, began to feel that they would not be disappointed.

"Let the Holy Ghost descend upon us now," the revivalist pleaded with restrained passion; and then, opening his eyes and looking at the clock in front of the gallery, he repeated, " Now, now, at twenty-one minutes past seven." Then his eyes, without shifting, seemed to ignore the clock, to gaze through it into some unworldly dimension, and he murmured in a soft dramatic whisper: " I see the Divine Dove——"

The doors, closed during prayer, were opened, and more people entered. A youth came into Anna's pew.

The superintendent minister gave out another hymn, and when this was finished the revivalist, who had been resting in a chair, came forward again. " Friends and fellow-sinners," he said, " a lot of you, fools that you are, have come here to-night to hear me play my cornet. Well, you have heard me. I have played the cornet, and I will play it again. I would play it on my head if by so doing I could bring sinners to Christ. I have been called a mountebank. I am one. I glory in it. I am God's mountebank, doing God's precious business in my own way. But God's precious business cannot be carried on, even by a mountebank, without money, and there will be a collection towards the expenses of the Revival. During the collection we will sing ' Rock of Ages,' and you shall hear my cornet again. If you feel willing to give us your sixpences, give; but if you resent a collection," here he adopted a tone of ferocious sarcasm, " keep your miserable sixpences and get six-penny-worth of miserable enjoyment out of them else-where."

As the meeting proceeded, submitting itself more and more to the imperious hypnotism of the revivalist, Anna gradually became oppressed by a vague sensation which was partly sorrow and partly an inexplicable dull anger—anger at her own penitence. She felt as if everything was wrong and could never by any possibility be righted. After two exhortations, from the minister and the revivalist, and another hymn, the revivalist once more prayed, and as he did so Anna looked stealthily about in a sick, preoccupied way. The youth at her side stared glumly in front of him. In the orchestra Henry Mynors was whispering to the organist. Down in the body of the chapel the atmosphere was electric, perilous, overcharged with spiritual emotion. She was glad she was not down there. The voice of the revivalist ceased, but he kept the attitude of supplication. Sobs were heard in various quarters, and here and there an elder of the chapel could be seen talking quietly to some convicted sinner. The revivalist began softly to sing " Jesu, lover of my soul," and most of the congregation, standing up, joined him; but the sinners stricken of the Spirit remained abjectly bent, tortured by conscience, pulled this way by Christ and that by Satan. A few rose and went to the Communion rails, there to kneel in the sight of all. Mr. Banks descended from the pulpit and opening the wicket which led to the Communion table spoke to these over the rails, reassuringly, as a nurse to a child. Other sinners, desirous of fuller and more intimate guidance, passed down the aisles and so into the preacher's vestry at the eastern end of the chapel, and were followed thither by class-leaders and other proved servants of God: among these last were Titus Price and Mr. Sutton.

" The blood of Christ atones," said the revivalist solemnly, at the end of the hymn. " The spirit of Christ is working among us. Let us engage in private prayer. Let us drive the devil out of this chapel."

More sighs and groans followed. Then someone cried out in sharp, shrill tones, " Praise Him "; and another cried, " Praise Him "; and an old woman's quavering voice sang the words, " I know that my Redeemer liveth." Anna was in despair at her own predicament, and the sense of sin was not more strong than the sense of being confused and publicly shamed. A man opened the pew-door, and sitting down by the youth's side began to talk with him. It was Henry Mynors. Anna looked steadily away at the wall, fearful lest he should address her too. Presently the youth got up with a frenzied gesture and walked out of the gallery, followed by Mynors. In a moment she saw the youth stepping awkwardly along the aisle beneath, towards the inquiry room, his head forward and the lower lip hanging as though he were sulky.

Anna was now in the profoundest misery. The weight of her sins, of her ingratitude to God, lay on her like a physical and intolerable load, and she lost all feeling of shame, as a seasick voyager loses shame after an hour of nausea. She knew then that she could no longer go on living as aforetime. She shuddered at the thought of her tremendous responsibility to Agnes—Agnes who took her for perfection. She recollected all her sins individually— lies, sloth, envy, vanity, even theft in her infancy. She heaped up all the wickedness of a lifetime, hysterically augmented it, and found a horrid pleasure in the exaggeration. Her virtuous acts shrank into nothingness.

A man, and then another, emerged from the vestry door with beaming, happy face. These were saved; they had yielded to Christ's persuasive invitation. Anna tried to imagine herself converted, or in the process of being converted. She could not. She could only sit moveless, dull, and abject. She did not stir, even when the congregation rose for another hymn. In what did conversion consist? Was it to say the words, " I believe "? She repeated to herself softly, " I believe; I believe." But nothing happened. Of course she believed. She had never doubted, nor dreamed of doubting, that Jesus died on the Cross to save her soul—*her* soul—from eternal damnation. She was probably unaware that any person in Christendom had doubted that fact so fundamental to her. What, then, was lacking? What was belief? What was faith?

A venerable class-leader came from the vestry, and, slowly climbing the pulpit stairs, whispered in the ear of the revivalist. The latter faced the congregation with a cry of joy. " Lord," he exclaimed, " we bless Thee that seventeen souls have found Thee! Lord, let the full crop be gathered, for the fields are white unto harvest." There was an exuberant chorus of praise to God.

The door of the pew was opened gently, and Anna started to see Mrs. Sutton at her side. She at once guessed that Mynors had sent to her this angel of consolation.

" Are you near the light, dear Anna? " Mrs. Sutton began.

Anna searched for an answer. She now sat huddled up in the corner of the pew, her face partially turned towards Mrs. Sutton, who looked mildly into her eyes. "I don't know," Anna stammered, feeling like a naughty schoolgirl. A doubt whether the whole affair was not after all absurd flashed through her, and was gone.

"But it is quite simple," said Mrs. Sutton. "I cannot tell you anything that you do not know. Cast out pride. Cast out pride—that is it. Nothing but earthly pride prevents you from realising the saving power of Christ. You are afraid, Anna, afraid to be humble. Be brave. It is so simple, so easy. If one will but submit."

Anna said nothing, had nothing to say, was conscious of nothing save excessive discomfort.

"Where do you feel your difficulty to be?" asked Mrs. Sutton.

"I don't know," she answered wearily.

"The happiness that awaits you is unspeakable. I have followed Christ for nearly fifty years, and my happiness increases daily. Sometimes I do not know how to contain it all. It surges above all the trials and disappointments of this world. Oh, Anna, if you will but believe!"

The aging woman's thin, distinguished face, crowned with abundant grey hair, glistened with love and compassion, and as Anna's eyes rested upon it Anna felt that there was something tangible, something to lay hold on.

"I think I do believe," she said weakly.

"You 'think'? Are you sure? Are you not deceiving yourself? Belief is not with the lips: it is with the heart."

There was a pause.   Mr. Banks could be heard praying.

" I will go home," Anna whispered at length, " and think it out for myself."

" Do, my dear girl, and God will help you."

Mrs. Sutton bent and kissed Anna affectionately, and then hurried away to offer her ministrations elsewhere.   As Anna left the chapel, she encountered the chapel-keeper pacing regularly to and fro across the length of the broad steps.   In the porch was a notice that cabinet photographs of the revivalist could be purchased on application, at one shilling each.

## VI: WILLIE

ANNA closed the bedroom door softly; through the open window came the tones of Cauldon church clock, famous for their sonority and richness, announcing eleven. Agnes lay asleep under the blue-and-white counterpane, on the side of the bed next the wall, the bed-clothes pushed down and disclosing the upper half of her nightgowned figure. She slept in absolute repose, with flushed cheek and every muscle lax, her hair by some chance drawn in a perfect straight line diagonally across the pillow. Anna glanced at her sister, the image of physical innocence and childish security, and then, depositing the candle, went to the window and looked out.

The bedroom was over the kitchen and faced south. The moon was hidden by clouds, but clear stretches of sky showed thick-studded clusters of stars brightly winking. To the far right across the fields the silhouette of Hillport Church could just be discerned on the ridge. In front, several miles away, the blast-furnaces of Cauldon Bar Ironworks shot up vast wreaths of yellow flame with canopies of tinted smoke. Still more distant were a thousand other lights crowning chimney and kiln, and nearer, on the waste lands west of Bleakridge, long fields of burning ironstone glowed with all the strange colours of decadence. The entire landscape was illuminated and transformed by these unique pyrotechnics of labour, atoning for its grime, and dull, weird sounds, as of the breathings and sighings of gigantic nocturnal creatures, filled the enchanted air. It was a romantic scene, a romantic summer night, balmy, delicate, and wrapped in meditation. But Anna saw nothing there save the repulsive evidences of manufacture, had never seen anything else.

She was still horribly, acutely miserable, exhausted by the fruitless search for some solution of the enigma of sin —her sin in particular—and of redemption. She had cogitated in a vain circle until she was no longer capable of reasoned ideas. She gazed at the stars and into the illimitable spaces beyond them, and thought of life and its inconceivable littleness, as millions had done before in the presence of that same firmament. Then, after a time, her brain resumed its nightmare-like task. She began to probe herself anew. Would it have availed if she had walked publicly to the penitential form at the Communion-rail, and, ranging herself with the working men and women, proved by that overt deed the sincerity of her contrition? She wished ardently that she had done so, yet knew well that such an act would always be impossible for her, even though the evasion of it meant eternal torture. Undoubtedly, as Mrs. Sutton had implied, she was proud, stiff-necked, obstinate in iniquity.

Agnes stirred slightly in her sleep, and Anna, aroused, dropped the blind, turned towards the room and began to undress, slowly, with reflective pauses. Her melancholy became grim, sardonic; if she was doomed to destruction, so let it be. Suddenly, half-clad, she knelt down and prayed, prayed that pride might be cast out, burying her face in the coverlet and caging the passionate effusion in a whisper lest Agnes should be disturbed. Having prayed, she still knelt quiescent; her eyes were dry and burning. The last car thundered up the road, shaking the house, and she rose, finished undressing, blew out the candle, and slipped into bed by Agnes's side.

She could not sleep, did not attempt to sleep, but abandoned herself meekly to despair. Her thoughts covered again the interminable round, and again, and yet, again. In the twilight of the brief summer night her accustomed eyes could distinguish every object in the room, all the bits of furniture which had been brought from Hanbridge and with which she had been familiar since her memory began: everything appeared mean, despicable, cheerless; there was nothing to inspire. She dreamed impossibly of a high spirituality which should metamorphose all, change her life, lend glamour to the most pitiful surroundings, ennoble the most ignominious burdens—a spirituality never to be hers.

At any rate she would tell her father in the morning that she was convicted of sin, and, however hopelessly, seeking salvation; she would tell both her father and Agnes at breakfast. The task would be difficult, but she swore to do it. So resolved, she endeavoured to sleep, and did sleep uneasily for a short period. When she woke the great business of the dawn had begun. She left the bed, and drawing up the blind looked forth. The furnace fires were paling; a few milky clouds sailed in the vast pallid blue.

It was cool just then, and she shivered. She went to the glass, and examined her face carefully, but it gave no signs whatever of the inward warfare. She saw her plain and mended night-gown. Suppose she were married to Mynors! Suppose he lay asleep in the bed where Agnes lay asleep! Involuntarily she glanced at Agnes to certify that the child and none else was indeed there, and got into bed hurriedly and hid herself because she was ashamed to have had such a fancy. But she continued to think of Mynors. She envied him for his cheerfulness, his joy, his goodness, his dignity, his tact, his sex. She envied every man. Even in the sphere of religion, men were not fettered like women. No man, she thought, would acquiesce in the futility to which she was already half resigned; a man would either wring salvation from the heavenly powers or race gloriously to hell. Mynors—Mynors was a god!

She recollected her resolution to speak to her father and Agnes at breakfast, and shudderingly confirmed it, but less stoutly than before. Then an announcement made by Mr. Banks in chapel on the previous evening presented itself, as though she was listening to it for the first time. It was the announcement of a prayer-meeting for workers in the Revival, to be held that (Saturday) morning at seven o'clock. She instantly decided to go to the meeting, and the decision seemed to give her new hope. Perhaps there she might find peace. On that faint expectancy she fell asleep again and did not wake till half-past six, after her usual hour. She heard noises in the yard; it was her father going towards the garden with a wheelbarrow. She dressed quickly, and when she had pinned on her hat she woke Agnes.

" Going out, Sis? " the child asked sleepily, seeing her attire.

" Yes, dear. I'm going to the seven o'clock prayer-meeting. And you must get breakfast. You can—can't you? "

The child assented, glad of the chance.

" But what are you going to the prayer-meeting for? "

Anna hesitated. Why not confess? No. " I must go," she said quietly at length. " I shall be back before eight."

" Does father know? " Agnes enquired apprehensively.

" No, dear."

Anna shut the door quickly, went softly downstairs and along the passage, and crept into the street like a thief.

Men and women and boys and girls were on their way to work, with hurried, clattering steps, some munching thick pieces of bread as they went, all self-centred, apparently morose and not quite awake. The dust lay thick in the arid gutters, and in drifts across the pavement, as the night-wind had blown it. Vehicular traffic had not begun, and blinds were still drawn; and though the footpaths were busy the street had a deserted and forlorn aspect. Anna walked hastily down the road, avoiding the glances of such as looked at her, but peering furtively at the faces of those who ignored her. All seemed callous—hoggishly careless of the everlasting verities. At first it appeared strange to her that the potent revival in the Wesleyan chapel had produced no effect on these preoccupied people. Bursley, then, continued its dull and even course. She wondered whether any of them guessed that she was going to the prayer-meeting and secretly sneered at her therefor.

When she had climbed Duck Bank she found, to her surprise, that the doors of the chapel were fast closed, though it was ten minutes past seven. Was there to be no prayer-meeting? A momentary sensation of relief flashed through her, and then she saw that the gate of the school-yard was open. She should have known that early morning prayers were never offered up in the chapel, but in the lecture-hall. She crossed the quadrangle with beating heart, feeling now that she had embarked on a frightful enterprise. The door of the lecture-hall was ajar; she pushed it and went in. At the other end of the hall a meagre handful of worshippers were collected, and on the raised platform stood Mr. Banks, vapid, perfunctory, and fatigued. He gave out a verse, and pitched the tune—too high, but the singers with a heroic effort accomplished the verse without breaking down. The singing was thin and feeble, and the eagerness of one or two voices seemed strained, as though with a determination to make the best of things. Mynors was not present, and Anna did not know whether to be sorry or glad of this. She recognised that, save herself, all present were old believers, tried warriors of the Lord. There was only one other woman, Miss Sarah Vodrey, an aged spinster who kept house for Titus Price and his son, and found her sole diversion in the variety of her religious experiences. Before the hymn was finished a young man joined the assembly; it was the youth who had sat near Anna on the previous night;

an ecstatic and naïve bliss shone from his face. In his prayer the minister drew the attention of the Deity to the fact that, although a score or more of souls had been ingathered at the first service, the Methodists of Bursley were by no means satisfied. They wanted more; they wanted the whole of Bursley; and they would be content with no less. He begged that their earnest work might not be shamed before the world by a partial success. In conclusion he sought the blessing of God on the revivalist and asked that this tireless enthusiast might be led to husband his strength: at which there was a fervent Amen.

Several men prayed, and a pause ensued, all still kneeling.

Then the minister said in a tone of oily politeness:

" Will a sister pray? "

Another pause followed.

" Sister Tellwright? "

Anna would have welcomed death and damnation. She clasped her hands tightly, and longed for the endless moment to pass. At last Sarah Vodrey gave a preliminary cough. Miss Vodrey was always happy to pray aloud, and her invocations usually began with the same phrase: " Lord, we thank Thee that this day finds us with our bodies out of the grave and our souls out of hell."

Afterwards the minister gave out another hymn, and as soon as the singing commenced Anna slipped away. Once in the yard, she breathed a sigh of relief. Peace at the prayer-meeting? It was like coming out of prison. Peace was farther off than ever. Nay, she had actually forgotten her soul in the sensations of shame and discomfort. She had contrived only to make herself ridiculous, and perhaps the pious at their breakfast-tables would discuss her and her father, and their money, and the queer life they led.

If Mynors had but been present!

She walked out into the street. It was twenty minutes to eight by the town-hall clock. The last workman's car of the morning was just leaving Bursley: it was packed inside and outside, and the conductor hung insecurely on the step. At the gates of the manufactory opposite the chapel, a man in a white smock stood placidly smoking a pipe. A prayer-meeting was a little thing, a trifle in the immense and regular activity of the town: this thought necessarily occurred to Anna. She hurried homewards, wondering what her father would say about that morning's unusual excursion. A couple of hundred yards distant from home she saw, to her astonishment, Agnes emerging from the front door of the house. The child ran rapidly down the street, not observing Anna till they were close upon each other.

" Oh, Anna! You forgot to buy the bacon yesterday. There isn't a *scrap*, and father's fearfully angry. He gave me sixpence, and I'm going down to Leal's to get some as quick as ever I can."

It was a thunderbolt to Anna, this seemingly petty misadventure. As she entered the house she felt a tear on her cheek. She was ashamed to weep, but she wept. This, after the fiasco of the prayer-meeting, was a climax

of woe; it overtopped and extinguished all the rest; her soul
was nothing to her now. She quickly took off her hat and
ran to the kitchen. Agnes had put the breakfast-things
on the tray ready for setting; the bread was cut, the coffee
portioned into the jug; the fire burned bright, and the
kettle sang. Anna took the cloth from the drawer in the
oak dresser, and went to the parlour to lay the table. Mr.
Tellwright was at the end of the garden, pointing the wall,
his back to the house. The table set, Anna observed that the
room was only partly dusted; there was a duster on the
mantelpiece; she seized it to finish, and at that moment
the kitchen clock struck eight. Simultaneously Mr. Tellwright dropped his trowel, and came towards the house.
She doggedly dusted one chair, and then, turning coward,
fled away upstairs; the kitchen was barred to her, since her
father would enter by the kitchen door.

She had forgotten to buy bacon, and breakfast would
be late: it was a calamity unique in her experience! She
stood at the door of her bedroom, and waited, vehemently,
for Agnes's return. At last the child raced breathlessly
in; Anna flew to meet her. With incredible speed the bacon
was whipped out of its wrapper, and Anna picked up the
knife. At the first stroke she cut herself, and Agnes was
obliged to bind her finger with rag. The clock struck the
half-hour like a knell. It was twenty minutes to nine,
forty minutes behind time, when the two girls hurried into
the parlour, Anna bearing the bacon and hot plates, Agnes
the bread and coffee. Mr. Tellwright sat upright and
ferocious in his chair, the image of offence and wrath. In-

stead of reading his letters he had fed full of this ineffable
grievance.  The meal began in a desolating silence.  The
male creature's terrible displeasure permeated the whole
room like an ether, invisible, but carrying vibrations to the
heart.  Then, when he had eaten one piece of bacon, and
cut his envelopes, the miser began to empty himself of
some of his anger in stormy tones that might have up-
rooted trees.  Anna ought to feel thoroughly ashamed.  He
could not imagine what she had been thinking of.  Why
didn't she tell him she was going to the prayer-meeting?
Why did she go to the prayer-meeting, disarranging the
whole household?  How came she to forget the bacon?  It
was gross carelessness.  A pretty example to her little sister!  The fact was that *since her birthday* she had gotten
above hersen.  She was careless and extravagant.  Look
how thick the bacon was cut.  He should not stand it much
longer.  And her finger all red, and the blood dropping on
the cloth: a nice sight at a meal!  Go and tie it up again.

Without a word she left the room to obey.  Of course
she had no defence.  Agnes, her tears falling, pecked her
food timidly like a bird, not daring to stir from her chair,
even to assist at the finger.

" What did Mr. Mynors say? "   Tellwright enquired
fiercely when Anna had come back into the room.

" Mr. Mynors? " she murmured, at a loss, but vaguely
apprehending further trouble.

" Did ye see him? "

" Yes, father."

" Did ye give him my message? "

" I forgot it." God in heaven! She had forgotten the message!

With a devastating grunt Mr. Tellwright walked speechless out of the room. The girls cleared the table, exchanging sympathy with a single mute glance. Anna's one satisfaction was that, even if she had remembered the message, she could not possibly have delivered it.

Ephraim Tellwright stayed in the front parlour till half-past ten o'clock, unseen but felt, like an angry god behind a cloud. The consciousness that he was there, unappeased and dangerous, remained uppermost in the minds of the two girls during the morning. At half-past ten he opened the door.

" Agnes! " he commanded, and Agnes ran to him from the kitchen with the speed of propitiation.

" Yes, father."

" Take this note down to Price's, and don't wait for an answer."

" Yes, father."

She was back in twenty minutes. Anna was sweeping the lobby.

" If Mr. Mynors calls while I'm out, you mun tell him to wait," Mr. Tellwright said to Agnes, pointedly ignoring Anna's presence. Then, having brushed his greenish hat on his sleeve he went off towards town to buy meat and vegetables. He always did Saturday's marketing himself. At the butcher's and in the St. Luke's covered market he was a familiar and redoubtable figure. Among the salespeople who stood the market was a wrinkled, hardy old potato-woman from the other side of Moorthorne: every Saturday the miser bested her in their higgling-match, and nearly every Saturday she scornfully threw at him the same joke: " Get thee along to th' post-office, Mester Terrick:* happen they'll give thee sixpenn'orth o' stamps for five-pence ha'penny." He seldom failed to laugh heartily at this.

At dinner the girls could perceive that the shadow of his displeasure had slightly lifted, though he kept a frown-ing silence. Expert in all the symptoms of his moods, they knew that in a few hours he would begin to talk again, at first in monosyllables, and then in short detached sentences. An intimation of relief diffused itself through the house like a hint of spring in February.

These domestic upheavals followed always the same course, and Anna had learnt to suffer the later stages of them with calmness and even with impassivity. Henry Mynors had not called. She supposed that her father had expected him to call for the answer which she had forgot-ten to give him, and she had a hope that he would come in the afternoon: once again she had the idea that something definite and satisfactory might result if she could only see him—that she might, as it were, gather inspiration from the mere sight of his face. After dinner, while the girls were washing the dinner things in the scullery, Agnes's quick ear caught the sound of voices in the parlour. They listened. Mynors had come. Mr. Tellwright must have seen him from the front window and opened the door to him before he could ring.

* *Terrick:* a corruption of Tellwright.

" It's him," said Agnes, excited.

" Who? " Anna asked self-consciously.

" Mr. Mynors, of course," said the child sharply, making it quite plain that this affectation could not impose on her for a single instant.

" Anna! " It was Mr. Tellwright's summons, through the parlour window. She dried her hands, doffed her apron, and went to the parlour, animated by a thousand fears and expectations. Why was she to be included in the colloquy?

Mynors rose at her entrance and greeted her with conspicuous deference, a deference which made her feel ashamed.

" Hum! " the old man growled, but he was obviously content. " I gave Anna a message for ye yesterday, Mr. Mynors, but her forgot to deliver it, wench-like. Ye might ha' been saved th' trouble o' calling. Now as ye're here, I've summat for tell ye. It 'll be Anna's money as 'll go into that concern o' yours. I've none by me; in fact, I'm a'most fast for brass, but her 'll have as near two thousand as makes no matter in a month's time, and her says her 'll go in wi' you on th' strength o' my recommendation."

This speech was evidently a perfect surprise for Henry Mynors. For a moment he seemed to be at a loss; then his face gave candid expression to a feeling of intense pleasure.

" You know all about this business then, Miss Mynors? "
She blushed. " Father has told me something about it,"

" And you are willing to be my partner? "

" Nay, I did na' say that," Tellwright interrupted. " It 'll be Anna's money, but i' my name."

" I see," said Mynors gravely. " But if it is Miss Anna's money, why should not she be the partner? " He offered one of his courtly diplomatic smiles.

" Oh—but——" Anna began in deprecation.

Tellwright laughed. " Ay!" he said, " Why not? It 'll be experience for th' lass."

" Just so," said Mynors.

Anna stood silent, like a child who is being talked about. There was a pause.

" Would you care for that arrangement, Miss Tell-wright? "

" Oh, yes!" she said.

" I shall try to justify your confidence. I needn't say that I think you and your father will have no reason to be disappointed. Two thousand pounds is of course only a trifle to you, but it is a great deal to me, and—and——" He hesitated. Anna did not surmise that he was too much moved by the sight of her and the situation to continue, but this was the fact.

" There's nobbut one point, Mr. Mynors," Tellwright said bluntly, " and that's the interest on th' capital, as must be deducted before reckoning profits. Us must have six per cent."

" But I thought we had settled it at five," said Mynors with sudden firmness.

" We 'n settled as you shall have five on your fifteen

hundred," the miser replied with imperturbable audacity, " but us mun have our six."

" I certainly thought we had thrashed that out fully, and agreed that the interest should be the same on each side." Mynors was alert and defensive.

" Nay, young man. Us mun have our six. We're takkin' a risk."

Mynors pressed his lips together. He was taken at a disadvantage. Mr. Tellwright, with unscrupulous cleverness, had utilised the effect on Mynors of his daughter's presence to regain a position from which the younger man had definitely ousted him a few days before. Mynors was annoyed, but he gave no sign of his annoyance.

" Very well," he said at length, with a private smile at Anna, to indicate that it was out of regard for her that he yielded.

Mr. Tellwright made no pretence of concealing his satisfaction. He, too, smiled at Anna sardonically : the last vestige of the morning's irritation vanished in a glow of triumph.

" I'm afraid I must go," said Mynors, looking at his watch. " There is a service at chapel at three. Our revivalist came down with Mrs. Sutton to look over the works this morning, and I told him I should be at his service. So I must. You coming, Mr. Tellwright? "

" Nay, my lad. I'm 'owd enough to leave it to young uns."

Anna forced her courage to the verge of rashness, moved by a swift impulse.

" Will you wait one minute? " she said to Mynors. " I am going to the service. If I'm late back, father, Agnes will see to the tea. Don't wait for me." She looked him straight in the face. It was one of the bravest acts of her life. After the episode of breakfast, to suggest a procedure which might entail any risk upon another meal was absolutely heroic. Tellwright glanced away from his daughter, and at Mynors. Anna hurried upstairs.

" Who's thy lawyer, Mr. Mynors? " Tellwright asked.

" Dane," said Mynors.

" That 'll be convenient. Dane does my bit o' business, too. I'll see him, and make a bargain wi' him for th' partnership deed. He always works by contract for me. I've no patience wi' six-and-eightpences."

Mynors assented.

" You must come down some afternoon and look over the works," he said to Anna as they were walking down Trafalgar Road towards chapel.

" I should like to," Anna replied. " I've never been over a works in my life."

" No? You are going to be a partner in the best works of its size in Bursley," Mynors said enthusiastically.

" I'm glad of that," she smiled, " for I do believe I own the worst."

" What—Price's, do you mean? "

She nodded.

" Ah!" he exclaimed, and seemed to be thinking. " I wasn't sure whether that belonged to you or your father. I'm afraid it isn't quite the best of properties. But perhaps I'd better say nothing about that. We had a grand meeting last night. Our little cornet-player quite lived up to his reputation, don't you think?"

"Quite," she said faintly.

"You enjoyed the meeting?"

"No," she blurted out, dismayed, but resolute to be honest.

There was a silence.

"But you were at the early prayer-meeting this morning, I hear."

She said nothing while they took a dozen paces, and then murmured, "Yes."

Their eyes met for a second, hers full of trouble.

"Perhaps," he said at length, "perhaps—excuse me saying this—but you may be expecting too much——"

"Well?" She encouraged him, prepared now to finish what had been begun.

"I mean," he said earnestly, "that I—we—cannot promise you any sudden change of feeling, any sudden relief and certainty, such as some people experience. At least, I never had it. What is called conversion can happen in various ways. It is a question of living, of constant endeavour, with the example of Christ always before us. It need not always be a sudden wrench, you know, from the world. Perhaps you have been expecting too much," he repeated, as though offering balm with that phrase.

She thanked him sincerely, but not with her lips, only with the heart. He had revealed to her an avenue of release from a situation which had seemed on all sides fatally closed. She sprang eagerly towards it. She realised afresh how frightful was the dilemma from which there was now a hope of escape, and she was grateful accordingly. Before, she had not dared steadily to face its terrors. She wondered that even her father's displeasure or the project of the partnership had been able to divert her from the plight of her soul. Putting these mundane things firmly behind her, she concentrated the activities of her brain on that idea of Christ-like living, day by day, hour by hour, of a gradual aspiration towards Christ and thereby an ultimate arrival at the state of being saved. This she thought she might accomplish; this gave opportunity of immediate effort, dispensing with the necessity of an impossible violent spiritual metamorphosis. They did not speak again until they had reached the gates of the chapel, when Mynors, who had to enter the choir from the back, bade her a quiet adieu. Anna enjoyed the service, which passed smoothly and uneventfully. At a Revival, night is the time of ecstasy and fervour and salvation; in the afternoon one must be content with preparatory praise and prayer.

That evening, while father and daughters sat in the parlour after supper, there was a ring at the door. Agnes ran to open, and found Willie Price. It had begun to rain, and the visitor, his jacket-collar turned up, was wet and draggled. Agnes left him on the mat and ran back to the parlour.

"Young Mr. Price wants to see you, father."

Tellwright motioned to her to shut the door.

" You'd best see him, Anna," he said. " It's none my business."

" But what has he come about, father? "

" That note as I sent down this morning. I told owd Titus as he mun pay us twenty pun' on Monday morning certain, or us should distrain. Them as can pay ten pun, especially in bank notes, can pay twenty pun, and thirty."

" And suppose he says he can't? "

" Tell him he must. I've figured it out and changed my mind about that works. Owd Titus isna' done for yet, though he's getting on that road. Us can screw another fifty out o' him; that 'll only leave six months' rent owing; then us can turn him out. He'll go bankrupt; us can claim for our rent afore th' other creditors, and us 'll have a hundred or a hundred and twenty in hand towards doing the owd place up a bit for a new tenant."

" Make him bankrupt, father? " Anna exclaimed. It was the only part of the ingenious scheme which she had understood.

" Ay ! " he said laconically.

" But——" (Would Christ have driven Titus Price into the bankruptcy court?)

" If he pays, well and good."

" Hadn't you better see Mr. William, father? "

" Whose property is it, mine or thine? " Tellwright growled. His good humour was still precarious, insecurely re-established, and Anna obediently left the room. After all, she said to herself, a debt is a debt, and honest people pay what they owe.

It was in an uncomplaisant tone that Anna invited Willie Price to the front parlour: nervousness always made her seem harsh, and moreover she had not the trick of hiding firmness under suavity.

"Will you come this way, Mr. Price?"

"Yes," he said with ingratiating, eager compliance. Dusk was falling, and the room in shadow. She forgot to ask him to take a chair, so they both stood up during the interview.

"A grand meeting we had last night," he began, twisting his hat. "I saw you there, Miss Tellwright."

"Yes."

"Yes. There was a splendid muster of teachers. I wanted to be at the prayer-meeting this morning, but couldn't get away. Did you happen to go, Miss Tellwright?"

She saw that he knew she had been present, and gave him another curt monosyllable. She would have liked to be kind to him, to reassure him, to make him happy and comfortable, so ludicrous and touching were his efforts after a social urbanity which should appease; but, just as much as he, she was unskilled in the subtle arts of converse.

"Yes," he continued, "and I was anxious to be at to-night's meeting, but the dad asked me to come up here. He said I'd better." That term, "the dad," uttered in William's slow, drawling voice, seemed to show Titus Price in a new light to Anna, as a human creature loved, not as a mere gross physical organism: the effect was quite surprising. William went on: " Can I see your father, Miss Tellwright? "

" Is it about the rent? "

" Yes," he said.

" Well, if you will tell me——"

" Oh! I beg pardon," he said quickly. " Of course I know it's your property, but I thought Mr. Tellwright always saw after it for you. It was he that wrote that letter this morning, wasn't it? "

" Yes," Anna replied. She did not explain the situation.

" You insist on another twenty pounds on Monday? "

" Yes," she said.

" We paid ten last Monday."

" But there is still over a hundred owing."

" I know, but—oh, Miss Tellwright, you mustn't be hard on us. Trade's bad."

" It says in the ' Signal ' that trade is improving," she interrupted sharply.

" Does it? " he said. " But look at prices; they're cut till there's no profit left. I assure you, Miss Tellwright, my father and me are having a hard struggle. Everything's against us, and the works in particular, as *you* know."

His tone was so earnest, so pathetic, that tears of compassion almost rose to her eyes as she looked at those simple naïve blue eyes of his. His lanky figure and clumsily-fitting clothes, his feeble placatory smile, the twitching movements of his long hands, all contributed to the effect of his defencelessness. She thought of the text: " Blessed are the meek," and saw in a flash the deep truth of it. Here were she and her father, rich, powerful, autocratic; and there were Willie Price and his father, commercial hares hunted by hounds of creditors, hares that turned in plaintive appeal to those greedy jaws for mercy. An yet, she, a hound, envied at that moment the hares. Blessed are the meek, blessed are the failures, blessed are the stupid, for they, unknown to themselves, have a grace which is denied to the haughty, the successful, and the wise. The very repulsiveness of old Titus, his underhand methods, his insincerities, only served to increase her sympathy for the pair. How could Titus help being himself any more than Henry Mynors could help being himself? And that idea led her to think of the prospective partnership, destined by every favourable sign to brilliant success, and to contrast it with the ignoble and forlorn undertaking in Edward Street.

She tried to discover some method of soothing the young man's fears, of being considerate to him without injuring her father's scheme.

" If you will pay what you owe," she said, " we will spend it all, every penny, on improving the works."

" Miss Tellwright," he answered with fatal emphasis, " we cannot pay."

Ah! She wished to follow Christ day by day, hour by hour—constantly to endeavour after saintlinesss. What was she to do? Left to herself, she might have said in a burst of impulsive generosity, " I forgive you all arrears. Start afresh." But her father had to be reckoned with. . .

" How much do you think you *can* pay on Monday? "
she asked coldly.

At that moment her father entered the room. His first
act was to light the gas. Willie Price's eyes blinked at
the glare, as though he were trembling before the anticipated decree of this implacable old man. Anna's heart
beat with sympathetic apprehension. Tellwright shook
hands grimly with the youth, who restated hurriedly what
he had said to Anna.

" It's o' this'n,' the old man began with finality, and
stopped. Anna caught a glance from him dismissing her.
She went out in silence. On the Monday Titus Price paid
another twenty pounds.

## VII: THE SEWING MEETING

ON an afternoon ten days later, Mr. Sutton's coachman, Barrett by name, arrived at Ephraim Tellwright's back-door with a note. The Tellwrights were having tea. The note could be seen in his enormous hand, and Agnes went out.

" An answer, if you please, miss," he said to her, touching his hat, and giving a pull to the leathern belt which, surrounding his waist, alone seemed to hold his frame together. Agnes, much impressed, took the note. She had never before seen that resplendent automaton apart from the equipage which he directed. Always afterwards, Barrett formally saluted her in the streets, affording her thus, every time, a thrilling moment of delicious joy.

" A letter, and there's an answer, and he's waiting," she cried, running into the parlour.

" Less row ! " said her father. " Here, give it me."

" It's for Miss Tellwright—that's Anna, isn't it? Oh! Scent ! " She put the grey envelope to her nose like a flower.

Anna, secretly as excited as her sister, opened the note and read: " Lansdowne House, Wednesday. Dear Miss Tellwright,—Mother gives tea to the Sunday-school Sewing Meeting here *to-morrow*. Will you give us the pleasure of your company? I do not think you have been to any of the S. S. S. meetings yet, but we should all be glad to see you and to have your assistance. Everyone is working very hard for the Autumn Bazaar, and mother has set her mind on the Sunday-school stall being the best. Do come, will you? Excuse this short notice. Yours sincerely, BEATRICE SUTTON. P.S.—We begin at 3.30."

" They want me to go to their sewing meeting to-morrow," she explained timidly to her father, pushing the note towards him across the table. " Must I go, father? "

" What dost ask me for? Please thysen. I've nowt do wi' it."

" I don't want to go——"

" Oh! Sis, *do* go," Agnes pleaded.

" Perhaps I'd better," she agreed, but with the misgivings of diffidence. " I haven't a rag to wear. I really must have a new dress, father, at once."

" Hast forgotten as that there coachman's waiting? " he remarked curtly.

" Shall I run and tell him you'll go? " Agnes suggested. " It 'll be splendid for you."

" Don't be silly, dear. I must write."

" Well, write then," said the child energetically. " I'll get you the ink and paper." She flew about and hovered over Anna while the answer to the invitation was being written. Anna made her reply as short and simple as possible, and then tendered it for her father's inspection. " Will that do? "

He pretended to be nonchalant, but in fact he was somewhat interested.

"Thou's forgotten to put th' date in," was all his comment, and he threw the note back.

"I've put Wednesday."

"That's not the date."

"Does it matter? Beatrice Sutton only puts Wednesday."

His response was to walk out of the room.

"Is he vexed?" Agnes asked anxiously. There had been a whole week of almost perfect amenity.

The next day at half-past three Anna, having put on her best clothes, was ready to start. She had seen almost nothing of social life, and the prospect of taking part in this entertainment at the Suttons' filled her with trepidation. Should she arrive early, in which case she would have to talk more, or late, in which case there would be the ordeal of entering a crowded room? She could not decide. She went into her father's bedroom, whose window overlooked Trafalgar Road, and saw from behind a curtain that small groups of ladies were continually passing up the street to disappear into Alderman Sutton's house. Most of the women she recognised; others she knew but vaguely by sight. Then the stream ceased, and suddenly she heard the kitchen clock strike four. She ran downstairs— Agnes, swollen by importance, was carrying her father's tea into the parlour—and hastened out by the back way. In another moment she was at the Suttons' front-door. A servant in black alpaca, with white wristbands, cap, streamers, and embroidered apron (each article a *dernier cri* from

Bostock's great shop at Hanbridge), asked her in a subdued and respectful tone to step within. Externally there had been no sign of the unusual, but once inside the house Anna found it a humming hive of activity. Women laden with stuffs and implements were crossing the picture-hung hall, their footsteps noiseless on the thick rugs which lay about in rich confusion. On either hand was an open door, and from each door came the sound of many eager voices. Beyond these doors a broad staircase rose majestically to unseen heights, closing the vista of the hall. As the servant was demanding Anna's name, Beatrice Sutton, radiant and gorgeous, came with a rush out of the room to the left, the dining-room, and, taking her by both hands, kissed her.

"My dear, we thought you were never coming. Everyone's here, except the men, of course. Come along upstairs and take your things off. I'm so glad you've kept your promise."

"Did you think I should break it?" said Anna, as they ascended the easy gradient of the stairs.

"Oh, no, my dear! But you're such a shy little bird."

The conception of herself as a shy little bird amused Anna. By a curious chain of ideas she came to wonder who could clean those stairs the better, she or this gay and flitting butterfly in a pale green tea-gown. Beatrice led the way to a large bedroom, crammed with furniture and knick-knacks. There were three mirrors in this spacious apartment—one in the wardrobe, a cheval-glass, and a third over the mantelpiece; the frame of the last was bordered with photographs.

" This is my room," said Beatrice. " Will you put your things on the bed? " The bed was already laden with hats, bonnets, jackets, and wraps.

" I hope your mother won't give me anything fancy to do," Anna said. " I'm no good at anything except plain sewing."

" Oh, that's all right," Beatrice answered carelessly. " It's all plain sewing." She drew a cardboard box from her pocket, and offered it to Anna. " Here, have one." They were choclate creams.

" Thanks," said Anna, taking one. Aren't they very expensive? I've never seen any like these before."

" Oh! Just ordinary. Four shillings a pound. Papa buys them for me: I simply dote on them. I love to eat them in bed, if I can't sleep." Beatrice made these statements with her mouth full. " Don't you adore chocolates? " she added.

" I don't know," Anna lamely replied. " Yes, I like them." She only adored her sister, and perhaps God; and this was the first time she had tasted chocolate.

" I couldn't *live* without them," said Beatrice. " Your hair is lovely. I never saw such a brown. What wash do you use? "

" Wash? " Anna repeated.

" Yes, don't you put anything on it? "

" No, never."

" Well! Take care you don't lose it, that's all. Now, will you come and have just a peep at my studio—where I paint, you know? I'd like you to see it before we go down."

They proceeded to a small room on the second floor, with a sloping ceiling and a dormer window.

" I'm obliged to have this room," Beatrice explained, " because it's the only one in the house with a north light, and of course you can't do without that. How do you like it? "

Anna said that she liked it very much.

The walls of the room were hung with various odd curtains of Eastern design. Attached somehow to these curtains some coloured plates, bits of pewter, and a few fans were hung high in apparently precarious suspense. Lower down on the walls were pictures and sketches, chiefly unframed, of flowers, fishes, loaves of bread, candlesticks, mugs, oranges and tea-trays. On an immense easel in the middle of the room was an unfinished portrait of a man.

" Who's that? " Anna asked, ignorant of those rules of caution which are observed by the practised frequenter of studios.

" Don't you know? " Beatrice exclaimed, shocked. " That's papa; I'm doing his portrait; he sits in that chair there. The silly old master at the school won't let me draw from life yet—he keeps me to the antique—so I said to myself I would study the living model at home. I'm dreadfully in earnest about it, you know—I really am. Mother says I work far too long up here."

Anna was unable to perceive that the picture bore any resemblance to Alderman Sutton, except in the matter of the aldermanic robe, which she could now trace beneath the portrait's neck. The studies on the wall pleased her much better. Their realism amazed her. One could make out not only that here, for instance, was a fish—there was no doubt that it was a halibut; the solid roundness of the oranges and the glitter on the tea-trays seemed miraculously achieved. " Have you actually done all these? " she asked, in genuine admiration. " I think they're splendid."

" Oh, yes, they're all mine; they're only still-life studies," Beatrice said contemptuously of them, but she was nevertheless flattered.

" I see now that that *is* Mr. Sutton," Anna said, pointing to the easel-picture.

" Yes, it's pa right enough. But I'm sure I'm boring you. Let's go down now, or perhaps we shall catch it from mother."

As Anna, in the wake of Beatrice, entered the drawing-room, a dozen or more women glanced at her with keen curiosity, and the even flow of conversation ceased for a moment, to be immediately resumed. In the centre of the room, with her back to the fire-place, Mrs. Sutton was seated at a square table, cutting out. Although the afternoon was warm, she had a white woollen wrap over her shoulders; for the rest she was attired in plain black silk, with a large stuff apron containing a pocket for scissors and chalk. She jumped up with the activity of which Beatrice had inherited a part, and greeted Anna, kissing her heartily.

" How are you, my dear? So pleased you have come." The time-worn phrases came from her thin, nervous lips full of a sincere and kindly welcome.  Her wrinkled face broke into a warm, life-giving smile.  " Beatrice, find Miss Anna a chair."   There were two chairs in the bay ‚ᶜ the window, and one of them was occupied by Miss Dickinson, whom Anna slightly knew.  The other, being empty, was assigned to the late-comer.

" Now you want something to do, I suppose," said Beatrice.

" Please."

" Mother, let Miss Tellwright have something to get on with at once.  She has a lot of time to make up."

Mrs. Sutton, who had sat down again, smiled across at Anna.  " Let me see, now, what can we give her? "

" There's several of those boys' nightgowns ready tacked," said Miss Dickinson, who was stitching at a boy's nightgown.  " Here's one half-finished," and she picked up an inchoate garment from the floor.  " Perhaps Miss Tellwright wouldn't mind finishing it."

" Yes, I will do my best at it," said Anna.

The thoughtless girl had arrived at the sewing meeting without needles or thimbles or scissors, but one lady or another supplied these deficiencies, and soon she was at work.  She stitched her best and her hardest, with head bent, and all her wits concentrated on the task.  Most of the others seemed to be doing likewise, though not to the detriment of conversation.   Beatrice sank down on a stool near her mother, and, threading a needle with coloured silk, took up a long piece of elaborate embroidery.

The general subjects of talk were the Revival, now over,

with a superb record of seventy saved souls, the school-treat shortly to occur, the summer holidays, the fashions, and the change of ministers which would take place in August. The talkers were the wives and daughters of tradesmen and small manufacturers, together with a few girls of a somewhat lower status, employed in shops: it was for the sake of these latter that the sewing meeting was always fixed for the weekly half-holiday. The splendour of Mrs. Sutton's drawing-room was a little dazzling to most of the guests, and Mrs. Sutton herself seemed scarcely of a piece with it. The fact was that the luxury of the abode was mainly due to Alderman Sutton's inability to refuse anything to his daughter, whose tastes lay in the direction of rich draperies, large or quaint chairs, occasional tables, dwarf screens, hand-painted mirrors, and an opulence of bric-à-brac. The hand of Beatrice might be perceived everywhere, even in the position of the piano, whose back, adorned with carelessly-flung silks and photographs, was turned away from the wall. The pictures on the wall had been acquired gradually by Mr. Sutton at auction sales: it was commonly held that he had an excellent taste in pictures, and that his daughter's aptitude for the arts came from him, and not from her mother. The gilt clock and side pieces on the mantelpiece were also peculiarly Mr. Sutton's, having been publicly presented to him by the directors of a local building society of which he had been chairman for many years.

Less intimidated by all this unexampled luxury than she was reassured by the atmosphere of combined and homely effort, the lowliness of several of her companions, and the kind, simple face of Mrs. Sutton, Anna quickly began to feel at ease. She paused in her work, and, glancing around her, happened to catch the eye of Miss Dickinson, who offered a remark about the weather. Miss Dickinson was head-assistant at a draper's in St. Luke's Square, and a pillar of the Sunday-school, which Sunday by Sunday and year by year had watched her develop from a rosy-cheeked girl into a confirmed spinster with sallow and warted face. Miss Dickinson supported her mother, and was a pattern to her sex. She was lovable, but had never been loved. She would have made an admirable wife and mother, but fate had decided that this material was to be wasted. Miss Dickinson found compensation for the rigour of destiny in gossip as innocent as indiscreet. It was said that she had a tongue.

" I hear," said Miss Dickinson, lowering her contralto voice to a confidential tone, " that you are going into partnership with Mr. Mynors, Miss Tellwright."

The suddenness of the attack took Anna by surprise. Her first defensive impulse was boldly to deny the statement, or at the least to say that it was premature. A fortnight ago, under similar circumstances, she would not have hesitated to do so. But for more than a week Anna had been " leading a new life," which chiefly meant a meticulous avoidance of the sins of speech. Never to deviate from the truth, never to utter an unkind or a thoughtless word, under whatever provocation: these were two of her self-imposed rules. " Yes," she answered Miss Dickinson, " I am."

"Rather a novelty, isn't it?" Miss Dickinson smiled amiably.

"I don't know," said Anna. "It's only a business arrangement; father arranged it. Really I have nothing to do with it, and I had no idea that people were talking about it."

"Oh! Of course I should never breathe a syllable," Miss Dickinson said with emphasis. "I make a practice of never talking about other people's affairs. I always find that best, don't you? But I happened to hear it mentioned in the shop."

"It's very funny how things get abroad, isn't it?" said Anna.

"Yes, indeed," Miss Dickinson concurred. "Mr. Mynors hasn't been to our sewing meetings for quite a long time, but I expect he'll turn up to-day."

Anna took thought. "Is this a sort of special meeting, then?"

"Oh, not at all. But we all of us said just now, while you were upstairs, that he would be sure to come," Miss Dickinson's features, skilful in innuendo, conveyed that which was too delicate for utterance. Anna said nothing.

"You see a good deal of him at your house, don't you?" Miss Dickinson continued.

"He comes sometimes to see father on business," Anna replied sharply, breaking one of her rules.

"Oh! Of course I meant that. You didn't suppose I meant anything else, did you?" Miss Dickinson smiled pleasantly. She was thirty-five years of age. Twenty of those years had passed in a desolating routine; she had existed in the midst of life and never lived; she knew no finer joy than that which she at that moment experienced.

Again Anna offered no reply. The door opened, and every eye was centred on the stately Mrs. Clayton Vernon, who, with Mrs. Banks, the minister's wife, was in charge of the other half of the sewing party in the dining-room. Mrs. Clayton Vernon had heroic proportions, a nose which everyone admitted to be aristocratic, exquisite tact, and the calm consciousness of social superiority. In Bursley she was a great lady; her instincts were those of a great lady; and she would have been a great lady no matter to what sphere her God had called her. She had abundant white hair, and wore a flowered purple silk, in the antique taste.

"Beatrice, my dear," she began, "you have deserted us."

"Have I, Mrs. Vernon?" the girl answered with involuntary deference. "I was just coming in."

"Well, I am sent as a deputation from the other room to ask you to sing something."

"I'm very busy, Mrs. Vernon. I shall never get this mantel-cloth finished in time."

"We shall all work better for a little music," Mrs. Clayton Vernon urged. "Your voice is a precious gift, and should be used for the benefit of all. We entreat, my dear girl."

Beatrice arose from the footstool and dropped her embroidery.

" Thank you," said Mrs. Clayton Vernon. " If both doors are left open we shall hear nicely."

" What would you like? " Beatrice asked.

" I once heard you sing 'Nazareth,' and I shall never forget it. Sing that. It will do us all good."

Mrs. Clayton Vernon departed with the large movement of an argosy, and Beatrice sat down to the piano and removed her bracelets. " The accompaniment is simply frightful towards the end," she said, looking at Anna with a grimace. " Excuse mistakes."

During the song, Mrs. Sutton beckoned with her finger to Anna to come and occupy the stool vacated by Beatrice. Glad to leave the vicinity of Miss Dickinson, Anna obeyed, creeping on tiptoe across the intervening space. " I thought I would like to have you near me, my dear," she whispered maternally. When Beatrice had sung the song and somehow executed that accompaniment which has terrorised whole multitudes of drawing-room pianists, there was a great deal of applause from both rooms. Mrs. Sutton bent down and whispered in Anna's ear: " Her voice has been very well trained, has it not? " " Yes, very," Anna replied. But, though " Nazareth " had seemed to her wonderful, she had neither understood it nor enjoyed it. She tried to like it, but the effect of it on her was bizarre rather than pleasing.

Shortly after half-past five the gong sounded for tea, and the ladies, bidden by Mrs. Sutton, unanimously thronged into the hall and towards a room at the back of the house. Beatrice came and took Anna by the arm. As they were crossing the hall there was a ring at the door. "There's father—and Mr. Banks, too," Beatrice exclaimed, opening to them. Everyone in the vicinity, animated suddenly by this appearance of the male sex, turned with welcoming smiles. "A greeting to you all," the minister ejaculated with formal suavity as he removed his low hat. The Alderman beamed a rather absent-minded goodwill on the entire company, and said: "Well! I see we're just in time for tea." Then he kissed his daughter, and she accepted from him his hat and stick. "Miss Tellwright, pa," Beatrice said, drawing Anna forward: he shook hands with her heartily, emerging for a moment from the benignant dream in which he seemed usually to exist.

That air of being rapt by some inward vision, common in very old men, probably signified nothing in the case of William Sutton: it was a habitual pose into which he had perhaps unconsciously fallen. But people connected it with his humble archæological, geological, and zoölogical hobbies, which had sprung from his membership of the Five Towns Field Club, and which most of his acquaintances regarded with amiable secret disdain. At a school-treat once, held at a popular rural resort, he had taken some of the teachers to a cave, and pointing out the wave-like formation of its roof, had told them that this particular phenomenon had actually been caused by waves of the sea. The discovery, valid enough and perfectly substantiated by an enquiry into the levels, was extremely creditable to the amateur geologist, but it seriously impaired his reputation among the Wesleyan community as a shrewd man of the world. Few believed the statement, or even tried to believe it, and nearly all thenceforth looked on him as a man who must be humoured in his harmless hallucinations and inexplicable curiosities. On the other hand, the collection of arrowheads, Roman pottery, fossils, and birds' eggs which he had given to the Museum in the Wedgwood Institution was always viewed with municipal pride.

The tea-room opened by a large French window into a conservatory, and a table was laid down the whole length of the room and the conservatory. Mr. Sutton sat at one end and the minister at the other, but neither Mrs. Sutton nor Beatrice occupied a distinctive place. The ancient clumsy custom of having tea-urns on the table itself had been abolished by Beatrice, who had read in a paper that carving was now never done at table, but by a neatly-dressed parlour-maid at the sideboard. Consequently the tea-urns were exiled to the sideboard, and the tea dispensed by a couple of maids. Thus, as Beatrice had explained to her mother, the hostess was left free to devote herself to the social arts. The board was richly spread with fancy breads and cakes, jams of Mrs. Sutton's own celebrated preserving, diverse sandwiches compiled by Beatrice, and one or two large examples of the famous Bursley pork-pie. Numerous as the company was, several chairs remained empty after everyone was seated. Anna found herself again next to Miss Dickinson, and five places from the minister, in the conservatory. Beatrice and her mother were higher up, in the room. Grace was sung, by request of

Mrs. Sutton.  At first, silence prevailed among the guests, and the enquiries of the maids about milk and sugar were almost painfully audible.  Then Mr. Banks, glancing up the long vista of the table and pretending to descry some object in the distance, called out:

" Worthy host, I doubt not you are there, but I can only see you with the eye of faith."

At this all laughed, and a natural ease was established. The minister and Mrs. Clayton Vernon, who sat on his right, exchanged badinage on the merits and demerits of pork-pies, and their neighbours formed an appreciative audience.  Then there was a sharp ring at the front door, and one of the maids went out.

" Didn't I tell you? " Miss Dickinson whispered to Anna.

" What? " asked Anna.

" That he would come to-day—Mr. Mynors, I mean."

" Who can that be? " Mrs. Sutton's voice was heard from the room.

" I dare say it's Henry, mother," Beatrice answered.

Mynors entered, joyous and self-possessed, a white rose in his coat: he shook hands with Mr. and Mrs. Sutton, sent a greeting down the table to Mr. Banks and Mrs. Clayton Vernon, and offered a general apology for being late.

" Sit here," said Beatrice to him  sharply, indicating a chair between Mrs. Banks and herself.  " Mrs. Banks has a word to say to you about the singing of that anthem last Sunday."

Mynors made some laughing rejoinder, and the voices sank so that Anna could not catch what was said.

" That's a new frock that Miss Sutton is wearing to-day," Miss Dickinson remarked in an undertone.

" It looks new," Anna agreed.

" Do you like it? "

" Yes. Don't you? "

" Hum! Yes. It was made at Brunt's at Hanbridge. It's quite the fashion to go there now," said Miss Dickinson, and added almost inaudibly, " She's put it on for Mr. Mynors. You saw how she saved that chair for him."

Anna made no reply.

" Did you know they were engaged once? " Miss Dickinson resumed.

" No," said Anna.

" At least people *said* they were. It was all over the town—oh! let me see, three years ago."

" I had not heard," said Anna.

During the rest of the meal she said little. On some natures Miss Dickinson's gossip had the effect of bringing them to silence. Anna had not seen Mynors since the previous Sunday, and now she was apparently unperceived by him. He talked gaily with Beatrice and Mrs. Banks: that group was a centre of animation. Anna envied their ease of manner, their smooth and sparkling flow of conversation. She had the sensation of feeling vulgar, clumsy, tongue-tied; Mynors and Beatrice possessed something which she would never possess. So they had been engaged! But had they? Or was it an idle rumour, manufactured by one who spent her life in such creations? Anna was conscious of misgivings. She had despised Beatrice once,

but now it seemed that, after all, Beatrice was the natural
equal of Henry Mynors. Was it more likely that Mynors
or she, Anna, should be mistaken in Beatrice? That
Beatrice had generous instincts she was sure. Anna lost
confidence in herself; she felt humbled, out-of-place, and
shamed.

" If our hostess and the company will kindly excuse me,"
said the minister with a pompous air, looking at his watch,
" I must go. I have an important appointment, or an
appointment which some people think is important."

He got up and made various adieux. The elaborate
meal, complex with fifty dainties, each of which had to be
savoured, was not nearly over. The parson stopped in his
course up the room to speak with Mrs. Sutton. After he
had shaken hands with her, he caught the admired violet
eyes of his slim wife, a lady of independent fortune whom
the wives of circuit stewards found it difficult to please in
the matter of furniture, and who, despite her forty years,
still kept something of the pose of a spoiled beauty. As
a minister's spouse this languishing, but impeccable and
invariably correct, dame was unique even in the experience
of Mrs. Clayton Vernon.

" Shall you not be home early, Rex? " she asked in the
tone of a young wife lounging amid the delicate odours
of a boudoir.

" My love," he replied with the stern fixity of a histrionic
martyr, " did you ever know me have a free evening? "

The Alderman accompanied his pastor to the door.

After tea Mynors was one of the first to leave the room,

and Anna one of the last, but he accosted her in the hall, on the way back to the drawing-room, and asked how she was, and how Agnes was, with such deference and sincerity of regard for herself and everything that was hers that she could not fail to be impressed. Her sense of humiliation and of uncertainty was effaced by a single word, a single glance. Uplifted by a delicious reassurance, she passed into the drawing-room, expecting him to follow: strange to say, he did not do so. Work was resumed, but with less ardour than before. It was in fact impossible to be strenuously diligent after one of Mrs. Sutton's teas, and in every heart, save those which beat over the most perfect and vigorous digestive organs, there was a feeling of repentance. The building society's clock on the mantelpiece intoned seven: all expressed surprise at the lateness of the hour, and Mrs. Clayton Vernon, pleading fatigue after her recent indisposition, quietly departed. As soon as she had gone, Anna said to Mrs. Sutton that she too must go.

" Why, my dear? " Mrs. Sutton asked.

" I shall be needed at home," Anna replied.

" Ah! In that case—I will come upstairs with you, my dear," said Mrs. Sutton.

When they were in the bedroom, Mrs. Sutton suddenly clasped her hand. " How is it with you, dear Anna? " she said, gazing anxiously into the girl's eyes. Anna knew what she meant, but made no answer. " Is it well? " the earnest old woman asked.

" I hope so," said Anna, averting her eyes. " I am trying."

Mrs. Sutton kissed her almost passionately. "Ah! my dear," she exclaimed with an impulsive gesture, "I am glad, so glad. I did so want to have a word with you. You must 'lean hard,' as Miss Havergal says. 'Lean hard' on Him. Do not be afraid." And then, changing her tone: "You are looking pale, Anna. You want a holiday. We shall be going to the Isle of Man in August or September. Would your father let you come with us?"

"I don't know," said Anna. She knew, however, that he would not. Nevertheless the suggestion gave her much pleasure.

"We must see about that later," said Mrs. Sutton, and they went downstairs.

"I must say good-bye to Beatrice. Where is she?" Anna said in the hall. One of the servants directed them to the dining-room. The Alderman and Henry Mynors were looking together at a large photogravure of Sant's "The Soul's Awakening," which Mr. Sutton had recently bought, and Beatrice was exhibiting her embroidery to a group of ladies: sundry stitchers were scattered about, including Miss Dickinson.

"It is a great picture—a picture that makes you think," Henry was saying seriously, and the Alderman, feeling as the artist might have felt, was obviously flattered by this sagacious praise.

Anna said good-night to Miss Dickinson and then to Beatrice. Mynors, hearing the words, turned round. "Well, I must go. Good-evening," he said suddenly to the astonished Alderman.

" What?   Now? " the latter enquired, scarcely pleased
to find that Mynors could tear himself away from the picture with so little difficulty.

" Yes."

" Good-night, Mr. Mynors," said Anna.

" If I may, I will walk down with you," Mynors imperturbably answered.

It was one of those dramatic moments which arrive without the slightest warning.   The gleam of joyous satisfaction in Miss Dickinson's eyes showed that she alone had
foreseen this declaration.   For a declaration it was, and a
formal declaration.   Mynors stood there calm, confident
with masculine superiority, and his glance seemed to say
to those swiftly alert women, whose faces could not disguise
a thrilling excitation: " Yes.   Let all know that I, Henry
Mynors, the desired of all, am honourably captive to this
shy and perfect creature, who is blushing because I have
said what I have said."   Even the Alderman forgot his
photogravure.   Beatrice hurriedly resumed her explanation
of the embroidery.

" How did you like the sewing meeting? " Mynors asked
Anna when they were on the pavement.

Anna paused.   " I think Mrs. Sutton is simply a splendid woman," she said enthusiastically.

When, in a moment too far short, they reached Tellwright's house, Mynors, obeying a mutual wish to which
neither had given expression, followed Anna up the side
entry, and so into the yard, where they lingered for a few
seconds.   Old Tellwright could be seen at the extremity

of the long narrow garden—a garden which consisted chiefly
of a grass-plot sown with clothes-props and a narrow
bordering of flower-beds without flowers.    Agnes was
invisible.    The kitchen-door stood ajar, and as this was
the sole means of ingress from the yard, Anna, humming an air, pushed it open and entered, Mynors in
her wake.    They stood on the threshold, happy, hesi-
tating, confused, and looked at the kitchen as at something they had not seen before.    Anna's kitchen
was the only satisfactory apartment in the house.    Its
furniture included a dresser of the simple and dignified
kind which is now assiduously collected by amateurs of
old oak.    It had four long narrow shelves holding plates
and saucers; the cups were hung in a row on small brass
hooks screwed into the fronts of the shelves.    Below the
shelves were three drawers in a line, with brass handles, and
below the drawers was a large recess which held stone jars,
a copper preserving-saucepan, and other receptacles.    Seventy years of continuous polishing by a dynasty of priest-
esses of cleanliness had given to this dresser a rich ripe tone
which the cleverest trade-trickster could not have imitated.
In it was reflected the conscientious labour of generations.
It had a soft and assuaged appearance, as though it had
never been new and could never have been new.    All its
corners and edges had long lost the asperities of manufacture, and its smooth surfaces were marked by slight hollows
similar in spirit to those worn by the naked feet of pilgrims
into the marble steps of a shrine.    The flat portion over
the drawers was scarred with hundreds of scratches, and

yet even all these seemed to be incredibly ancient, and in some distant past to have partaken of the mellowness of the whole. The dark woodwork formed an admirable background for the crockery on the shelves, and a few of the old plates, hand-painted according to some vanished secret in pigments which time could only improve, had the look of relationship by birth to the dresser. There must still be thousands of exactly similar dressers in the kitchens of the people, but they are gradually being transferred to the dining-rooms of curiosity-hunters. To Anna this piece of furniture, which would have made the most taciturn collector vocal with joy, was merely " the dresser." She had always lamented that it contained no cupboard. In front of the fireless range was an old steel kitchen fender with heavy fire-irons. It had in the middle of its flat top a circular lodgment for saucepans, but on this polished disc no saucepan was ever placed. The fender was perhaps as old as the dresser, and the profound depths of its polish served to mitigate somewhat the newness of the patent coal-economising range which Tellwright had had put in when he took the house. On the high mantelpiece were four tall brass candlesticks which, like the dresser, were silently awaiting their apotheosis at the hands of some collector. Beside these were two or three common mustard tins, polished to counterfeit silver, containing spices; also an abandoned coffee-mill and two flat-irons. A grandfather's clock, of oak to match the dresser, stood to the left of the fireplace; it had a very large white dial with a grinning face in the centre. Though it would only run for twenty-four hours, its leisured movement seemed to have the certainty of a natural law, especially to Agnes, for Mr. Tellwright never forgot to wind it before going to bed. Under the window was a plain deal table, with white top and stained legs. Two windsor chairs completed the catalogue of furniture. The glistening floor was of red and black tiles, and in front of the fender lay a list hearthrug, made by attaching innumerable bits of black cloth to a canvas base. On the painted walls were several grocers' almanacs, depicting sailors in the arms of lovers, children crossing brooks, or monks swelling themselves with Gargantuan repasts. Everything in this kitchen was absolutely bright and spotless, as clean as a cat in pattens, except the ceiling, darkened by fumes of gas. Everything was in perfect order, and had the humanised air of use and occupation which nothing but use and occupation can impart to senseless objects. It was a kitchen where, in the housewife's phrase, you might eat off the floor, and to any Bursley matron it would have constituted the highest possible certificate of Anna's character, not only as housewife, but as elder sister—for in her absence Agnes had washed the tea-things and put them away.

" This is the nicest room, I know," said Mynors at length.

" Whatever do you mean? " Anna smiled, incapable, of course, of seeing the place with his eye.

" I mean there is nothing to beat a clean straight kitchen," Mynors replied, " and there never will be. It wants only the mistress in a white apron to make it complete. Do you know, when I came in here the other night, and you were sitting at the table there, I thought the place was like a picture."

"How funny!" said Anna, puzzled but well satisfied. "But won't you come into the parlour?"

The Persian with one ear met them in the lobby, his tail flying, but cautiously sidled upstairs at sight of Mynors. When Anna opened the door of the parlour she saw Agnes seated at the table over her lessons, frowning and preoccupied. Tears were in her eyes.

"Why, what's the matter, Agnes?" she exclaimed.

"Oh! Go away," said the child crossly. "Don't bother."

"But what's the matter? You're crying."

"No, I'm not. I'm doing my sums, and I can't get it— can't——" The child burst into tears just as Mynors entered. His presence was a complete surprise to her. She hid her face in her pinafore, ashamed to be thus caught.

"Where is it?" said Mynors. "Where is this sum that won't come right?" He picked up the slate and examined it while Agnes was finding herself again. "Practice!" he exclaimed. "Has Agnes got as far as practice?" She gave him an instant's glance and murmured "Yes." Before she could shelter her face he had kissed her. Anna was enchanted by his manner, and as for Agnes, she surrendered happily to him at once. He worked the sum, and she copied the figures into her exercise-book. Anna sat and watched.

"Now I must go," said Mynors.

"But surely you'll stay and see father," Anna urged.

"No. I really had not meant to call. Good-night, Agnes." In a moment he was gone out of the room and the house. It was as if, in obedience to a sudden impulse, he had forcibly torn himself away.

"Was *he* at the sewing meeting?" Agnes asked, adding in parenthesis, "I never dreamt he was here, and I was frightfully vexed. I felt such a baby."

"Yes. At least, he came for tea."

"Why did he call here like that?"

"How can I tell?" Anna said. The child looked at her.

"It's awfully queer, isn't it?" she said slowly. "Tell me all about the sewing meeting. Did they have cakes or was it a plain tea? And did you go into Beatrice Sutton's bedroom?"

# VIII: ON THE BANK

ANNA began to receive her July interest and dividends. During a fortnight remittances, varying from a few pounds to a few hundreds of pounds, arrived by post almost daily. They were all addressed to her, since the securities now stood in her own name; and upon her, under the miser's superintendence, fell the new task of entering them in a book and paying them into the Bank. This mysterious begetting of money by money—a strange process continually going forward for her benefit, in various parts of the world, far and near, by means of activities of which she was completely ignorant and would always be completely ignorant—bewildered her and gave her a feeling of its unreality. The elaborate mechanism by which capital yields interest without suffering diminution from its original bulk is one of the commonest phenomena of modern life, and one of the least understood. Many capitalists never grasp it, nor experience the slightest curiosity about it until the mechanism through some defect ceases to revolve. Tellwright was of these; for him the interval between the outlay of capital and the receipt of interest was nothing but an efflux of time: he planted capital as a gardener plants rhubarb, tolerably certain of a particular result, but not dwelling even in thought on that which is hidden. The productivity of capital was to him the greatest achievement of social progress—indeed, the social organism justified its existence by that achievement; nothing could be more equitable than this productivity, nothing more natural. He would as soon have enquired into it as Agnes would have enquired into the ticking of the grandfather's clock. But to Anna, who had some imagination, and whose imagination had been stirred by recent events, the arrivals of moneys out of space, unearned, unasked, was a disturbing experience, affecting her as a conjuring trick affects a child, whose sensations hesitate between pleasure and apprehension. Practically, Anna could not believe that she was rich; and in fact she was not rich—she was merely a fixed point through which moneys that she was unable to arrest passed with the rapidity of trains. If money is a token, Anna was denied the satisfaction of fingering even the token: drafts and cheques were all that she touched (touched only to abandon)—the doubly tantalising and insubstantial tokens of a token. She wanted to test the actuality of this apparent dream by handling coin and causing it to vanish over counters and into the palms of the necessitous. And moreover, quite apart from this curiosity, she really needed money for pressing requirements of Agnes and herself. They had yet had no new summer clothes, and Whitsuntide, the time prescribed by custom for the refurnishing of wardrobes, was long since past. The intercourse with Henry Mynors, the visit to the Suttons, had revealed to her more plainly than ever the intolerable shortcomings of her wardrobe, and similar imperfections. She was more painfully awake to these, and yet, by an unhappy paradox, she was even less in a position to remedy them than in previous years.  For now, she possessed her own fortune; to ask her father's bounty was therefore, she divined, a sure way of inviting a rebuff. But, even if she had dared, she might not use the income that was privately hers, for was not every penny of it already allocated to the partnership with Mynors?  So it happened that she never once mentioned the matter to her father; she lacked the courage, since by whatever avenue she approached it circumstances would add an illogical and adventitious force to the brutal snubs which he invariably dealt out when petitioned for money.  To demand his money, having fifty thousand of her own!  To spend her own in the face of that agreement with Mynors!  She could too easily guess his bitter and humiliating retorts to either proposition, and she kept silence, comforting herself with timid visions of a far distant future.  The balance at the bank crept up to sixteen hundred pounds.  The deed of partnership was drawn; her father pored over the blue draft, and several times Mynors called and the two men discussed it together.  Then one morning her father summoned her into the front parlour, and handed to her a piece of parchment on which she dimly deciphered her own name coupled with that of Henry Mynors, in large letters.

" You mun sign, seal, and deliver this," he said, putting a pen in her hand.

She sat down obediently to write, but he stopped her with a scornful gesture.

" Thou'lt sign blind then, eh?   Just like a woman! "

" I left it to you," she said.

" Left it to me! Read it."

She read through the deed, and after she had accomplished the feat one fact only stood clear in her mind, that the partnership was for seven years, a period extensible by consent of both parties to fourteen or twenty-one years. Then she affixed her signature, the pen moving awkwardly over the rough surface of the parchment.

" Now put thy finger on that bit 'o wax, and say: ' I deliver this as my act and deed.' "

" I deliver this as my act and deed."

The old man signed as witness. " Soon as I give this to Lawyer Dane," he remarked, " thou'rt bound, willy-nilly. Law's law, and thou'rt bound."

On the following day she had to sign a cheque which reduced her bank-balance to about three pounds. Perhaps it was the knowledge of this reduction that led Ephraim Tellwright to resume at once and with fresh rigour his new policy of " squeezing the last penny " out of Titus Price (despite the fact that the latter had already achieved the incredible by paying thirty pounds in little more than a month), thus causing the catastrophe which soon afterwards befell. What methods her father was adopting Anna did not know, since he said no word to her about the matter: she only knew that Agnes had twice been dispatched with notes to Edward Street. One day, about noon, a clay-soiled urchin brought a letter addressed to herself; she guessed that it was some appeal for mercy from the Prices, and wished that her father had been at home. The old man was away for the whole day, attending a sale of property at Axe, the agricultural town in the north of the county, locally styled " the metropolis of the moorlands." Anna read: " My dear Miss Tellwright,—Now that our partnership is an accomplished fact, will you not come and look over the works? I should much like you to do so. I shall be passing your house this afternoon about two, and will call on the chance of being able to take you down with me to the works. If you are unable to come no harm will be done, and some other day can be arranged; but of course I shall be disappointed.—Believe me, yours most sincerely, Hy. Mynors."

She was charmed with the idea—to her so audacious—and relieved that the note was not after all from Titus or Willie Price: but again she had to regret that her father was not at home. He would be capable of thinking and saying that the projected expedition was a truancy, contrived to occur in his absence. He might grumble at the house being left without a keeper. Moreover, according to a tacit law, she never departed from the fixed routine of her existence without first obtaining Ephraim's approval, or at least being sure that such a departure would not make him violently angry. She wondered whether Mynors knew that her father was away, and, if so, whether he had chosen that afternoon purposely. She did not care that Mynors should call for her—it made the visit seem so formal; and as in order to reach the works, down at Shawport, by the canalside, they would necessarily go through the middle of the town, she foresaw infinite gossip and rumour as one result.

Already, she knew, the names of herself and Mynors were everywhere coupled, and she could not even enter a shop without being made aware, more or less delicately, that she was an object of piquant curiosity. A woman is profoundly interesting to women at two periods only—before she is betrothed and before she becomes the mother of her firstborn. Anna was in the first period; her life did not comprise the second.

When Agnes came home to dinner from school, Anna said nothing of Mynors' note until they had begun to wash up the dinner-things, when she suggested that Agnes should finish this operation alone.

" Yes," said Agnes, ever compliant. " But why? "

" I'm going out, and I must get ready."

" Going out? And shall you leave the house all empty? What will father say? Where are you going to? "

Agnes's tendency to anticipate the worst, and never to blink their father's tyranny, always annoyed Anna, and she answered rather curtly: " I'm going to the works—Mr. Mynors' works. He's sent word he wants me to." She despised herself for wishing to hide anything, and added, " He will call here for me about two o'clock."

" Mr. Mynors! How splendid! " And then Agnes's face fell somewhat. " I suppose he won't call *before* two? If he doesn't I shall be gone to school."

" Do you want to see him? "

" Oh, no! I don't want to see him. But—I suppose you'll be out a long time, and he'll bring you back."

" Of course he won't, you silly girl.    And I shan't be out long.    I shall be back for tea."

Anna ran upstairs to dress.    At ten minutes to two she was ready.    Agnes usually left at a quarter to two, but the child had not yet gone.    At five minutes to two, Anna called downstairs to her to ask her when she meant to depart.

" I'm just going now," Agnes shouted back.    She opened the front door and then returned to the foot of the stairs. " Anna, if I meet him down the road, shall I tell him you're ready waiting for him? "

" Certainly not.    Whatever are you dreaming of? " the elder sister reproved.    " Besides, he isn't coming from the town."

" Oh!    All right.    Good-bye."    And the child at last went.

It was something after two—every siren and hooter had long since finished the summons to work—when Mynors rang the bell.    Anna was still upstairs.    She examined herself in the glass, and then descended slowly.

" Good-afternoon," he said.    " I see you are ready to come.    I'm very glad.    I hope I haven't inconvenienced you, but just this afternoon seemed to be a good opportunity for you to see the works, and you know you ought to see it. Father in? "

" No," she said.    " I shall leave the house to take care of itself.    Do you want to see him? "

" Not specially," he replied.    " I think we have settled everything."

She banged the door behind her, and they started. As he held open the gate for her exit, she could not ignore the look of passionate admiration on his face. It was a look disconcerting by its mere intensity. The man could control his tongue, but not his eyes. His demeanour, as she viewed it, aggravated her self-consciousness as they braved the streets. But she was happy in her perturbation. When they reached Duck Bank Mynors asked her whether they should go through the market-place or along King Street, by the bottom of St. Luke's Square. "By the market-place," she said. The shop where Miss Dickinson was employed was at the bottom of St. Luke's Square, and all the eyes of the market-place were preferable to the chance of those eyes.

Probably no one in the Five Towns takes a conscious pride in the antiquity of the potter's craft, nor in its unique and intimate relation to human life, alike civilised and uncivilised. Man hardened clay into a bowl before he spun flax and made a garment, and the last lone man will want an earthen vessel after he has abandoned his ruined house for a cave, and his woven rags for an animal's skin. This supremacy of the most ancient of crafts is in the secret nature of things, and cannot be explained. History begins long after the period when Bursley was first the central seat of that honoured manufacture: it is the central seat still— "the mother of the Five Towns," in our local phrase—and though the townsmen, absorbed in a strenuous daily struggle, may forget their heirship to an unbroken tradition of

countless centuries, the seal of their venerable calling is upon
their foreheads. If no other relic of an immemorial past
is to be seen in these modernised sordid streets, there is at
least the living legacy of that extraordinary kinship between
workman and work, that instinctive mastery of clay, which
the past has bestowed upon the present. The horse is less
to the Arab than clay is to the Bursley man. He exists in
it and by it; it fills his lungs and blanches his cheek; it keeps
him alive and it kills him. His fingers close round it as
round the hand of a friend. He knows all its tricks and
aptitudes; when to coax and when to force it, when to rely
on it and when to distrust it. The weavers of Lancashire
have dubbed him with an obscene epithet on account of it,
an epithet whose hasty use has led to many a fight, but
nothing could be more illuminatively descriptive than that
epithet, which names his vocation in terms of another vocation. A dozen decades of applied science have of course resulted in the interposition of elaborate machinery between
the clay and the man; but no great vulgar handicraft has
lost less of the human than potting. Clay is always clay,
and the steam-driven contrivance that will mould a basin
while a man sits and watches has yet to be invented. Moreover, if in some coarser process the hands are superseded,
the number of processes has been multiplied tenfold: the
ware in which six men formerly collaborated is now produced by sixty; and thus, in one sense, the touch of finger
on clay is more pervasive than ever before.

Mynors' works was acknowledged to be one of the best,
of its size, in the district—a model three-oven bank, and it

must be remembered that of the hundreds of banks in the Five Towns the vast majority are small, like this: the large manufactory with its corps of jacket-men,* one of whom is detached to show visitors round so much of the works as it is deemed advisable for them to see, is the exception. Mynors paid three hundred pounds a year in rent, and produced nearly three hundred pounds' worth of work a week. He was his own manager, and there was only one jacket-man on the place, a clerk at eighteen shillings. He employed about a hundred hands, and devoted all his ingenuity to prevent that wastage which is at once the easiest to overlook and the most difficult to check, the wastage of labour. No pains were spared to keep all departments in full and regular activity, and owing to his judicious firmness the feast of St. Monday, that canker eternally eating at the root of the prosperity of the Five Towns, was less religiously observed on his bank than perhaps anywhere else in Bursley. He had realised that when a workshop stands empty the employer has not only ceased to make money, but has begun to lose it. The architect of " Providence Works " (Providence stands godfather to many commercial enterprises in the Five Towns) knew his business and the business of the potter, and he had designed the works with a view to the strictest economy of labour. The various shops were so arranged that in the course of its metamorphosis the clay travelled naturally in a circle from the slip-house by the

---

* *Jacket-man*: the artisan's satiric term for anyone who does not work in shirtsleeves, who is not actually a producer, such as a clerk or a pretentious foreman.

canal to the packing-house by the canal: there was no carrying to and fro.    The steam installation was complete: steam
once generated had no respite; after it had exhausted itself in vitalising fifty machines, it was killed by inches in
order to dry the unfired ware and warm the dinners of the
workpeople.

Henry took Anna to the canal-entrance, because the buildings looked best from that side.

" Now how much is a crate worth? " she asked, pointing
to a crate which was being swung on a crane direct from the
packing-house into a boat.

" That? " Mynors answered.  " A crateful of ware may be
worth anything.    At Minton's I have seen a crate worth
three hundred pounds.    But that one there is only worth
eight or nine pounds.    You see you and I make cheap
stuff."

" But don't you make any really good pots—are they
all cheap? "

" All cheap," he said.

" I suppose that's business? "    He detected a note of regret in her voice.

" I don't know," he said, with the slightest impatient
warmth.   " We make the stuff as good as we can for the
money.   We supply what everyone wants.   Don't you think
it's better to please a thousand folks than to please ten?
I like to feel that my ware is used all over the country and
the colonies.   I would sooner do as I do than make swagger
ware for a handful of rich people."

" Oh, yes! " she exclaimed, eagerly accepting the point of

view, " I quite agree with you." She had never heard him in that vein before, and was struck by his enthusiasm. And Mynors was in fact always very enthusiastic concerning the virtues of the general markets. He had no sympathy with specialities, artistic or otherwise. He found his satisfaction in honestly meeting the popular taste. He was born to be a manufacturer of cheap goods on a colossal scale. He could dream of fifty ovens, and his ambition blinded him to the present absurdity of talking about a three-oven bank spreading its productions all over the country and the colonies; it did not occur to him that there were yet scarcely enough plates to go round.

" I suppose we had better start at the start," he said, leading the way to the slip-house. He did not need to be told that Anna was perfectly ignorant of the craft of pottery, and that every detail of it, so stale to him, would acquire freshness under her naïve and enquiring gaze.

In the slip-house begins the long manipulation which transforms raw porous friable clay into the moulded, decorated, and glazed vessel. The large whitewashed place was occupied by ungainly machines and receptacles through which the four sorts of clay used in a common " body "— ball clay, China clay, flint clay, and stone clay—were compelled to pass before they became a white putty-like mixture meet for shaping by human hands. The blunger crushed the clay, the sifter extracted the iron from it by means of a magnet, the press expelled the water, and the pug-mill expelled the air. From the last reluctant mouth slowly emerged a solid stream nearly a foot in diameter, like a huge white snake. Already the clay had acquired the uniformity characteristic of a manufactured product.

Anna moved to touch the bolts of the enormous twenty-four-chambered press.

" Don't stand there," said Mynors. " The pressure is tremendous, and if the thing were to burst——"

She fled hastily. " But isn't it dangerous for the workmen? " she asked.

Eli Machin, the engineman, the oldest employee on the works, a moneyed man and the pattern of reliability, allowed a vague smile to flit across his face at this remark. He had ascended from the engine-house below in order to exhibit the tricks of the various machines, and that done he disappeared. Anna was awed by the sensation of being surrounded by terrific forces always straining for release and held in check by the power of a single will.

" Come and see a plate made: that is one of the simplest things, and the batting-machine is worth looking at," said Mynors, and they went into the nearest shop, a hot interior in the shape of four corridors round a solid square middle. Here men and women were working side by side, the women subordinate to the men. All were preoccupied, wrapped up in their respective operations, and there was the sound of irregular whirring movements from every part of the big room. The air was laden with a whitish dust, and clay was omnipresent—on the floor, the walls, the benches, the windows, on clothes, hands, and faces. It was in this shop, where both hollowware pressers and flat pressers were busy as only craftsmen on piecework can be busy, that more than

anywhere else clay was to be seen " in the hand of the potter." Near the door a stout man with a good-humoured
face flung some clay on to a revolving disc, and even as
Anna passed a jar sprang into existence. One instant the
clay was an amorphous mass, the next it was a vessel perfectly circular, of a prescribed width and a prescribed
depth; the fat and apparently clumsy fingers of the crafts-
man had seemed to lose themselves in the clay for a fraction of time, and the miracle was accomplished. The man
threw these vessels with the rapidity of a Roman candle
throwing off coloured stars, and one woman was kept busy
in supplying him with material and relieving his bench of
the finished articles. Mynors drew Anna along to the batting-machines for plate-makers, at that period rather a novelty and the latest invention of the dead genius whose brain
has reconstituted a whole industry on new lines. Confronted
with a piece of clay, the batting-machine descended upon it
with the ferocity of a wild animal, worried it, stretched it,
smoothed it into the width and thickness of a plate, and then
desisted of itself and waited inactive for the flat presser to
remove its victim to his more exact shaping machine. Sev--
eral men were producing plates, but their rapid labours
seemed less astonishing than the preliminary feat of the
batting-machine. All the ware, as it was moulded, disappeared into the vast cupboards occupying the centre of the
shop, where Mynors showed Anna innumerable rows of
shelves full of pots in process of steam-drying. Neither
time nor space nor material was wasted in this ant-heap of
industry. In order to move to and fro, the women were

compelled to insinuate themselves past the stationary bodies of the men. Anna marvelled at the careless accuracy with which they fed the batting-machines with lumps precisely calculated to form a plate of a given diameter. Everyone exerted himself as though the salvation of the world hung on the production of so much stuff by a certain hour; dust, heat, and the presence of a stranger were alike unheeded in the mad creative passion.

" Now," said Mynors the cicerone, opening another door which gave into the yard, " when all that stuff is dried and fettled—smoothed, you know—it goes into the biscuit oven: that's the first firing. There's the biscuit oven, but we can't inspect it because it's just being drawn."

He pointed to the oven near by, in whose dark interior the forms of men, naked to the waist, could dimly be seen struggling with the weight of saggars* full of ware. It seemed like some release of martyrs, this unpacking of the immense oven, which, after being flooded with a sea of flame for fifty-four hours, had cooled for two days, and was yet hotter than the Equator. The inertness and pallor of the saggars seemed to be the physical result of their fiery trial, and one wondered that they should have survived the trial. Mynors went into the place adjoining the oven and brought back a plate out of an open saggar; it was still quite warm. It had the *matt* surface of a biscuit, and adhered slightly to the fingers: it was now a " crook "; it had exchanged malleability for brittleness, and nothing mortal could undo what

* *Saggars:* large oval receptacles of coarse clay, in which the ware is placed for firing.

the fire had done. Mynors took the plate with him to the biscuit-warehouse, a long room where one was forced to keep to narrow alleys amid parterres of pots. A solitary biscuit-warehouseman was examining the ware, in order to determine the remuneration of the pressers.

They climbed a flight of stairs to the printing-shop, where, by means of copperplates, printing-presses, mineral colours, and transfer-papers, most of the decoration was done. The room was filled by a little crowd of people— oldish men, women, and girls, divided into printers, cutters, transferrers, and apprentices. Each interminably repeated some trifling process, and every article passed through a succession of hands until at length it was washed in a tank and rose dripping therefrom with its ornament of flowers and scrolls fully revealed. The room smelt of oil and flannel and humanity; the atmosphere was more languid, more like that of a family party, than in the pressers' shop: the old women looked stern and shrewish, the pretty young women pert and defiant, the younger girls meek. The few men seemed out of place. By what trick had they crept into the very centre of that mass of femineity? It seemed wrong, scandalous that they should remain. Contiguous with the printing-shop was the painting-shop, in which the labours of the former were taken to a finish by the brush of the paintress, who filled in outlines with flat colour, and thus converted mechanical printing into handiwork. The paint-resses form the *noblesse* of the banks. Their task is a light one, demanding deftness first of all; they have delicate fin-gers, and enjoy a general reputation for beauty: the wages they earn may be estimated from their finery on Sundays. They come to business in cloth jackets, carrying dinner in little satchels; in the shop they wear white aprons, and look startlingly neat and tidy. Across the benches over which they bend their coquettish heads gossip flies and returns like a shuttle; they are the source of a thousand intrigues, and one or other of them is continually getting married or omitting to get married. On the bank they constitute " the sex." An infinitesimal proportion of them, from among the branch known as ground-layers, die of lead-poisoning—a fact which adds pathos to their frivolous charm. In a sub-sidiary room off the painting-shop a single girl was seated at a revolving table actuated by a treadle. She was doing the " band-and-line " on the rims of saucers. Mynors and Anna watched her as with her left hand she flicked saucer after saucer into the exact centre of the table, moved the treadle, and, holding a brush firmly against the rim of the piece, produced with infallible exactitude the band and the line. She was a brunette, about twenty-eight: she had a calm, vacuously contemplative face; but God alone knew whether she thought. Her work represented the summit of monotony; the regularity of it hypnotised the observer, and Mynors himself was impressed by this stupendous phe-nomenon of absolute sameness, involuntarily assuming towards it the attitude of a showman.

" She earns as much as eighteen shillings a week some-times," he whispered.

" May I try? " Anna timidly asked of a sudden, curious to experience what the trick was like.

" Certainly," said Mynors, in eager assent. " Priscilla, let this lady have your seat a moment, please."

The girl got up, smiling politely. Anna took her place.

" Here, try on this," said Mynors, putting on the table the plate which he still carried.

" Take a full brush," the paintress suggested, not attempting to hide her amusement at Anna's unaccustomed efforts. " Now push the treadle. There! It isn't in the middle yet. Now!"

Anna produced a most creditable band, and a trembling but passable line, and rose, flushed with the small triumph.

" You have the gift," said Mynors; and the paintress respectfully applauded.

" I felt I could do it," Anna responded. " My mother's mother was a paintress, and it must be in the blood."

Mynors smiled indulgently. They descended again to the ground floor, and following the course of manufacture came to the " hardening-on " kiln, a minor oven where for twelve hours the oil is burnt out of the colour in decorated ware. A huge, jolly man in shirt and trousers, with an enormous apron, was in the act of drawing the kiln, assisted by two thin boys. He nodded a greeting to Mynors and exclaimed, " Warm!" The kiln was nearly emptied. As Anna stopped at the door, the man addressed her.

" Step inside, miss, and try it."

" No, thanks!" she laughed.

" Come now," he insisted, as if despising this hesitation. " An ounce of experience——" The two boys grinned and wiped their foreheads with their bare skeleton-like arms.

Anna, challenged by the man's look, walked quickly into the kiln. A blasting heat seemed to assault her on every side, driving her back; it was incredible that any human being could support such a temperature.

" There ! " said the jovial man, apparently summing her up with his bright, quizzical eyes. " You know summat as you didn't know afore, miss. Come along, lads," he added with brisk heartiness to the boys, and the drawing of the kiln proceeded.

Next came the dipping-house, where a middle-aged woman, enveloped in a protective garment from head to foot, was dipping jugs into a vat of lead-glaze, a boy assisting her. The woman's hands were covered with the grey slimy glaze. She alone of all the employees appeared to be cool.

" That is the last stage but one," said Mynors. " There is only the glost-firing," and they passed out into the yard once more. One of the glost-ovens was empty ; they entered it and peered into the lofty inner chamber, which seemed like the cold crater of an exhausted volcano, or like a vault, or like the ruined seat of some forgotten activity. The other oven was firing, and Anna could only look at its exterior, catching glimpses of the red glow at its twelve mouths, and guess at the Tophet within, where the lead was being fused into glass.

" Now for the glost-warehouse, and you will have seen all," said Mynors, " except the mould-shop, and that doesn't matter."

The warehouse was the largest place on the works, a room

sixty feet long and twenty broad, low, whitewashed, bare,
and clean. Piles of ware occupied the whole of the walls
and of the immense floor-space, but there was no trace here
of the soilure and untidiness incident to manufacture; all
processes were at one end, clay vanished into crock: and the
calmness and the whiteness atoned for the disorder, noise,
and squalor which had preceded. Here was a sample of the
total and final achievement towards which the thousands of
small, disjointed efforts that Anna had witnessed were
directed. And it seemed a miraculous, almost impossible,
result; so definite, precise, and regular after a series of acts
apparently variable, inexact, and casual; so unhuman after
all that intensely human labour; so vast in comparison with
the minuteness of the separate endeavours. As Anna looked,
for instance, at a pile of tea-sets, she found it difficult even
to conceive that, a fortnight or so before, they had been
nothing but lumps of dirty clay. No stage of the manufacture was incredible by itself, but the result was incredible.
It was the result that appealed to the imagination, authen-
ticating the adage that fools and children should never see
anything till it is done.

Anna pondered over the organising power, the fore-
thought, the wide vision, and the sheer ingenuity and cleverness which were implied by the contents of this warehouse.
"What brains!" she thought, of Mynors; "what quan-
tities of all sorts of things he must know!" It was a humble
and deeply-felt admiration.

Her spoken words gave no clue to her thoughts. "You
seem to make a fine lot of tea-sets," she remarked.

" Oh, no ! " he said carelessly. " These few that you see here are a special order. I don't go in much for tea-sets: they don't pay; we lose fifteen per cent. of the pieces in making. It's toilet-ware that pays, and that is our leading line." He waved an arm vaguely towards rows and rows of ewers and basins in the distance. They walked to the end of the warehouse, glancing at everything.

" See here," said Mynors, " isn't that pretty? " He pointed through the last window to a view of the canal, which could be seen thence in perspective, finishing in a curve. On one side, close to the water's edge, was a ruined and fragmentary building, its rich browns reflected in the smooth surface of the canal. On the other side were a few grim, grey trees bordering the towpath. Down the vista moved a boat steered by a woman in a large mob-cap. " Isn't that picturesque? " he said.

" Very," Anna assented willingly. " It's really quite strange, such a scene right in the middle of Bursley."

" Oh! There are others," he said. " But I always take a peep at that whenever I come into the warehouse."

" I wonder you find time to notice it—with all this place to see after," she said. " It's a splendid works ! "

" It will do—to be going on with," he answered, satisfied. " I'm very glad you've been down. You must come again. I can see you would be interested in it, and there are plenty of things you haven't looked at yet, you know."

He smiled at her. They were alone in the warehouse.

" Yes," she said; " I expect so. Well, I must go, at once; I'm afraid it's very late now. Thank you for showing me round, and explaining, and—I'm frightfully stupid and ignorant. Good-bye."

Vapid and trite phrases: what unimaginable messages the hearer heard in you!

Anna held out her hand, and he seized it almost convulsively, his incendiary eyes fastened on her face.

" I must see you out," he said, dropping that ungloved hand.

It was ten o'clock that night before Ephraim Tellwright returned home from Axe. He appeared to be in a bad temper. Agnes had gone to bed. His supper of bread-and-cheese and water was waiting for him, and Anna sat at the table while he consumed it. He ate in silence, somewhat hungrily, and she did not deem the moment propitious for telling him about her visit to Mynors' works.

" Has Titus Price sent up? " he asked at length, gulping down the last of the water.

" Sent up? "

" Yes. Art fond, lass? I told him as he mun send up some more o' thy rent to-day—twenty-five pun. He's not sent? "

" I don't know," she said timidly. " I was out this afternoon."

" Out, wast? "

" Mr. Mynors sent word to ask me to go down and look over the works; so I went. I thought it would be all right."

" Well, it was'na all right. And I'd like to know what business thou hast gadding out, as soon as my back's turned.

How can I tell whether Price sent up or not? And what's more, thou know's as th' house hadn't ought to be left."

" I'm sorry," she said pleasantly, with a determination to be meek and dutiful.

He grunted. " Happen he didna' send. And if he did, and found th' house locked up, he should ha' sent again. Bring me th' inkpot, and I'll write a note as Agnes must take when her goes to school to-morrow morning."

Anna obeyed. " They'll never be able to pay twenty-five pounds, father," she ventured. " They've paid thirty already, you know."

" Less gab," he said shortly, taking up the pen. " Here —write it thysen." He threw the pen towards her. " Tell Titus if he doesn't pay five-and-twenty this wik, us 'll put bailiffs in."

" Won't it come better from you, father? " she pleaded.

" Whose property is it? " The laconic question was final. She knew she must obey, and began to write. But, realising that she would perforce meet both Titus Price and Willie on Sunday, she merely demanded the money, omitting the threat. Her hand trembled as she passed the note to him to read.

" Will that do? "

His reply was to tear the paper across. " Put down what I tell ye," he ordered, " and don't let's have any more paper wasted." Then he dictated a letter which was an ultimatum in three lines. " Sign it," he said.

She signed it, weeping. She could see the wistful reproach in Willie Price's eyes.

" I suppose," her father said, when she bade him " Good-night," " I suppose if I had'na asked, I should ha' heard nowt o' this gadding-about wi' Mynors? "

" I was going to tell you I had been to the works, father," she said.

" Going to! " That was his final blow, and having delivered it, he loosed his victim. " Get to bed," he said.

She went upstairs, resolutely read her Bible, and resolutely prayed.

## IX: THE TREAT

**T**HIS surly and terrorising ferocity of Tellwright's was as instinctive as the growl and spring of a beast of prey. He never considered his attitude towards the women of his household as an unusual phenomenon which needed justification, or as being in the least abnormal. The women of a household were the natural victims of their master: in his experience it had always been so. In his experience the master had always, by universal consent, possessed certain rights over the self-respect, the happiness, and the peace of the defenceless souls set under him—rights as unquestioned as those exercised by Ivan the Terrible. Such rights were rooted in the secret nature of things. It was futile to discuss them, because their necessity and their propriety were equally obvious. Tellwright would not have been angry with any man who impugned them: he would merely have regarded the fellow as a crank and a born fool, on whom logic or indignation would be entirely wasted. He did as his father and uncles had done. He still thought of his father as a grim customer, infinitely more redoubtable than himself. He really believed that parents spoiled their children nowadays: to be knocked down by a single blow was one of the punishments of his own generation. He could recall the fearful timidity of his mother's eyes without a trace of compassion. His treatment of his daughters was no part of a system, nor obedient to any defined principles, nor the expression of a brutal disposition, nor the result of gradually-acquired habit. It came to him like eating, and like parsimony. He belonged to the great and powerful class of house-tyrants, the backbone of the British nation, whose views on income-tax cause ministries to tremble. If you had talked to him of the domestic graces of life, your words would have conveyed to him no meaning. If you had indicted him for simple, unprovoked rudeness, he would have grinned, well knowing that, as the King can do no wrong, so a man cannot be rude in his own house. If you had told him that he inflicted purposeless misery not only on others, but on himself, he would have grinned again, vaguely aware that he had not tried to be happy, and rather despising happiness as a sort of childish gewgaw. He had, in fact, never been happy at home: he had never known that expansion of the spirit which is called joy; he existed continually under a grievance. The atmosphere of Manor Terrace afflicted him, too, with a melancholy gloom—him, who had created it. Had he been capable of self-analysis, he would have discovered that his heart lightened whenever he left the house, and grew dark whenever he returned; but he was incapable of the feat. His case, like every similar case, was irremediable.

The next morning his preposterous displeasure lay like a curse on the house; Anna was silent, and Agnes moved on timid feet. In the afternoon Willie Price called in answer to the note. The miser was in the garden, and Agnes at school. Willie's craven and fawning humility was inexpressibly touching and shameful to Anna. She longed to

say to him, as he stood hesitant and confused in the parlour:
" Go in peace.    Forget this despicable rent.    It sickens me
to see you so."    She foresaw, as the effect of her father's
vindictive pursuit of her tenants, an interminable succession
of these mortifying interviews.

" You're rather hard on us," Willie Price began, using
the old phrases, but in a tone of forced and propitiatory
cheerfulness, as though he feared to bring down a storm of
anger, which should ruin all.    " You'll not deny that we've
been doing our best."

" The rent is due, you know, Mr. William," she replied,
blushing.

" Oh, yes!" he said quickly.    " I don't deny that.    I
admit that.    I—did you happen to see Mr. Tellwright's
postscript to your letter? "

" No," she answered, without thinking.

He drew the letter, soiled and creased, from his pocket,
and displayed it to her.    At the foot of the page she read, in
Ephraim's thick and clumsy characters: " P. S.    This is
final."

" My father," said Willie, " was a little put about.    He
said he'd never received such a letter before in the whole of
his business career.    It isn't as if——"

"·I needn't tell you," she interrupted, with a sudden determination to get to the worst without more suspense, " that
of course I am in father's hands."

" Oh!    Of course, Miss Tellwright; we quite understand
that—quite.    It's just a matter of business.    We owe a
debt and we must pay it.    All we want is time."    He smiled

piteously at her, his blue eyes full of appeal. She was obliged to gaze at the floor.

" Yes," she said, tapping her foot on the rug.. " But father means what he says." She looked up at him again, trying to soften her words by means of something more subtle than a smile.

" He means what he says," Willie agreed; " and I admire him for it."

The obsequious, truckling lie was odious to her.

" Perhaps I could see him," he ventured.

" I wish you would," Anna said sincerely.  " Father, you're wanted," she called curtly through the window.

" I've got a proposal to make to him," Price continued, while they awaited the presence of the miser, " and I can't hardly think he'll refuse it."

" Well, young sir," Tellwright said blandly, with an air almost insinuating, as he entered.  Willie Price, the simpleton, was deceived by it, and, taking courage, adopted another line of defence.  He thought the miser was a little ashamed of his postscript.

" About your note, Mr. Tellwright; I was just telling Miss Tellwright that my father said he had never received such a letter in the whole of his business career."  The youth assumed a discreet indignation.

" Thy feyther's had dozens o' such letters, lad," the miser said with cold emphasis, " or my name's not Tellwright. Dunna tell me as Titus Price's never heard of a bumbailiff afore,"

Willie was crushed at a blow, and obliged to retreat.   He smiled painfully.   " Come, Mr. Tellwright.   Don't talk like that.   All we want is time."

" Time is money," said Tellwright, " and if us give you time us give you money.   'Stead o' that, it's you as mun give us money.   That's right reason."

Willie laughed with difficulty.   " See here, Mr. Tell-wright.   To cut a long story short, it's like this.   You ask for twenty-five pounds.   I've got in my pocket a bill of exchange drawn by us on Mr. Sutton and endorsed by him, for thirty pounds, payable in three months.   Will you take that?   Remember it's for thirty, and you only ask for twenty-five."

" So Mr. Sutton has dealings with ye, eh? " Tellwright remarked.

" Oh, yes! " Willie answered proudly.   " He buys off us regularly.   We've done business for years."

" And pays i' bills at three months, eh? "   The miser grinned.

" Sometimes," said Willie.

" Let's see it," said the miser.

" What—the bill? "

" Ay! "

" Oh!   The bill's all right."   Willie took it from his pocket, and opening out the blue paper, gave it to old Tell-wright.   Anna perceived the anxiety on the youth's face. He flushed and his hand trembled.   She dared not speak, but she wished to tell him to be at ease.   She knew from infallible signs that her father would take the bill.   Ephraim gazed at the stamped paper as at something strange and unprecedented in his experience.

" Father would want you not to negotiate that bill," said Willie. " The fact is, we promised Mr. Sutton that that particular bill should not leave our hands—unless it was absolutely necessary. So father would like you not to discount it, and he will redeem it before it matures. You quite understand—we don't care to offend an old customer like Mr. Sutton."

" Then this bit o' paper's worth nowt for welly* three months? " the old man said, with an affectation of bewildered simplicity.

Happily inspired for once, Willie made no answer, but put the question: " Will you take it? "

" Ay! Us 'll tak' it," said Tellwright, " though it is but a promise." He was well pleased.

Young Price's face showed his relief. It was now evident that he had been passing through an ordeal. Anna guessed that perhaps everything had depended on the acceptance by Tellwright of that bill. Had he refused it, Prices, she thought, might have come to sudden disaster. She felt glad and disburdened for the moment; but immediately it occurred to her that her father would not rest satisfied for long; a few weeks, and he would give another turn to the screw.

The Tellwrights were destined to have other visitors that afternoon. Agnes, coming from school, was accompanied by a lady. Anna, who was setting the tea-table, saw a

* *Welly*: nearly.

double shadow pass the window, and heard voices.    She ran
into the kitchen, and found Mrs. Sutton seated on a chair,
breathing quickly.

" You'll excuse me coming in so unceremoniously, Anna,"
she said, after having kissed her heartily.    " But Agnes
said that *she* always came in by the back way, so I came that
way too.    Now I'm resting a minute.    I've had to walk
to-day.    Our horse has gone lame."

This kind heart radiated a heavenly good will, even in the
most ordinary phrases.    Anna began to expand at once.

" Now do come into the parlour," she said, " and let me
make you comfortable."

" Just a minute, my dear," Mrs. Sutton begged, fanning
herself with her handkerchief.    " Agnes's legs are so long."

" Oh, Mrs. Sutton," Agnes protested, laughing, " how
can you?    I could scarcely keep up with you ! "

" Well, my dear, I never could walk slowly.    I'm one of
them that go till they drop.    It's very silly."    She smiled,
and the two girls smiled happily in return.

" Agnes," said the housewife, " set another cup and
saucer and plate."    Agnes threw down her hat and satchel
of books, eager to show hospitality.

" It still keeps very warm," Anna remarked, as Mrs. Sutton was silent.

" It's beautifully cool here," said Mrs. Sutton.    " I see
you've got your kitchen like a new pin, Anna, if you'll excuse me saying so.    Henry was very enthusiastic about this
kitchen the other night, at our house."

" What!    Mr. Mynors? "    Anna reddened to the eyes.

" Yes, my dear; and he's a very particular young man, you know."

The kettle conveniently boiled at that moment, and Anna went to the range to make the tea.

" Tea is all ready, Mrs. Sutton," she said at length. " I'm sure you could do with a cup."

" That I could," said Mrs. Sutton. " It's what I've come for."

" We have tea at four. Father will be glad to see you." The clock struck, and they went into the parlour, Anna carrying the tea-pot and the hot-water jug. Agnes had preceded them. The old man was sitting expectant in his chair.

" Well, Mr. Tellwright," said the visitor, " you see I've called to see you, and to beg a cup of tea. I overtook Agnes coming home from school—overtook her, mind—me, at my age!" Ephraim rose slowly and shook hands.

" You're welcome," he said curtly, but with a kindliness that amazed Anna. She was unaware that in past days he had known Mrs. Sutton as a young and charming girl, a vision that had stirred poetic ideas in hundreds of prosaic breasts, Tellwright's included. There was scarcely a middle-aged male Wesleyan in Bursley and Hanbridge who had not a peculiar regard for Mrs. Sutton, and who did not think that he alone truly appreciated her.

" What an' you bin tiring yourself with this afternoon? " he asked, when they had begun tea, and Mrs. Sutton had refused a second piece of bread-and-butter.

" What have I been doing? I've been seeing to some inside repairs to the superintendent's house. Be thankful you aren't a circuit-steward's wife, Anna."

" Why, does she have to see to the repairs of the minister's house? " Anna asked, surprised.

" I should just think she does.   She has to stand between the minister's wife and the funds of the society.   And Mrs. Reginald Banks has been used to the very best of everything.   She's just a bit exacting, though I must say she's willing enough to spend her own money too.   She wants a new boiler in the scullery now, and I'm sure her boiler is a great deal better than ours.   But we must try to please her.   She isn't used to us rough folks and our ways.   Mr. Banks said to me this afternoon that he tried always to shield her from the worries of this world."   She smiled almost imperceptibly.

There was a ring at the bell, and Agnes, much perturbed by the august arrival, let in Mr. Banks himself.

" Shall I enter, my little dear? " said Mr. Banks.  " Your father, your sister, in? "

" It ne'er rains but it pours," said Tellwright, who had caught the minister's voice.

" Speak of angels——" said Mrs. Sutton, laughing quietly.

The minister came grandly into the parlour.  " Ah! How do you do, brother Tellwright, and you, Miss Tellwright?   Mrs. Sutton, we two seem happily fated to meet this afternoon.   Don't let me disturb you, I beg—I cannot stay.   My time is very limited.   I wish I could call oftener, brother Tellwright; but really the new *régime* leaves no time for pastoral visits. I was saying to my wife only this morning that I haven't had a free afternoon for a month." He accepted a cup of tea.

" Us'n having a tea-party this afternoon," said Tellwright *quasi*-privately to Mrs. Sutton.

" And now," the minister resumed, " I've come to beg. The special fund, you know, Mr. Tellwright, to clear off the debt on the new school-buildings. I referred to it from the pulpit last Sabbath. It's not in my province to go round begging, but someone must do it."

" Well, for me, I'm beforehand with you, Mr. Banks," said Mrs. Sutton, " for it's on that very errand that I've called to see Mr. Tellwright this afternoon. His name is on my list."

" Ah! Then I leave our brother to your superior persuasions."

" Come, Mr. Tellwright," said Mrs. Sutton, " you're between two fires, and you'll get no mercy. What will you give? "

The miser foresaw a probable discomfiture, and sought for some means of escape.

" What are others giving? " he asked

" My husband is giving fifty pounds, and you could buy him up, lock, stock, and barrel."

" Nay, nay! " said Tellwright, aghast at this sum. He had underrated the importance of the Building Fund.

" And I," said the parson solemnly, " I have but fifty pounds in the world, but I am giving twenty to this fund."

" Then you're giving too much," said Tellwright with quick brusqueness. " You canna' afford it."

" The Lord will provide," said the parson.

" Happen He will, happen not. It's as well you've gotten a rich wife, Mr. Banks."

The parson's dignity was obviously wounded, and Anna wondered timidly what would occur next. Mrs. Sutton interposed. " Come now, Mr. Tellwright," she said again, " to the point: what will you give? "

" I'll think it over and let you hear," said Ephraim.

" Oh, no! That won't do at all, will it, Mr. Banks? I, at any rate, am not going away without a definite promise. As an old and good Wesleyan, of course you will feel it your duty to be generous with us."

" You used to be a pillar of the Hanbridge circuit—was it not so? " said Mr. Banks to the miser, recovering himself.

" So they used to say," Tellwright replied grimly. " That was because I cleared 'em of debt in ten years. But they've slipped into th' ditch again sin' I left 'em."

" But, if I am right, you do not meet* with us," the minister pursued imperturbably.

" No."

" My own class is at three on Saturdays," said the minister. " I should be glad to see you."

" I tell you what I'll do," said the miser to Mrs. Sutton. " Titus Price is a big man at th' Sunday School. I'll give as much as he gives to th' school buildings. That's fair."

---

* *Meet:* meet in class—a gathering for the exchange of religious counsel and experience.

" Do you know what Mr. Price is giving? " Mrs. Sutton asked the minister.

" I saw Mr. Price yesterday. He is giving twenty-five pounds."

" Very well, that's a bargain," said Mrs. Sutton, who had succeeded beyond her expectations.

Ephraim was the dupe of his own scheming. He had made sure that Price's contribution would be a small one. This ostentatious munificence on the part of the beggared Titus filled him with secret anger. He determined to demand more rent at a very early date.

" I'll put you down for twenty-five pounds as a first subscription," said the minister, taking out a pocket-book. " Perhaps you will give Mrs. Sutton or myself the cheque to-day? "

" Has Mr. Price paid? " the miser asked warily.

" Not yet."

" Then come to me when he has." Ephraim perceived the way of escape.

When the minister was gone, as Mrs. Sutton seemed in no hurry to depart, Anna and Agnes cleared the table.

" I've just been telling your father, Anna," said Mrs. Sutton, when Anna returned to the room, " that Mr. Sutton and myself and Beatrice are going to the Isle of Man soon for a fortnight or so, and we should very much like you to come with us."

Anna's heart began to beat violently, though she knew there was no hope for her. This, then, doubtless, was the main object of Mrs. Sutton's visit! "Oh, but I couldn't, really!" said Anna, scarcely knowing what she did say.

"Why not?" asked Mrs. Sutton.

"Well—the house."

"The house? Agnes could see to what little housekeeping your father would want. The schools will break up next week."

"What do these young folks want holidays for?" Tellwright inquired with philosophic gruffness. "I never had one. And what's more, I wouldn't thank ye for one. I'll pig on at Bursley. When ye've gotten a roof of your own, where's the sense o' going elsewhere and pigging?"

"But we really want Anna to go," Mrs. Sutton went on. "Beatrice is very anxious about it. Beatrice is very short of suitable friends."

"I should na' ha' thought it," said Tellwright. "Her seems to know everyone."

"But she is," Mrs. Sutton insisted.

"I think as you'd better leave Anna out this year," said the miser stubbornly.

Anna wished profoundly that Mrs. Sutton would abandon the futile attempt. Then she perceived that the visitor was signalling to her to leave the room. Anna obeyed, going into the kitchen to give an eye to Agnes, who was washing up.

"It's all right," said Mrs. Sutton contentedly, when Anna returned to the parlour. "Your father has consented to your going with us. It is very kind of him, for I'm sure he'll miss you."

Anna sat down, limp, speechless. She could not believe the news.

" You are awfully good," she said to Mrs. Sutton in the lobby, as the latter was leaving the house. " I'm ever so grateful—you can't think." And she threw her arms round Mrs. Sutton's neck.

Agnes ran up to say good-bye.

Mrs. Sutton kissed the child. " Agnes will be the little housekeeper, eh? " The little housekeeper was almost as pleased at the prospect of housekeeping as if she, too, had been going to the Isle of Man. " You'll both be at the school-treat next Tuesday, I suppose," Mrs. Sutton said, holding Agnes by the hand. Agnes glanced at her sister in enquiry.

" I don't know," Anna replied. " We shall see."

The truth was that, not caring to ask her father for the money for the tickets, she had given no thought to the school-treat.

" Did I tell you that Henry Mynors will most likely come with us to the Isle of Man? " said Mrs. Sutton from the gate.

Anna retired to her bedroom to savour an astounding happiness in quietude. At supper the miser was in a mood not unbenevolent. She expected a reaction the next morning, but Ephraim, strange to say, remained innocuous. She ventured to ask him for the money for the treat tickets, two shillings. He made no immediate reply. Half an hour afterwards, he ejaculated: " What i' th' name o' fortune dost thee want wi' school-treats? "

" It's Agnes," she answered; " of course Agnes can't go alone."

In the end he threw down a florin. He became perilous for the rest of the day, but the florin was an indisputable fact in Anna's pocket.

The school-treat was held in a twelve-acre field near Sneyd, the seat of a marquis, and a Saturday afternoon resort very popular in the Five Towns. The children were formed at noon on Duck Bank into a procession, which marched to the railway station to the singing of " Shall we gather at the river? " Thence a special train carried them, in seething compartments, excited and strident, to Sneyd, where the procession was re-formed along a country road. There had been two sharp showers in the morning, and the vacillating sky threatened more rain; but because the sun had shone dazzlingly at eleven o'clock all the women and girls, too easily tempted by the glory of the moment, blossomed forth in pale blouses and parasols. The chattering crowd, bright and defenceless as flowers, made at Sneyd a picture at once gay and pathetic. It had rained there at half-past twelve; the roads were wet; and among the 250 children and 30 teachers there were less than a score umbrellas.

The excursion was theoretically in charge of Titus Price, the Senior Superintendent, but this dignitary had failed to arrive on Duck Bunk, and Mynors had taken his place. In the train Anna heard that someone had seen Mr. Price, wearing a large grey wideawake, leap into the guard's van at the very instant of departure. He had not been at school on the previous Sunday, and Anna was somewhat perturbed at the prospect of meeting the man who had defined her letter to him as unique in the whole of his business career. She caught a glimpse of the grey wideawake on the platform at Sneyd, and steered her own scholars so as to avoid its vicinity. But on the march to the field Titus reviewed the procession, and she was obliged to meet his eyes and return his salutation. The look of the man was a shock to her. He seemed thinner, nervous, restless, preoccupied, and terribly careworn; except the new brilliant hat, all his summer clothes were soiled and shabby. It was as though he had forced himself, out of regard for appearances, to attend the fête, but had left his thoughts in Edward Street. His uneasy and hollow cheerfulness was painful to watch. Anna realised the intensity of the crisis through which Mr. Price was passing. She perceived in a single glance, more clearly than she could have done after a hundred interviews with the young and unresponsible William—however distressing these might be—that Titus must for weeks have been engaged in a truly frightful struggle. His face was a proof of the tragic sincerity of William's appeals to herself and to her father. That Price should have contrived to pay seventy pounds of rent in a little more than a month seemed to her, imperfectly acquainted alike with Ephraim's ruthless compulsions and with the financial jugglery often practiced by hard-pressed debtors, to be an almost miraculous effort after honesty. Her conscience smote her for conniving at what she now saw to be a persecution. She felt as sorry for Titus as she had felt for his son. The obese man, with his reputation in rags about him, was acutely wistful in her eyes, as a child might have been.

A carriage rolled by, raising the dust in places where the strong sun had already dried the road.  It was Mr. Sutton's landau, driven by Barrett.  Beatrice, in white, sat solitary amid cushions, while two large hampers occupied most of the coachman's box.  The carriage seemed to move with lordly ease and rapidity, and the teachers, already weary and fretted by the endless pranks of the children, bitterly envied the enthroned maiden who nodded and smiled to them with such charming condescension.  It was a social triumph for Beatrice.  She disappeared ahead like a goddess in a cloud, and scarcely a woman who saw her from the humble level of the roadway but would have married a satyr to be able to do as Beatrice did.  Later, when the field was reached, and the children, bursting through the gate, had spread like a flood over the daisied grass, the landau was to be seen drawn up near the refreshment tent; Barrett was unpacking the hampers, which contained delicate creamy confectionery for the teachers' tea; Beatrice explained that these were her mother's gift, and that she had driven down in order to preserve the fragile pasties from the risks of a railway journey.  Gratitude became vocal, and Beatrice's success was perfected.

Then the more conscientious teachers set themselves seriously to the task of amusing the smaller children, and the smaller children consented to be amused according to the recipes appointed by long custom for school-treats.  Many round-games, which invariably comprised singing or kissing, being thus annually resuscitated by elderly people from the deeps of memory, were preserved for a posterity which otherwise would never have known them. Among these was Bobby-Bingo. For twenty-five years Titus Price had played at Bobby-Bingo with the infant classes at the school-treat, and this year he was bound by the expectations of all to continue the practice. Another diversion which he always took care to organise was the three-legged race for boys. Also, he usually joined in the tut-ball, a quaint game, which owes its surprising longevity to the fact that it is equally proper for both sexes. Within half an hour the treat was in full career; football, cricket, rounders, tick, leap-frog, prison-bars, and round games, transformed the field into a vast arena of complicated struggles and emulations. All were occupied, except a few of the women and older girls, who strolled languidly about in the *rôle* of spectators. The sun shone generously on scores of vivid and frail toilettes, and parasols made slowly-moving hemispheres of glowing colour against the rich green of the grass. All around were yellow cornfields, and meadows where cows of a burnished brown indolently meditated upon the phenomena of a school-treat. Every hedge and ditch and gate and stile was in that ideal condition of plenary correctness which denotes that a great landowner is exhibiting the beauties of scientific farming for the behoof of his villagers. The sky, of an intense blue, was a sea in which large white clouds sailed gently but capriciously; on the northern horizon a low range of smoke marked the sinister region of the Five Towns.

"Will you come and help with the bags and cups?" Henry Mynors asked Anna.   She was standing by herself, watching Agnes at play with some other girls.   Mynors had evidently walked across to her from the refreshment tent, which was at the opposite extremity of the field.   In her eyes he was once more the exemplar of style.   His suit of grey flannel, his white straw hat, became him to admiration. He stood at ease with his hands in his coat-pockets, and smiled contentedly.

"After all," he said, "the tea is the principal thing, and, although it wants two hours to tea-time yet, it's as well to be beforehand."

"I should like something to do," Anna replied.

"How are you?" he said familiarly, after this abrupt opening, and then shook hands.   They traversed the field together, with many deviations to avoid trespassing upon areas of play.

The flapping refreshment-tent seemed to be full of piles of baskets and piles of bags and piles of cups, which the contractor had brought in a waggon.   Some teachers were already beginning to put the paper bags into the baskets; each bag contained bread-and-butter, currant cake, an Eccles-cake, and a Bath-bun.   At the far end of the tent Beatrice Sutton was arranging her dainties on a small trestle-table.

"Come along quick, Anna," she exclaimed," and taste my tarts, and tell me what you think of them.   I do hope the good people will enjoy them."   And then, turning to Mynors, "Hello!   Are you seeing after the bags and things?

I thought that was always William Price's favourite job!"

"So it is," said Mynors. "But, unfortunately, he isn't here to-day."

"How's that, pray? I never knew *him* miss a school-treat before."

"Mr. Price told me they couldn't both be away from the works just now. Very busy, I suppose."

"Well, William would have been more use than his father, anyhow."

"Hush, hush!" Mynors murmured with a subdued laugh.

Beatrice was in one of her "downright" moods, as she herself called them.

Mynors' arrangements for the prompt distribution of tea at the appointed hour were very minute, and involved a considerable amount of back-bending and manual labour. But, though they were enlivened by frequent intervals of gossip, and by excursions into the field to observe this and that amusing sight, all was finished half an hour before time.

"I will go and warn Mr. Price," said Mynors. "He is quite capable of forgetting the clock." Mynors left the tent, and proceeded to the scene of an athletic meeting, at which Titus Price, in shirt-sleeves, was distributing prizes of sixpences and pennies. The famous three-legged race had just been run. Anna followed at a saunter, and shortly afterwards Beatrice overtook her.

"The great Titus looks better than he did when he came on the field," Beatrice remarked. And indeed the superintendent had put on quite a merry appearance—flushed, excited, and jocular in his elephantine way—it seemed as if he had not a care in the world. The boys crowded appreciatively round him. But this was his last hour of joy.

"Why! Willie Price *is* here," Anna exclaimed, perceiving William in the fringe of the crowd. The lanky fellow stood hesitatingly, his left hand busy with his moustache.

"So he is," said Beatrice. "I wonder what that means."

Titus had not observed the newcomer, but Henry Mynors saw William, and exchanged a few words with him. Then Mr. Mynors advanced into the crowd and spoke to Mr. Price, who glanced quickly round at his son. The girls, at a distance of forty yards, could discern the swift change in the man's demeanour. In a second he had reverted to the deplorable Titus of three hours ago. He elbowed his way roughly to William, getting into his coat as he went. The pair talked, William glanced at his watch, and in another moment they were leaving the field. Henry Mynors had to finish the prize distribution. So much Anna and Beatrice plainly saw. Others, too, had not been blind to this sudden and dramatic departure. It aroused universal comment among the teachers.

"Something must be wrong at Price's works," Beatrice said, "and Willie has had to fetch his papa." This was the conclusion of all the gossips. Beatrice added: "Dad has mentioned Price's several times lately, now I think of it."

Anna grew extremely self-conscious and uncomfortable. She felt as though all were saying of her: "There goes the oppressor of the poor!" She was fairly sure, however, that her father was not responsible for this particular incident. There must, then, be other implacable creditors. She had been thoroughly enjoying the afternoon, but now her pleasure ceased.

The treat ended disastrously. In the middle of the children's meal, while yet the enormous double-handled tea-cans were being carried up and down the thirsty rows, and the boys were causing their bags to explode with appalling detonations, it began to rain sharply. The fickle sun withdrew his splendour from the toilettes, and was seen no more for a week afterwards. " It's come at last," ejaculated Mynors, who had watched the sky with anxiety for an hour previously. He mobilised the children and ranked them under a row of elms. The teachers, running to the tent for their own tea, said to one another that the shower could only be a brief one. The wish was father to the thought, for they were a little ashamed to be under cover while their charges precariously sheltered beneath dripping trees—yet there was nothing else to be done; the men took turns in the rain to keep the children in their places. The sky was completely overcast. " It's set in for a wet evening, and so we may as well make the best of it," Beatrice said grimly, and she sent the landau home empty. She was right. A forlorn and disgusted snake of a procession crawled through puddles to the station. The platform resounded with sneezes. None but a dressmaker could have discovered a silver lining to that black and all-pervading cloud which had ruined so many dozens of fair costumes. Anna, melancholy and taciturn, exerted herself to minimise the discomfort of her scholars. A word from Mynors would have been balm to her; but Mynors, the general of a routed army, was parleying by telephone with the traffic-manager of the railway for the expediting of the special train.

# X: THE ISLE

ABOUT this time Anna was not seeing very much of Henry Mynors. At twenty a man is rash in love, and again, perhaps, at fifty; a man of middle-age enamoured of a young girl is capable of sublime follies. But the man of thirty who loves for the first time is usually the embodiment of cautious discretion. He does not fall in love with a violent descent, but rather lets himself gently down, continually testing the rope. His social value, especially if he have achieved worldly success, is at its highest, and, without conceit, he is aware of it. He has lost many illusions concerning women; he has seen more than one friend wrecked in the sea of foolish marriage; he knows the joys of a bachelor's freedom, without having wearied of them; he perceives risks where the youth perceives only ecstasy, and the oldster only a blissful release from solitude. Instead of searching, he is sought for; accordingly he is selfish and exacting. All these things combine to tranquillize passion at thirty. Mynors was in love with Anna, and his love had its ardent moments; but in the main it was a temperate affection, an affection that walked circumspectly, with its eyes open, careful of its dignity, too proud to seem in a hurry; if, by impulse, it chanced now and then to leap forward, the involuntary movement was mastered and checked. Mynors called at Manor Terrace once a week, never on the same day of the week, not without discussing

175

business with the miser.   Occasionally he accompanied Anna
from school or chapel.   Such methods were precisely to
Anna's taste.   Like him, she loved prudence and decorum,
preferring to make haste slowly.   Since the Revival they
had only once talked together intimately; on that sole occasion Henry had suggested to her that she might care to
join Mrs. Sutton's class, which met on Monday nights; she
accepted the hint with pleasure, and found a well of spiritual inspiration in Mrs. Sutton's modest and simple, yet fervent, homilies.   Mynors was not guilty of blowing both hot
and cold.   She was sure of him.   She waited calmly for
events, existing, as her habit was, in the future.

The future, then, meant the Isle of Man.   Anna dreamed
of an enchanted isle and hours of unimaginable rapture.
For a whole week after Mrs. Sutton had won Ephraim's
consent, her vision never stooped to practical details.   Then
Beatrice called to see her; it was the morning after the treat,
and Anna was brushing her muddy frock; she wore a large
white apron, and held a clothes-brush in her hand as she
opened the door.

" You're busy? " said Beatrice.

" Yes," said Anna, " but come in.   Come into the kitchen
—do you mind? "

Beatrice was covered from neck to heel with a long mack-
intosh, which she threw off when entering the kitchen.

" Anyone else in the house? " she asked.

" No," said Anna, smiling, as Beatrice seated herself, with
a sigh of content, on the table.

" Well, let's talk, then."   Beatrice drew from her pocket

the indispensable chocolates and offered them to Anna. " I say, wasn't last night perfectly awful? Henry got wet through in the end, and mother made him stop at our house, as he was at the trouble to take me home. Did you see him go down this morning? "

" No; why? " said Anna stiffly.

" Oh—no reason. Only I thought perhaps you did. I simply can't tell you how glad I am that you're coming with us to the Isle of Man; we shall have rare fun. We go every year, you know—to Port Erin, a lovely little fishing village. All the fishermen know us there. Last year Henry hired a yacht for the fortnight, and we all went mackerel-fishing, every day; except sometimes pa. Now and then pa had a tendency to go fiddling in caves and things. I do hope it will be fine weather again by then, don't you? "

" I am looking forward to it, I can tell you," Anna said. " What day are we supposed to start? "

" Saturday week."

" So soon? " Anna was surprised at the proximity of the event.

" Yes; and quite late enough, too. We should start earlier, only the dad always makes out he can't. Men always pretend to be so frightfully busy, and I believe it's all put on." Beatrice continued to chat about the holiday, and then of a sudden she asked: " What are you going to wear? "

" Wear! " Anna repeated; and then added, with hesitation: " I suppose one will want some new clothes? "

" Well, just a few! Now let me advise you. Take a blue

serge skirt. Sea-water won't harm it, and if it's dark enough it will look well to any mortal blouse. Secondly, you can't have too many blouses; they're always useful at the seaside. Plain straw-hats are my tip. A coat for nights, and thick boots. There! Of course no one ever *dresses* at Port Erin. It isn't like Llandudno, and all that sort of thing. You don't have to meet your young man on the pier, because there isn't a pier."

There was a pause. Anna did not know what to say. At length she ventured: " I'm not much for clothes, as I dare say you've noticed."

" I think you always look nice, my dear," Beatrice responded. Nothing was said as to Anna's wealth, no reference made as to the discrepancy between that and the style of her garments. By a fiction, there was supposed to be no discrepancy.

" Do you make your own frocks? " Beatrice asked, later.

" Yes."

" Do you know I thought you did. But they do you great credit. There's few people can make a plain frock look decent."

This conversation brought Anna with a shock to the level of the earth. She perceived—only too well—a point which she had not hitherto fairly faced in her idyllic meditations: that her father was still a factor in the case. Since Mrs. Sutton's visit both Anna and the miser avoided the subject of the holiday. " You can't have too many blouses." Did Beatrice. then, have blouses by the dozen? A coat, a serge skirt, straw hats (how many?)—the catalogue frightened her. She began to suspect that she would not be able to go to the Isle of Man.

" About me going with Suttons to the Isle of Man? " she accosted her father, in the afternoon, outwardly calm, but with secret trembling.

" Well? " he exclaimed savagely.

" I shall want some money—a little." She would have given much not to have added that " little," but it came out of itself.

" It's a waste o' time and money—that's what I call it. I can't think why Suttons asked ye. Ye aren't ill, are ye? " His savagery changed to sullenness.

" No, father; but as it's arranged, I suppose I shall have to go."

" Well, I'm none so set up with the idea mysen."

" Sha'n't you be all right with Agnes? "

" Oh, yes! *I* shall be all right. *I* don't want much. *I*'ve no fads and fal-lals. How long art going to be away? "

" I don't know. Didn't Mrs. Sutton tell you? You arranged it."

" That I didna'. Her said nowt to me."

" Well, anyhow I shall want some clothes."

" What for? Art naked? "

" I must have some money." Her voice shook. She was getting near tears.

" Well, thou's gotten thy own money, hast na'? "

" All I want is that you shall let me have some of my own money. There's forty odd pounds now in the bank."

" Oh! " he repeated, sneering, " all ye want is as I shall let thee have some o' thy own money. And there's forty odd pound i' the bank. Oh! "

" Will you give me my cheque-book out of the bureau? And I'll draw a cheque; I know how to." She had conquered the instinct to cry, and unwillingly her tones became somewhat peremptory. Ephraim seized the chance.

" No, I won't give ye the cheque-book out o' th' bureau," he said flatly. " And I'll thank ye for less sauce."

That finished the episode. Proudly she took an oath with herself not to re-open the question, and resolved to write a note to Mrs. Sutton, saying that on consideration she found it impossible to go to the Isle of Man.

The next morning there came to Anna a letter from the secretary of a limited company, enclosing a post-office order for ten pounds. Some weeks previously her father had discovered an error of that amount in the deduction of income-tax from the dividend paid by this company, and had instructed Anna to demand the sum. She had obeyed, and then forgotten the affair. Here was the answer. Desperate at the thought of missing the holiday, she cashed the order, bought and made her clothes in secret, and then, two days before the arranged date for departure, told her father what she had done. He was enraged; but since his anger was too illogical to be rendered effectively coherent in words, he had the wit to keep silence. With bitterness Anna reflected that she owed her holiday to the merest accident—for if the remittance had arrived a little earlier or a little later, or in the form of a cheque, she could not have utilised it.

It was an incredible day, the following Saturday, a warm and benign day of earliest autumn. The Suttons, in a hired cab, called for Anna at half-past eight, on the way to the main-line station at Shawport. Anna's tin box was flung on to the roof of the cab amid the trunks and portmanteaux already there.

" Why should not Agnes ride with us to the station? " Beatrice suggested.

" Nay, nay; there's no room," said Tellwright, who stood at the door, impelled by an unacknowledged awe of Mrs. Sutton thus to give official sanction to Anna's departure.

" Yes, yes," Mrs. Sutton exclaimed. " Let the little thing come, Mr. Tellwright."

Agnes, far more excited than any of the rest, seized her straw hat, and slipping the elastic under her small chin, sprang into the cab, and found a haven between Mr. Sutton's short, fat legs. The driver drew his whip smartly across the aged neck of the cream mare. They were off. What a rumbling, jolting, delicious journey, down the first hill, up Duck Bank, through the market-place, and down the steep declivity of Oldcastle Street! Silent and shy, Agnes smiled ecstatically at the others. Anna answered remarks in a dream. She was conscious only of present happiness and happy expectation. All bitterness had disappeared. At least thirty thousand Bursley folk were not going to the Isle of Man that day—their preoccupied and cheerless faces swam in a continuous stream past the cab window—and Anna sympathised with every unit of them. Her spirit overflowed with universal compassion. What haste and exquisite confusion at the station! The train was signalled, and the porter, crossing the line with the luggage, ran his truck perilously under the very buffers of the incoming engine. Mynors was awaiting them, admirably attired as a tourist. He had got the tickets, and secured a private compartment in the through-coach for Liverpool; and he found time to arrange with the cabman to drive Agnes home on the box-seat. Certainly there was none like Mynors. From the footboard of the carriage Anna bent down to kiss Agnes. The child had been laughing and chattering. Suddenly, as Anna's lips touched hers, she burst into tears, sobbed passionately as though overtaken by some terrible and unexpected misfortune. Tears stood also in Anna's eyes. The sisters had never been parted before.

" Poor little thing!" Mrs. Sutton murmured; and Beatrice told her father to give Agnes a shilling to buy chocolates at Stevenson's in St. Luke's Square, that being the best shop. The shilling fell between the footboard and the platform. A scream from Beatrice! The attendant porter promised to rescue the shilling in due course. The engine whistled, the silver-mounted guard asserted his authority, Mynors leaped in, and amid laughter and tears the brief and unique joy of Anna's life began.

In a moment, so it seemed, the train was thundering through the mile of solid rock which ends at Lime Street Station, Liverpool. Thenceforward, till she fell asleep that night, Anna existed in a state of blissful bewilderment, stupefied by an overdose of novel and wondrous sensations. They lunched in amazing magnificence at the Bear's Paw, and then walked through the crowded and prodigious streets to Prince's landing-stage. The luggage had disappeared by some mysterious agency—Mynors said that they would find it safe at Douglas; but Anna could not banish the fear that her tin box had gone forever.

The great, wavy river, churned by thousands of keels; the monstrous steamer—the " Mona's Isle "—whose side rose like solid wall out of the water; the vistas of its decks; its vast saloons, story under story, solid and palatial (could all this float?); its high bridge; its hawsers as thick as trees; its funnels like sloping towers; the multitudes of passengers; the whistles, hoots, cries; the far-stretching panorama of wharves and docks; the squat ferry-craft carrying horses and carts, and no one looking twice at the feat—it was all too much, too astonishing, too lovely. She had not guessed at this.

" They call Liverpool the slum of Europe," said Mynors.

" How can you! " she exclaimed, shocked.

Beatrice, seeing her radiant and rapt face, walked to and fro with Anna, proud of the effect produced on her friend's inexperience by these sights. One might have thought that Beatrice had built Liverpool and created its trade by her own efforts.

Suddenly the landing-stage and all the people on it moved away bodily from the ship; there was green water between; a tremor like that of an earthquake ran along the deck; handkerchiefs were waved. The voyage had commenced. Mynors found chairs for all the Suttons, and tucked them up on the lee-side of a deck-house; but Anna did not stir. They passed New Brighton, Seaforth, and the Crosby and Formby lightships.

"Come and view the ship," said Mynors, at her side. "Suppose we go round and inspect things a bit?"

"It's a very big one, isn't it?" she asked.

"Pretty big," he said; "of course not as big as the Atlantic liners—I wonder we didn't meet one in the river— but still pretty big. Three hundred and twenty feet over all. I sailed on her last year on her maiden voyage. She was packed, and the weather very bad."

"Will it be rough to-day?" Anna inquired timidly.

"Not if it keeps like this," he laughed. "You don't feel queer, do you?"

"Oh, no! It's as firm as a house. No one could be ill with this."

"Couldn't they?" he exclaimed. "Beatrice could be."

They descended into the ship, and he explained all its internal economy, with a knowledge that seemed to her encyclopædic. They stayed a long time watching the engines, so Titanic, ruthless, and deliberate; even the smell of the oil was pleasant to Anna. When they came on deck again the ship was at sea. For the first time Anna beheld the ocean. A strong breeze blew from prow to stern, yet the sea was absolutely calm, the unruffled mirror of effulgent sunlight. The steamer moved along on the waters, exultantly, leaving behind it an endless track of white froth in the green, and the shadow of its smoke. The sun, the salt breeze, the living water, the proud gaiety of the ship, produced a feeling of intense, inexplicable joy, a profound satisfaction with the present, and a negligence of past and future. To exist was enough, then. As Anna and Henry leaned over the starboard quarter and watched the torrent of foam rush madly and ceaselessly from under the paddle-box to be swallowed up in the white wake, the spectacle of the wild torrent almost hypnotised them, destroying thought and reason, and all sense of their relation to other things. With difficulty Anna raised her eyes, and perceived the dim receding line of the Lancashire coast.

" Shall we get quite out of sight of land? " she asked.

" Yes, for a little while, about half an hour or so. Just as much out of sight of land as if we were in the middle of the Atlantic."

" I can scarcely believe it."

" Believe what? "

" Oh! The idea of that—of being out of sight of land —nothing but sea."

When at last it occurred to them to reconnoitre the Suttons, they found all three still in their deck-chairs, enwrapped and languid. Mr. Sutton and Beatrice were apparently dozing. This part of the deck was occupied by somnolent, basking figures.

" Don't wake them," Mrs. Sutton enjoined, whispering out of her hood. Anna glanced curiously at Beatrice's yellow face.

" Go away, do," Beatrice exclaimed, opening her eyes and shutting them again, wearily.

So they went away, and discovered two empty deck-chairs on the fore-deck. Anna was innocently vain of her immunity from *malaise*. Mynors appeared to appoint himself little errands about the deck, returning frequently to his chair.

" Look over there. Can you see anything? "

Anna ran to the rail, with the infantile idea of getting nearer, and Mynors followed, laughing. What looked like a small slate-coloured cloud lay on the horizon.

" I seem to see something," she said.

" That is the Isle of Man."

By insensible gradations the contours of the land grew clearer in the afternoon haze.

" How far are we off now? "

" Perhaps twenty miles."

Twenty miles of uninterrupted flatness, and the ship steadily invading that separating solitude, yard by yard, furlong by furlong! The conception awed her. There, a morsel in the waste of the deep, a speck under the infinite sunlight, lay the island, mysterious, enticing, enchanted, a glinting jewel on the sea's bosom, a remote entity fraught with strange secrets. It was all unspeakable.


" Anna, you have covered yourself with glory," said Mrs. Sutton, when they were in the diminutive and absurd train which by breathless plunges annihilates the sixteen miles between Douglas and Port Erin in sixty-five minutes.

" Have I? " she answered. " How? "

" By not being ill."

" That's always the beginner's luck," said Beatrice, pale

and dishevelled. They all relapsed into the silence of fatigue. It was growing dusk when the train stopped at the
tiny terminus. The station was a hive of bustling activity,
the arrival of this train being the daily event at that end of
the world. Mynors and the Suttons were greeted familiarly
by several sailors, and one of these, Tom Kelly, a tall,
middle-aged man, with grey beard, small grey eyes, a
wrinkled skin of red mahogany, and an enormous fist, was
introduced to Anna. He raised his cap, and shook hands.
She was touched by the sad, kind look on his face, the melancholy impress of the sea. Then they drove to their lodging, and here again the party was welcomed as being old and
tried friends. A fire was burning in the parlour. Throwing herself down in front of it, Mrs. Sutton breathed, " At
last! Oh, for some tea." Through the window, Anna had
a glimpse of a deeply indented bay at the foot of cliffs below
them, with a bold headland to the right. Fishing vessels
with flat red sails seemed to hang undecided just outside
the bay. From cottage chimneys beneath the road blue
smoke softly ascended.

All went early to bed, for the weariness of Mr. and Mrs.
Sutton seemed to communicate itself to the three young
people, who might otherwise have gone forth into the village in search of adventures. Anna and Beatrice shared a
room. Each inspected the other's clothes, and Beatrice made
Anna try on the new serge skirt. Through the thin wall
came the sound of Mr. and Mrs. Sutton talking, a high
voice, then a bass reply, in continual alternation. Beatrice said that these two always discussed the day's doings

in such manner. In a few moments Beatrice was snoring; she had the subdued, but steady and serious, snore characteristic of some muscular men. Anna felt no inclination to sleep. She lived again hour by hour through the day, and beneath Beatrice's snore her ear caught the undertone of the sea.

The next morning was as lovely as the last. It was Sunday, and every activity of the village was stilled. Sea and land were equally folded in a sunlit calm. During breakfast —a meal abundant in fresh herrings, fresh eggs, and fresh rolls, eaten with the window wide open—Anna was puzzled by the singular amenity of her friends to one another and to her. They were as polite as though they had been strangers; they chatted amiably, were full of good will, and as anxious to give happiness as to enjoy it. She thought at first, so unusual was it to her as a feature of domestic privacy, that this demeanour was affected, or at any rate a somewhat exaggerated punctilio due to her presence; but she soon came to see that she was mistaken. After breakfast Mr. Sutton suggested that they should attend the Wesleyan Chapel on the hill leading to the Chasms. Here they met the sailors of the night before, arrayed now in marvellous blue Melton coats with velveteen collars. Tom Kelly walked back with them to the beach, and showed them the yacht " Fay," which Mynors had arranged to hire for mackerel-fishing; it lay on the sand, speckless in new white paint. All afternoon they dozed on the cliffs, doing nothing whatever, for this Sunday was tacitly regarded, not as part of the holiday, but as a preparation for the holiday; all felt that the holiday, with its proper exertions and appointed delights, would really begin on Monday morning.

" Let us go for a walk," said Mynors, after tea, to Beatrice and Anna. They stood at the gate of the lodging-house. The old people were resting within.

" You two go," Beatrice replied, looking at Anna. " You know I hate walking, Henry. I'll stop with mother and dad."

Throughout the day Anna had been conscious of the fact that all the Suttons showed a tendency, slight but percept-ible, to treat Henry and herself as a pair desirous of oppor-tunities for being alone together. She did not like it. She flushed under the passing glance with which Beatrice accom-panied the words: " You two go." Nevertheless, when My-nors placidly remarked: " Very well," and his eyes sought hers for a consent, she could not refuse it. One part of her nature would have preferred to find an excuse for staying at home; but another, and a stronger, part insisted on seiz-ing this offered joy.

They walked straight up out of the village towards the high coast-range which stretches, peak after peak, from Port Erin to Peel. The stony and devious lanes wound about the bleak hillside, passing here and there small, solitary cottages of whitewashed stone, with children, fowls, and dogs at the doors, all embowered in huge fuchsia trees. Presently they had surmounted the limit of habitation and were on the naked flank of Bradda, following a narrow track which crept upwards amid short mossy turf of the most vivid green. Nothing seemed to flourish on this exposed height except bracken, sheep, and boulders that, from a distance, resembled sheep; there was no tree, scarcely a shrub; the immense contours, stark, grim, and unrelieved, rose in melancholy and defiant majesty against the sky: the hand of man could coax no harvest from these smooth, but obdurate, slopes; they had never relented and they would never relent. The spirit was braced by the thought that here, to the furthest eternity of civilisations more and more intricate, simple and strong souls would always find solace and repose.

Mynors bore to the left for a while, striking across the moor in the direction of the sea. Then he said:

" Look down, now."

The little bay lay like an oblong swimming-bath five hundred feet below them. The surface of the water was like glass; the strand, with its phalanx of boats drawn up in Sabbath tidiness, glittered like marble in the dying light, and over this marble black dots moved slowly to and fro; behind the boats were the houses—doll's houses—each with a curling wisp of smoke; further away the railway and the high-road ran out in a black and a white line to Port St. Mary; the sea, a pale grey, encompassed all; the southern sky had a faint sapphire tinge, rising to delicate azure. The sight of this haven at rest, shut in by the restful sea and by great moveless hills, a calm within a calm, aroused profound emotion.

" It's lovely," said Anna, as they stood gazing. Tears came to her eyes and hung there. She wondered that scenery should cause tears, felt ashamed, and turned her face so that Mynors should not see. But he had seen.

"Shall we go on to the top?" he suggested, and they set their faces northwards, to climb still higher. At length they stood on the rocky summit of Bradda, seven hundred feet from the sea. The Hill of the Night Watch lifted above them to the north, but on east, south, and west, the prospect was bounded only by the ocean. The coast-line was revealed for thirty miles, from Peel to Castletown. Far to the east was Castletown Bay, large, shallow, and inhospitable, its floor strewn with a thousand unseen wrecks; the lighthouse at Scarlet Point flashed dimly in the dusk; thence the beach curved nearer in an immense arc, without a sign of life, to the little cove of Port St. Mary, and jutted out again into a tongue of land, at the end of which lay the Calf of Man, with its single white cottage and cart-track. The dangerous Calf Sound, where the vexed tide is forced to run nine hours one way and three the other, seemed like a grey ribbon, and the Chicken Rock like a tiny pencil on a vast slate. Port Erin was hidden under their feet. They looked westward. The darkening sky was a labyrinth of purple and crimson scarves drawn pellucid, as though by the finger of God, across a sheet of pure saffron. These decadent tints of the sunset faded in every direction to the same soft azure which filled the south, and one star twinkled in the illimitable field. Thirty miles off, on the horizon, could be discerned the Mourne Mountains of Ireland.

"See!" Mynors exclaimed, touching her arm.

The huge disc of the moon was rising in the east, and as

this mild lamp passed up the sky, the sense of universal quiescence increased. Lovely, Anna had said. It was the loveliest sight her eyes had ever beheld, a panorama of pure beauty transcending all imagined visions. It overwhelmed her, thrilled her to the heart, this revelation of the loveliness of the world. Her thoughts went back to Hanbridge and Bursley and her life there; and all the remembered scenes, bathed in the glow of a new ideal, seemed to lose their pain. It was as if she had never been really unhappy, as if there was no real unhappiness on the whole earth. She perceived that the monotony, the austerity, the melancholy of her existence had been sweet and beautiful of its kind, and she recalled, with a sort of rapture, hours of companionship with the beloved Agnes, when her father was equable and pacific. Nothing was ugly nor mean. Beauty was everywhere, in everything.

In silence they began to descend, perforce walking quickly because of the steep gradient. At the first cottage they saw a little girl in a mob-cap, playing with two kittens.

" How like Agnes! " Mynors said.

" Yes, I was just thinking so," Anna answered.

" I thought of her up on the hill," he continued. " She will miss you, won't she? "

" I know she cried herself to sleep last night. You mightn't guess it, but she is extremely sensitive."

" Not guess it? Why not? I am sure she is. Do you know—I am very fond of your sister. She's a simply delightful child. And there's a lot in her, too. She's so quick and bright, and somehow like a little woman."

" She's exactly like a woman sometimes," Anna agreed.
" Sometimes I fancy she's a great deal older than I am."

" Older than any of us," he corrected.

" I'm glad you like her," Anna said, content. " She
thinks all the world of you." And she added: " My word,
wouldn't she be vexed if she knew I had told you that!"

This appreciation of Agnes brought them into closer intimacy, and they talked the more easily of other things.

" It will freeze to-night," Mynors said; and then, suddenly looking at her in the twilight: " You are feeling
chill."

" Oh, no!" she protested.

" But you are. Put this muffler round your neck." He
took a muffler from his pocket.

" Oh, no, really! You will need it yourself." She drew
a little away from him, as if to avoid the muffler.

" Please take it."

She did so, and thanked him, tying it loosely and untidily
round her throat. That feeling of the untidiness of the
muffler, of its being something strange to her skin, something with the rough virtue of masculinity, which no one
could detect in the gloom, was in itself pleasant.

" I wager Mrs. Sutton has a good fire burning when we
get in," he said.

She thought with joyous anticipation of the warm, bright
sitting-room, the supper, and the vivacious, good-natured
conversation. Though the walk was nearly at an end, other
delights were in store. Of the holiday, thirteen complete
days yet remained, each to be happy as the one now clos-

ing. It was an age! At last they entered the human cosi-
ness of the village. As they walked up the steps of their
lodging, and he opened the door for her, she quickly drew
off the muffler and returnèd it to him with a word of thanks.

On Monday morning, when Beatrice and Anna came
downstairs, they found the breakfast odorously cooling on
the table, and nobody in the room.

" Where are they all, I wonder. Any letters? " Beatrice
said.

" There's your mother, out on the front—and Mr. Mynors, too."

Beatrice threw up the window, and called: " Come along,
Henry; come along, mother. Everything's going cold."

" Is it? " Mynors cheerfully replied. " Come out here,
both of you, and begin the day properly with a dose of
ozone."

" I loathe cold bacon," said Beatrice, glancing at the
table, and they went out into the road, where Mrs. Sutton
kissed them with as much fervour as if they had arrived from
a long journey.

" You look pale, Anna," she remarked.

" Do I? " said Anna, " I don't feel pale."

" It's that long walk last night," Beatrice put in.
" Henry always goes too far."

" I don't——" Anna began; but at that moment Mr.
Sutton, lumbering and ponderous, joined the party.

" Henry," he said, without greeting anyone, " hast
noticed those half-finished houses down the road yonder by
the ' Falcon '? I've been having a chat with Kelly, and he

tells me the fellow that was building them has gone bankrupt, and they're at a standstill. The receiver wants to sell 'em. In fact Kelly says they're going cheap. I believe they'd be a good spec."

" Eh, dear ! " Mrs. Sutton interrupted him. " Father, I wish you would leave your specs alone when you're on your holiday."

" Now, missis ! " he affectionately protested, and continued: " They're fairly well-built, seemingly, and the rafters are on the roof. Anna," he turned to her quickly, as if counting on her sympathy, " you must come with me and look at 'em after breakfast. Happen they might suit your father—or you. I know your father's fond of a good spec."

She assented with a ready smile. This was the beginning of a fancy which the Alderman always afterwards showed for Anna.

After breakfast, Mrs. Sutton, Beatrice, and Anna arranged to go shopping.

" Father—brass," Mrs. Sutton ejaculated in two monosyllables to her husband.

" How much will content ye? " he asked mildly.

" Give me five or ten pounds to go on with."

He opened the left-hand front pocket of his trousers— a pocket which fastened with a button; and leaning back in the chair drew out a fat purse, and passed it to his wife with a preoccupied air. She helped herself, and then Beatrice intercepted the purse and lightened it of half a sovereign.

" Pocket-money," Beatrice said ; " I'm ruined."

The Alderman's eyes requested Anna to observe how he was robbed. At last the purse was safely buttoned up again.

Mrs. Sutton's purchases of food at the three principal shops of the village seemed startlingly profuse to Anna, but gradually she became accustomed to the scale, and to the amazing habit of always buying the very best of everything, from beefsteak to grapes. Anna calculated that the housekeeping could not cost less than six pounds a week for the five. At Manor Terrace three people existed on a pound. With her half-sovereign Beatrice bought a belt and a pair of sand-shoes, and some cigarettes for Henry. Mrs. Sutton bought a pipe with a nickel cap, such as is used by sailors. When they returned to the house, Mr. Sutton and Henry were smoking in the front. All five walked in a row down to the harbour, the Alderman giving an arm each to Beatrice and Anna. Near the " Falcon " the procession had to be stopped in order to view the unfinished houses. Tom Kelly had a cabin partly excavated out of the rock behind the little quay. Here they found him entangled amid nets, sails, and oars. All crowded into the cabin and shook hands with its owner, who remarked with severity on their pallid faces, and insisted that a change of complexion must be brought about. Mynors offered him his tobacco-pouch, but on seeing the light colour of the tobacco he shook his head and refused it, at the same time taking from within his jersey a lump of something that resembled leather.

" Give him this, Henry," Mrs. Sutton whispered, handing Mynors the pipe which she had bought.

" Mrs. Sutton wishes you to accept this," said Mynors.

" Eh, thank ye," he exclaimed. " There's a leddy that knows my taste." He cut some shreds from his plug with a clasp-knife and charged and lighted the pipe, filling the cabin with asphyxiating fumes.

" I don't know how you can smoke such horrid, nasty stuff," said Beatrice, coughing.

He laughed condescendingly at Beatrice's petulant manner. " That stuff of Henry's is boy's tobacco," he said shortly.

It was decided that they should go fishing in the " Fay." There was a light southerly breeze, a cloudy sky, and smooth water. Under charge of young Tom Kelly, a sheepish lad of sixteen, with his father's smile, they all got into an inconceivably small dinghy, loading it down till it was almost awash. Old Tom himself helped Anna to embark, told her where to tread, and forced her gently into a seat at the stern. No one else seemed to be disturbed, but Anna was in a state of desperate fear. She had never committed herself to a boat before, and the little waves spat up against the sides in a most alarming way as young Tom jerked the dinghy along with the short sculls. She went white, and clung in silence fiercely to the gunwale. In a few moments they were tied up to the " Fay," which seemed very big and safe in comparison with the dinghy. They clambered on board, and in the deep well of the two-ton yacht Anna contrived to collect her wits. She was reassured by the painted legend in

the well, " Licensed to carry eleven." Young Tom and
Henry busied themselves with ropes, and suddenly a huge
white sail began to ascend the mast; it flapped like thunder
in the gentle breeze.    Tom pulled up the anchor, curling
the chain round and round on the forward deck, and
then Anna noticed that, although the wind was scarcely
perceptible, they were gliding quickly past the embankment.
Henry was at the tiller.    The next minute Tom had set the
jib, and by this time the " Fay " was approaching the breakwater at a great pace.    There was no rolling or pitching,
but simply a smooth, swift progression over the calm surface.    Anna thought it the ideal of locomotion.    As soon
as they were beyond the breakwater and the sails caught
the breeze from the Sound, the " Fay " lay over as if shot,
and a little column of green water flung itself on the lee
coaming of the well.    Anna screamed as she saw the water
and felt the angle of the floor suddenly change, but when
everyone laughed, she laughed too.    Henry, noticing the
whiteness of her knuckles as she gripped the coaming, explained the disconcerting phenomena.    Anna tried to be at
ease, but she was not.    She could not for a long time dismiss
the suspicion that all these people were foolishly blind to a
peril which she alone had the sagacity to perceive.

They cruised about while Tom prepared the lines.    The
short waves chopped cheerfully against the carvel sides of
the yacht; the clouds were breaking at a hundred points; the
sea grew lighter in tone; gaiety was in the air; no one could
possibly be indisposed in that innocuous weather.    At
length the lines were ready, but Tom said the yacht was

making at least a knot too much for serious fishing, so Henry took a reef in the mainsail, showing Anna how to tie the short strings. The Alderman, lying on the fore-deck, was placidly smoking. The lines were thrown out astern, and Mrs. Sutton and Beatrice each took one. But they had no success; young Tom said it was because the sun had appeared.

"Caught anything?" Mr. Sutton inquired at intervals. After a time he said:

"Suppose Anna and I have a try?"

It was agreed.

"What must I do?" asked Anna, brave now.

"You just hold the line—so. And if you feel a little jerk-jerk, that's a mackerel." These were the instructions of Beatrice. Anna was becoming excited. She had not held the line ten seconds before she cried out:

"I've got one."

"Nonsense," said Beatrice. "Everyone thinks at first that the motion of the waves against the line is a fish."

"Well," said Henry, giving the tiller to young Tom. "Let's haul in and see, anyway." Before doing so he held the line for a moment, testing it, and winked at Anna. While Anna and Henry were hauling in, the Alderman, dropping his pipe, began also to haul in his own line with great fury.

"Got one, father?" Mrs. Sutton asked.

"Ay!"

Both lines came in together, and on each was a pounder. Anna saw her fish gleam and flash like silver in the clear water as it neared the surface. Henry held the line short, letting the mackerel plunge and jerk, and then seized and unhooked the catch.

"How cruel!" Anna cried, startled at the nearness of the two fish as they sprang about in an old sugar-box at her feet. Young Tom laughed loud at her exclamation. "They cairn't feel, miss," he sniggered. Anna wondered that a mouth so soft and kind could utter such heartless words.

In an hour the united efforts of the party had caught nine mackerel; it was not a multitude, but the sun, in perfecting the weather, had spoilt the sport. Anna had ceased to commiserate the captured fish. She was obliged, however, to avert her head when Tom cut some skin from the side of one of the mackerel to provide fresh bait; this device seemed to her the extremest refinement of cruelty. Beatrice grew ominously silent and inert, and Mrs. Sutton glanced first at her daughter and then at her husband; the latter nodded.

"We'd happen better be getting back, Henry," said the Alderman.

The "Fay" swept home like a bird. They were at the quay, and Kelly was dragging them one by one from the black dinghy on to what the Alderman called *terra-firma*. Henry had the fish on a string.

"How many did ye catch, Miss Tellwright?" Kelly asked benevolently.

"I caught four," Anna replied. Never before had she felt so proud, elated, and boisterous. Never had the blood

so wildly danced in her veins. She looked at her short blue
skirt which showed three inches of ankle, put forward her
brown-shod foot like a vain coquette, and darted a covert
look at Henry. When he caught it she laughed instead of
blushing.

" Ye're doing well," Tom Kelly approved. " Ye'll make
a famous mackerel-fisher."

Five of the mackerel were given to young Tom. The
other four preceded a fowl in the menu of dinner. They
were called Anna's mackerel, and all the diners agreed that
better mackerel had never been lured out of the Irish sea.

In the afternoon the Alderman and his wife slept as usual,
Mr. Sutton with a bandanna handkerchief over his face.
The rest went out immediately; the invitation of the sun and
the sea was far too persuasive to be resisted.

" I'm going to paint," said Beatrice, with a resolute mien.
" I want to paint Bradda Head frightfully. I tried last
year, but I got it too dark, somehow. I've improved since
then. What are you going to do? "

" We'll come and watch you," said Henry.

" Oh, no, you won't. At least *you* won't; you're such
a critic. Anna can, if she likes."

" What! And me be left all afternoon by myself? "

" Well, suppose you go with him, Anna, just to keep
him from being bored? "

Anna hesitated. Once more she had the uncomfortable
suspicion that Mynors and herself were being manœuvred.

" Look here," said Mynors to Beatrice. " Have you decided absolutely to paint? "

" Absolutely." The finality of the answer seemed to have a touch of resentment.

" Then "—he turned to Anna—" let's go and get that dinghy and row about the bay.   Eh? "

She could offer no rational objection, and they were soon putting off from the jetty, impelled seaward by a mighty push from Kelly's arm.   It was very hot.   Mynors wore white flannels.   He removed his coat, and turned up his sleeves, showing thick, hairy arms.   He sculled in a manner almost dramatic, and the dinghy shot about like a water-spider on a brook.   Anna had nothing to do except to sit still and enjoy.   Everything was drowned in dazzling sun-light, and both Henry and Anna could feel the process of tanning on their faces.   The bay shimmered with a million diamond-points; it was impossible to keep the eyes open without frowning, and soon Anna could see the beads of sweat on Henry's crimson brow.

" Warm? "  she said.   This was the first word of con-versation.   He merely smiled in reply.   Presently they were at the other side of the bay, in a cave whose sandy and rock-strewn floor trembled clear under a fathom of blue water.

They landed on a jutting rock; Henry pushed his straw hat back, and wiped his forehead.   " Glorious! glorious! "  he exclaimed.   " Do you swim?   No?   You should get Beatrice to teach you.   I swam out here this morning at seven o'clock.   It was chilly enough then.   Oh! I forgot, I told you at breakfast."

She could see him in the translucent water, swimming with

long, powerful strokes. Dozens of boats were moving lazily in the bay, each with a cargo of parasols.

" There's a good deal of the sunshade afloat," he remarked. " Why haven't you got one? You'll get as brown as Tom Kelly."

" That's what I want," she said.

" Look at yourself in the water there," he said, pointing to a little pool left on the top of the rock by the tide. She did so, and saw two fiery cheeks, and a forehead divided by a horizontal line into halves of white and of crimson; the tip of the nose was blistered.

" Isn't it disgraceful? " he suggested.

" Why," she exclaimed, " they'll never know me when I get home! "

It was in such wise that they talked, endlessly exchanging trifles of comment. Anna thought to herself: " Is this love-making? " It could not be, she decided; but she infinitely preferred it so. She was content. She wished for nothing better than this apparently frivolous and irresponsible dalliance. She felt that if Mynors were to be tender, sentimental, and serious, she should become wretchedly self-conscious.

They re-embarked, and, skirting the shore, gradually came round to the beach. Up above them, on the cliffs, they could discern the industrious figure of Beatrice, with easel and sketching-umbrella, and all the panoply of the earnest amateur.

" Do you sketch? " she asked him.

" Not I! " he said scornfully.

" Don't you believe in that sort of thing, then? "

" It's all right for professional artists," he said; " people who *can* paint. But—— Well, I suppose it's harmless for the amateurs—finds them something to do."

" I wish I could paint, anyway," she retorted.

" I'm glad you can't," he insisted.

When they got back to the cliffs, towards tea-time, Beatrice was still painting, but in a new spot. She seemed entirely absorbed in her work, and did not hear their approach.

" Let's creep up and surprise her," Mynors whispered. " You go first, and put your hands over her eyes."

" Oh! " exclaimed Beatrice, blindfolded; " how horrid you are, Henry! I know who it is—I know who it is."

" You just don't, then," said Henry, now in front of her. Anna removed her hands.

" Well, you told her to do it, I'm sure of that. And I was getting on so splendidly! I sha'n't do another stroke now."

" That's right," said Henry. " You've wasted quite enough time as it is."

Beatrice pouted. She was evidently annoyed with both of them. She looked from one to the other, jealous of their mutual understanding and agreement. Mr. and Mrs. Sutton issued from the house, and the five stood chatting till tea was ready; but the shadow remained on Beatrice's face. Mynors made several attempts to laugh it away, and at dusk these two went for a stroll to Port St. Mary. They returned in a state of deep intimacy. During supper Bea-

trice was consciously and elaborately angelic, and there was
that in her voice and eyes, when sometimes she addressed
Mynors, which almost persuaded Anna that he might once
have loved his cousin. At night, in the bedroom, Anna
imagined that she could detect in Beatrice's attitude the
least shade of condescension. She felt hurt, and despised
herself for feeling hurt.

So the days passed, without much variety, for the Suttons
were not addicted to excursions. Anna was profoundly
happy; she had forgotten care. She agreed to every suggestion for amusement; each moment had its pleasure, and
this pleasure was quite independent of the thing done; it
sprang from all activities and idlenesses. She was at special pains to fraternise with Mr. Sutton. He made an interesting companion, full of facts about strata, outcrops,
and breaks, his sole weakness being the habit of quoting
extremely sentimental scraps of verse when walking by the
seashore. He frankly enjoyed Anna's attention to him,
and took pride in her society. Mrs. Sutton, that simple
heart, devoted herself to the attainment of absolute quiescence. She had come for a rest, and she achieved her purpose. Her kindliness became for the time passive instead of
active. Beatrice was a changing quantity in the domestic
equation. Plainly her parents had spoiled their only child,
and she had frequent fits of petulance, particularly with
Mynors; but her energy and spirits atoned well for these.
As for Mynors, he behaved exactly as on the first Monday.
He spent many hours alone with Anna—(Beatrice appeared
to insist on leaving them together, even while showing a

faint resentment at the loneliness thus entailed on herself)
—and his attitude was such as Anna, ignorant of the ways
of brothers, deemed a brother might adopt.

On the second Monday an incident occurred. In the
afternoon Mr. Sutton had asked Beatrice to go with him
to Port St. Mary, and she had refused on the plea that the
light was of a suitable grey for painting. Mr. Sutton had
slipped off alone, unseen by Anna and Henry, who had
meant to accompany him in place of Beatrice. Before tea,
while Anna, Beatrice, and Henry were awaiting the meal
in the parlour, Mynors referred to the matter.

" I hope you've done some decent work this afternoon,"
he said to Beatrice.

" I haven't," she replied shortly; " I haven't done a
stroke."

" But you said you were going to paint hard!"

" Well, I didn't."

" Then why couldn't you have gone to Port St. Mary,
instead of breaking your fond father's heart by a refusal? "

" He didn't want me, really."

·Anna interjected: " I think he did, Bee."

" You know you're very self-willed, not to say selfish,"
Mynors said.

" No, I'm not,"·Beatrice protested seriously. " Am I,
Anna? "

" Well——" Anna tried to think of a diplomatic pro-
nouncement. Beatrice took offence at the hesitation.

" Oh! You two are bound to agree, of course. You're
as thick as thieves."

She gazed steadily out of the window, and there was a silence. Mynors' lip curled.

"Oh! There's the loveliest yacht just coming into the bay," Beatrice cried suddenly, in a tone of affected enthusiasm. "I'm going out to sketch it." She snatched up her hat and sketching-block, and ran hastily from the room. The other two saw her sitting on the grass, sharpening a pencil. The yacht, a large and luxurious craft, had evidently come to anchor for the night.

Mrs. Sutton arrived from her bedroom, and then Mr. Sutton also came in. Tea was served. Mynors called to Beatrice through the window and received no reply. Then Mrs. Sutton summoned her.

"Go on with your tea," Beatrice shouted, without turning her head. "Don't wait for me. I'm bound to finish this now."

"Fetch her, Anna dear," said Mrs. Sutton after another interval. Anna rose to obey, half-fearful.

"Aren't you coming in, Bee?" She stood by the sketcher's side, and observed nothing but a few meaningless lines on the block.

"Didn't you hear what I said to mother?"

Anna retired in discomfiture.

Tea was finished. They went out, but kept at a discreet distance from the artist, who continued to use her pencil until dusk had fallen. Then they returned to the sitting-room, where a fire had been lighted, and Beatrice at length followed. As the others sat in a circle round the fire, Beatrice, who occupied the sofa in solitude, gave a shiver.

" Beatrice, you've taken cold," said her mother, " sitting out there like that."

" Oh, nonsense, mother—what a fidget you are! "

" A fidget I certainly am not, my darling, and that you know very well.   As you've had no tea, you shall have some gruel at once, and go to bed and get warm."

" Oh, no, mother! "    But Mrs. Sutton was resolved, and in half an hour she had taken Beatrice to bed and tucked her up.

When Anna went to the bedroom Beatrice was awake.

" Can't you sleep? " she inquired kindly.

" No," said Beatrice, in a feeble voice, " I'm restless, somehow."

" I wonder if it is influenza," said Mrs. Sutton, on the following morning, when she learnt from Anna that Beatrice had had a bad night, and would take breakfast in bed.   She carried the invalid's food upstairs herself.   " I hope it isn't influenza," she said later.   " The girl is very hot."

" You haven't a clinical thermometer? " Mynors suggested.

" Go, see if you can buy one at the little chemist's," she replied eagerly.   In a few minutes he came back with the instrument.

" She's at over a hundred," Mrs. Sutton reported, having used the thermometer.   " What do you say, father?   Shall we send for a doctor?   I'm not so set up with doctors as a general rule," she added, as if in defence, to Anna.   " I brought Beatrice through measles and scarlet fever without a doctor—we never used to think of having a doctor in those days for ordinary ailments; but influenza—that's different. Eh, I dread it; you never know how it will end. And poor Beatrice had such a bad attack last Martinmas."

"If you like, I'll run for a doctor now," said Mynors.

"Let be till to-morrow," the Alderman decided. "We'll see how she goes on. Happen it's nothing but a cold."

"Yes," assented Mrs. Sutton; "it's no use crying out before you're hurt."

Anna was struck by the placidity with which they covered their apprehension. Towards noon, Beatrice, who said that she felt better, insisted on rising. A fire was lighted at once in the parlour, and she sat in front of it till tea-time, when she was obliged to go to bed again. On the Wednesday morning, after a night which had been almost sleepless for both the girls, her temperature stood at 103°, and Henry fetched the doctor, who pronounced it a case of influenza, severe, demanding very careful treatment. Instantly the normal movement of the household was changed. The sick-room became a mysterious centre round which everything revolved, and the parlour, without the alteration of a single chair, took on a deserted, forlorn appearance. Meals were eaten like the passover, with loins girded for any sudden summons. Mrs. Sutton and Anna, as nurses, grew important in the eyes of the men, who instinctively effaced themselves, existing only like messenger-boys whose business it is to await a call. Yet there was no alarm, flurry, nor excitement. In the evening the doctor returned. The patient's temperature had not fallen. It was part of the treatment that a medicine should be administered every two hours with absolute regularity, and Mrs. Sutton said that she should sit up through the night.

" I shall do that," said Anna.

" Nay, I won't hear of it," Mrs. Sutton replied, smiling.

But the three men (the doctor had remained to chat in the parlour), recognising Anna's capacity and reliability, and perhaps impressed also by her business-like appearance as, arrayed in a white apron, she stood with firm lips before them, gave a unanimous decision against Mrs. Sutton.

" We'st have you ill next, lass," said the Alderman to his wife; " and that 'll never do."

" Well," Mrs. Sutton surrendered, " if I can leave her to anyone, it's Anna."

Mynors smiled appreciatively.

On the Thursday morning there was still no sign of recovery. The temperature was 104°, and the patient slightly delirious. Anna left the sickroom at eight o'clock to preside at breakfast, and Mrs. Sutton took her place.

" You look tired, my dear," said the Alderman affectionately.

" I feel perfectly well," she replied with cheerfulness.

" And you aren't afraid of catching it? " Mynors asked.

" Afraid? " she said; " there's no fear of me catching it."

" How do you know? "

" I know, that's all. I'm never ill."

" That's the right way to keep well," the Alderman remarked.

The quiet admiration of these two men was very pleasant to her. She felt that she had established herself forever in their esteem. After breakfast, in obedience to them, she slept for several hours on Mrs. Sutton's bed. In the afternoon Beatrice was worse. The doctor called, and found her temperature at 105°.

" This can't last," he remarked briefly.

" Well, Doctor," Mr. Sutton said, " it's i' your hands."

" Nay," Mrs. Sutton murmured with a smile, " I've left it with God. It's with Him."

This was the first and only word of religion, except grace at table, that Anna heard from the Suttons during her stay in the Isle of Man. She had feared lest vocal piety might form a prominent feature of their daily life, but her fear had proved groundless. She too, from reason rather than instinct, had tried to pray for Beatrice's recovery. She had, however, found much more satisfaction in the activity of nursing.

Again that night she sat up, and on the Friday morning Beatrice was better. At noon all immediate danger was past; the patient slept; her temperature was almost correct. Anna went to bed in the afternoon and slept soundly till supper-time, when she awoke very hungry. For the first time in three days Beatrice could be left alone. The other four had supper together, cheerful and relieved after the tension.

" She'll be as right as a trivet in a few days," said the Alderman.

" A few weeks," said Mrs. Sutton.

" Of course," said Mynors, " you'll stay on here now? "

" We shall stay until Beatrice is quite fit to travel," Mr.

Sutton answered. " I might have to run over to th' Five Towns for a day or two middle of next week, but I can come back immediately."

" Well, I must go to-morrow," Mynors sighed.

" Surely you can stay over Sunday, Henry? "

" No; I've no one to take my place at school."

" And I must go to-morrow, too," said Anna suddenly.

" Fiddle-de-dee, Anna ! " the Alderman protested.

" I must," she insisted. " Father will expect me. You know I came for a fortnight. Besides, there's Agnes."

" Agnes will be all right."

" I must go." They saw that she was fixed.

" Won't a short walk do you good? " Mynors suggested to her, with singular gravity, after supper. " You've not been outside for two days."

She looked inquiringly at Mrs. Sutton.

" Yes, take her, Henry; she'll sleep better for it. Eh, Anna, but it's a shame to send you home with those rings round your eyes."

She went upstairs for a jacket. Beatrice was awake.

" Anna," she exclaimed in a weak voice, without any preface, " I was awfully silly and cross the other afternoon, before all this business. Just now, when you came into the room, I was feeling quite ashamed."

" Oh ! Bee ! " she answered, bending over her, " what nonsense ! Now go off to sleep at once." She was very happy. Beatrice, victim of a temperament which had the childishness and the impulsiveness of the artist without his higher and sterner traits, sank back in facile content.

The night was still and very dark. When Anna and Mynors got outside they could distinguish neither the sky nor the sea; but the faint, restless murmur of the sea came up the cliffs. Only the lights of the houses disclosed the direction of the road.

" Suppose we go down to the jetty, and then along as far as the breakwater?" he said, and she concurred. " Won't you take my muffler—again?" he added, pulling this ever-present article from his pocket.

" No, thanks," she said, almost coldly, " it's really quite warm." She regarded the offer of the muffler as an indiscretion—his sole indiscretion during their acquaintance. As they walked down the hill to the shore she thought how Beatrice's illness had sharply interrupted their relations. If she had come to the Isle of Man with a vague idea that he would possibly propose to her, the expectation was disappointed; but she felt no disappointment. She felt that events had lifted her to a higher plane than that of lovemaking. She was filled with the proud satisfaction of a duty accomplished. She did not seek to minimise to herself the fact that she had been of real value to her friends in the last few days, had probably saved Mrs. Sutton from illness, had certainly laid them all under an obligation. Their gratitude, unexpressed, but patent on each face, gave her infinite pleasure. She had won their respect by the manner in which she had risen to the height of an emergency that demanded more than devotion. She had proved, not merely to them, but to herself, that she could be calm under stress, and could exert moral force when occasion needed.

Such were the joyous and exultant reflections which passed through her brain—unnaturally active in the factitious wakefulness caused by excessive fatigue. She was in an extremely nervous and excitable condition—and never guessed it, fancying indeed that her emotions were exceptionally tranquil that night. She had not begun to realise the crisis through which she had just lived.

The uneven road to the ruined breakwater was quite deserted. Having reached the limit of the path, they stood side by side, solitary, silent, gazing at the black and gently heaving surface of the sea. The eye was foiled by the intense gloom; the ear could make nothing of the strange night-noises of the bay and the ocean beyond; but the imagination was stimulated by the appeal of all this mystery and darkness. Never had the water seemed so wonderful, terrible, and austere.

" We are going away to-morrow," he said at length.

Anna started and shook with apprehension at the tremor in his voice. She had read that a woman was always well warned by her instincts when a man meant to propose to her. But here was the proposal imminent, and she had not suspected. In a flash of insight she perceived that the very event which had separated them for three days had also impelled the lover forward in his course. It was the thought of her vigils, her fortitude, her compassion, that had fanned the flame. She was not surprised, only made uncomfortable, when he took her hand.

" Anna," he said, " it's no use making a long story of it. I'm tremendously in love with you; you know I am."

He stepped back, still holding her hand. She could say nothing.

" Well? " he ventured. " Didn't you know? "

" I thought—I thought," she murmured stupidly, " I thought you liked me."

" I can't tell you how I admire you. I'm not going to praise you to your face, but I simply never met anyone like you. From the very first moment I saw you, it was the same. It's something in your face, Anna—— Anna, will you be my wife? "

The actual question was put in a precise, polite, somewhat conventional tone. To Anna he was never more himself than at that moment.

She could not speak; she could not analyse her feelings; she could not even think. She was adrift. At last she stammered: " We've only known each other—— "

" Oh, dear," he exclaimed masterfully, " what does that matter? If it had been a dozen years instead of one, that would have made no difference." She drew her hand timidly away, but he took it again. She felt that he dominated her, and would decide for her. " Say yes."

" Yes," she said.

She saw pictures of her career as his wife, and resolved that one of her first acts of her freedom should be to release Agnes from the more ignominious of her father's tyrannies.

They walked home almost in silence. She was engaged, then. Yet she experienced no new sensation. She felt as she had felt on the way down, except that she was sorely perturbed. There was no ineffable rapture, no ecstatic bliss. Suddenly the prospect of happiness swept over her like a flood.

At the gate she wished to make a request to him, but hesitated, because she could not bring herself to use his Christian name. It was proper for her to use his Christian name, however, and she would do so, or perish.

" Henry," she said, " don't tell anyone here." He merely kissed her once more. She went straight upstairs.

## XI: THE DOWNFALL

I N order to catch the Liverpool steamer at Douglas it was necessary to leave Port Erin at half-past six in the morning. The freshness of the morning, and the smiles of the Alderman and his wife as they waved God-speed from the door-step, filled Anna with a serene content which she certainly had not felt during the wakeful night. She forgot, then, the hours passed with her conscience in realising how serious and solemn a thing was this engagement, made in an instant on the previous evening. All that remained in her mind, as she and Henry walked quickly down the road, was the tonic sensation of high resolves to be a worthy wife. The duties, rather than the joys, of her condition, had lain nearest her heart until that moment of setting out, giving her an anxious and almost worried mien which at breakfast neither Henry nor the Suttons could quite understand. But now the idea of duty ceased for a time to be paramount, and she loosed herself to the pleasures of the day in store. The harbour was full of low wandering mists, through which the brown sails of the fishing-smacks played at hide-and-seek. High above them the round forms of immense clouds were still carrying the colours of sunrise. The gentle salt wind on the cheek was like the touch of the life-giver. It was impossible, on such a morning, not to exult in life, not to laugh childishly from irrational glee, not to dismiss the memory of grief and the apprehension of grief as morbid hallucinations. Mynors' face expressed the double happiness of present and anticipated pleasure. He had once again succeeded, he who never failed; and the voyage back to England was for him a triumphal progress. Anna responded eagerly to his mood. The day was an ecstasy, a bright expanse unstained. To Anna in particular it was a unique day, marking the apogee of her existence. In the years that followed she could always return to it and say to herself: " That day I was happy, foolishly, ignorantly, but utterly. And all that I have since learnt cannot alter it—I was happy."

When they reached Shawport station a cab was waiting for Anna. Unknown to her, Henry had ordered it by telegraph. This considerateness was of a piece, she thought, with his masterly conduct of the entire journey—on the steamer, at Liverpool, in the train; nothing that an experienced traveller could devise had been lacking to her comfort. She got into the cab alone, while Mynors, followed by a boy and his bag, walked to his rooms in Mount Street. It had been arranged, at Anna's wish, that he should not appear at Manor Terrace till supper-time. Ephraim opened for her the door of her home. It seemed to her that he was pleased.

" Well, father, here I am again, you see."

" Ay, lass." They shook hands, and she indicated to the cabman where to deposit her tin box. She was glad and relieved to be back. Nothing had changed, except herself, and this absolute sameness was at once pleasant and pathetic to her.

" Where's Agnes? " she asked, smiling at her father.   In
the glow of arrival she had a vague notion that her relations with him had been permanently softened by absence.

" I see thou's gotten into th' habit o' flitting about in
cabs," he said, without answering her question.

" Well, father," she said, smiling yet, " there was the
box.   I couldn't carry the box."

" I reckon thou couldst ha' hired a lad to carry it for
sixpence."

She did not reply.   The cabman had gone to his vehicle.

" Art'na going to pay th' cabby? "

" I've paid him, father."

" How much? "

She paused.   " Eighteenpence, father."   It was a lie;
she had paid two shillings.

She went eagerly into the kitchen, and then into the parlour, where tea was set for one.   Agnes was not there.
" Her's upstairs," Ephraim said, meeting Anna as she came
into the lobby again.   She ran softly upstairs, and into
the bedroom.   Agnes was replacing ornaments on the mantelpiece with mathematical exactitude; under her arm was
a duster.   The child turned, startled, and gave a little
shriek.

" Eh, I didn't know you'd come.   How early you are! "

They rushed towards each other, embraced, and kissed.
Anna was overcome by the pathos of her sister's loneliness
in that grim house for fourteen days, while she, the elder,
had been absorbed in selfish gaiety.   The pale face, large,
melancholy eyes, and long, thin arms, were a silent accusa-

tion. She wondered that she could ever have brought herself to leave Agnes even for a day. Sitting down on the bed, she drew the child on her knee in a fury of love, and kissed her again, weeping. Agnes cried too, from sympathy.

" Oh, my dear, dear Anna, I'm so glad you've come back! " She dried her eyes, and in quite a different tone of voice asked: " Has Mr. Mynors proposed to you? "

Anna could not avoid a blush at this simple and astounding query. She said: " Yes." It was the one word of which she was capable, under the circumstances. That was not the moment to tax Agnes with too much precocity and abruptness.

" You're engaged, then? Oh, Anna, does it feel nice? It must. I knew you would be! "

" How did you know, Agnes? "

" I mean I knew he would ask you, some time. All the girls at school knew too."

" I hope you didn't talk about it," said the elder sister.

" Oh, *no!* But they did; they always talking about it."

" You never told me that."

" I—I didn't like to. Anna, shall I have to call him Henry now? "

" Yes, of course. When we're married he will be your brother-in-law."

" Shall you be married soon, Anna? "

" Not for a very long time."

" When you are—shall I keep house alone? I can, you know—— I shall never *dare* to call him Henry. But he's awfully nice; isn't he, Anna? Yes, when you are married, I shall keep house here, but I shall come to see you every day. Father will *have* to let me do that. Does father know you're engaged?"

"Not yet. And you mustn't say anything. Henry is coming up for supper. And then father will be told."

"Did he kiss you, Anna?"

"Who—father?"

"No, silly! Henry, of course—I mean when he'd asked you?"

"I think you are asking all the questions. Suppose I ask you some now. How have you managed with father? Has he been nice?"

"Some days—yes," said Agnes, after thinking a moment. "We have had some new cups and saucers up from Mr. Mynors' works. And father has swept the kitchen chimney. And, oh Anna! I asked him to-day if I'd kept house well, and he said 'Pretty well,' and he gave me a penny. Look! It's the first money I've ever had, you know. I wanted you at nights, Anna—and all the time, too. I've been frightfully busy. I cleaned silvers all afternoon. Anna, I *have* tried—— And I've got some tea for you. I'll go down and make it. Now you mustn't come into the kitchen. I'll bring it to you in the parlour."

"I had my tea at Crewe," Anna was about to say, but refrained, in due course drinking the cup prepared by Agnes. She felt passionately sorry for Agnes, too young to feel the shadow which overhung her future. Anna would marry into freedom, but Agnes would remain the serf.

Would Agnes marry? Could she? Would her father allow it? Anna had noticed that in families the youngest, petted in childhood, was often sacrificed in maturity. It was the last maid who must keep her maidenhood, and, vicariously filial, pay out of her own life the debt of all the rest.

"Mr. Mynors is coming up for supper to-night. He wants to see you," Anna said to her father, as calmly as she could. The miser grunted. But at eight o'clock, the hour immutably fixed for supper, Henry had not arrived. The meal proceeded, of course, without him. To Anna his absence was unaccountable and disturbing, for none could be more punctilious than he in the matter of appointments. She expected him every moment, but he did not appear. Agnes, filled full of the great secret confided to her, was more openly impatient than her sister. Neither of them could talk, and a heavy silence fell upon the family group, a silence which her father, on that particular evening of Anna's return, resented.

"You dunna' tell us much," he remarked, when the supper was finished.

She felt that the complaint was a just one. Even before supper, when nothing had occurred to preoccupy her, she had spoken little. There had seemed so much to tell— at Port Erin, and now there seemed nothing to tell. She ventured into a flaccid, perfunctory account of Beatrice's illness, of the fishing, of the unfinished houses which had caught the fancy of Mr. Sutton; she said the sea had been smooth, that they had had something to eat at Liverpool, that the train for Crewe was very prompt; and then she could think of no more. Silence fell again. The supper-things were cleared away and washed up. At a quarter-past nine, Agnes, vainly begging permission to stay up in order to see Mr. Mynors, was sent to bed, only partially comforted by a clothes-brush, long-desired, which Anna had brought for her as a present from the Isle of Man.

"Shall you tell father yourself, now Henry hasn't come?" the child asked Anna, who had gone upstairs to un-pack her box.

"Yes," said Anna briefly.

"I wonder what he'll say," Agnes reflected, with that habit, always annoying to Anna, of meeting trouble half-way.

At a quarter to ten Anna ceased to expect Mynors, and finally braced herself to the ordeal of a solemn interview with her father, well knowing that she dared not leave him any longer in ignorance of her engagement. Already the old man was locking and bolting the door; he had wound up the kitchen clock. When he came back to the parlour to extinguish the gas she was standing by the mantel-piece.

"Father," she began, "I've something I must tell you."

"Eh, what's that ye say?" His hand was on the gas-tap. He dropped it, examining her face curiously.

"Mr. Mynors has asked me to marry him; he asked me last night. We settled he should come up to-night to see you—I can't think why he hasn't. It must be something very unexpected and important, or he'd have come." She trembled, her heart beat violently; but the words were out, and she thanked God.

" Asked ye to marry him, did he? "  The miser gazed at her quizzically out of his small blue eyes.

" Yes, father."

" And what didst say? "

" I said I would."

" Oh!  Thou saidst thou wouldst!  I reckon it was for thatten as thou must go gadding off to sea-side, eh? "

" Father, I never dreamt of such a thing when Suttons asked me to go.  I do wish Henry "—the cost of that Christian name!—" had come.  He quite meant to come to-night."  She could not help insisting on the propriety of Henry's intentions.

" Then I am for be consulted, eh? "

" Of course, father."

" Ye've soon made it up, between ye."

His tone was, at the best, brusque; but she breathed more easily, divining instantly from his manner that he meant to offer no violent objection to the engagement.  She knew that only tact was needed now.  The miser had, indeed, foreseen the possibility of this marriage for months past, and had long since decided in his own mind that Henry would make a satisfactory son-in-law.  Ephraim had no social ambitions—with all his meanness, he was above them; he had nothing but contempt for rank, style, luxury, and " the theory of what it is to be a lady and a gentleman." Yet, by a curious contradiction, Henry's smartness of ap-

pearance—the smartness of an unrivalled commercial traveller—pleased him. He saw in Henry a young and sedate
man of remarkable shrewdness, a man who had saved money,
had made money for others, and was now making it for himself; a man who could be trusted absolutely to perform that
feat of " getting on "; a " safe " and profoundly respectable man, at the same time audacious and imperturbable.
He was well aware that Henry had really fallen in love with
Anna, but nothing would have convinced him that Anna's
money was not the primal cause of Henry's genuine passion
for Anna's self.

" You like Henry, don't you, father? " Anna said. It was
a failure in the desired tact, for Ephraim had never been
known to admit that he liked anyone or anything. Such
natures are capable of nothing more positive than tolera-
tion.

" He's a hard-headed chap, and he knows the value o'
money. Ay! that he does; he knows which side his bread's
buttered on." A sinister emphasis marked the last sentence.

Instead of remaining silent, Anna, in her nervousness,
committed another imprudence. " What do you mean,
father? " she asked, pretending that she thought it impossible he could mean what he obviously did mean.

" Thou knows what I'm at, lass. Dost think he isna'
marrying thee for thy brass? Dost think as he canna' make
a fine guess what thou'rt worth? But that wunna' bother
thee as long as thou'st hooked a good-looking chap."

" Father! "

" Ay! thou mayst bridle; but it's true. Dunna' tell me."

Securely conscious of the perfect purity of Mynors' affection, she was not in the least hurt. She even thought that her father's attitude was not quite sincere, an attitude partially due to mere wilful churlishness. " Henry has never even mentioned money to me," she said mildly.

" Happen not; he isna' such a fool as that." He paused, and continued: " Thou'rt free to wed, for me. Lasses will do it, I reckon, and thee among th' rest." She smiled, and on that smile he suddenly turned out the gas. Anna was glad that the colloquy had ended so well. Congratulations, endearments, loving regard for her welfare: she had not expected these things, and was in no wise grieved by their absence. Groping her way towards the lobby, she considered herself lucky, and only wished that nothing had happened to keep Mynors away. She wanted to tell him at once that h.r father had proved tractable.

The next morning, Tellwright, whose attendance at chapel was losing the strictness of its old regularity, announced that he should stay at home. Sunday's dinner was to be a cold repast, and so Anna and Agnes went to chapel. Anna's thoughts were wholly occupied with the prospect of seeing Mynors, and hearing the explanation of his absence on Saturday night.

" There he is! " Agnes exclaimed loudly, as they were approaching the chapel.

" Agnes," said Anna, " when will you learn to behave in the street? "

Mynors stood at the chapel-gates; he was evidently await-ing them. He looked grave, almost sad. He raised his hat and shook hands, with a particular friendliness for Agnes, who was speculating whether he would kiss Anna, as his betrothed, or herself, as being only a little girl, or both, or neither of them. Her eyes already expressed a sort of ownership in him.

" I should like to speak to you a moment," Henry said. " Will you come into the school-yard? "

" Agnes, you had better go straight into chapel," said Anna. It was ignominious disaster to the child, but she obeyed.

" I didn't give you up last night till nearly ten o'clock," Anna remarked as they passed into the school-yard. She was astonished to discover in herself an inclination to pout, to play the offended fair one, because Mynors had failed in his appointment. Contemptuously she crushed it.

" Have you heard about Mr. Price? " Mynors began.

" No. What about him? Has anything happened? "

" A very sad thing has happened. Yes——" He stopped, from emotion. " Our superintendent has com-mitted suicide! "

" Killed himself? " Anna gasped.

" He hanged himself yesterday afternoon at Edward Street, in the slip-house, after the works were closed. Willie had gone home, but he came back, when his father didn't turn up for dinner, and found him. Mr. Price was quite dead. He ran into my place to fetch me just as I was get-ting my tea. That was why I never came last night."

Anna was speechless.

" I thought I would tell you myself," Henry resumed. " It is an awful thing for the Sunday School, and the whole society, too. He, a prominent Wesleyan, a worker among us! An awful thing!" he repeated, dominated by the idea of the blow thus dealt to the Methodist connexion by the man now dead.

" Why did he do it? " Anna demanded curtly.

Mynors shrugged his shoulders, and ejaculated: " Business troubles, I suppose; it couldn't be anything else. At school this morning I simply announced that he was dead." Henry's voice broke, but he added after a pause: " Young Price bore himself splendidly last night."

Anna turned away in silence. " I shall come up for tea, if I may," Henry said, and then they parted, he to the singing-seat, she to the portico of the chapel. People were talking in groups on the broad steps and in the vestibule. All knew of the calamity, and had received from it a new interest in life. The town was aroused as if from a lethargy. Consternation and eager curiosity were on every face. Those who arrived in ignorance of the event were informed of it in impressive tones, and with intense satisfaction to the informer; nothing of equal importance had happened in the society for decades. Anna walked up the aisle to her pew, filled with one thought:

" We drove him to it, father and I."

Her fear was that the miser had renewed his terrible insistence during the previous fortnight. She forgot that she had disliked the dead man, that he had always seemed to her mean, pietistic, and two-faced. She forgot that in pressing him for rent many months overdue she and her father had acted within their just rights—acted as Price himself would have acted in their place. She could think only of the strain, the agony, the despair that must have preceded the miserable tragedy. Old Price had atoned for all in one sublime sin, the sole deed that could lend dignity and repose to such a figure as his. Anna's feverish imagination reconstituted the scene in the slip-house: she saw it as something grand, accusing, and unanswerable; and she could not dismiss a feeling of acute remorse that she should have been engaged in pleasure at that very hour of death. Surely some instinct should have warned her that the hare which she had helped to hunt was at its last gasp!

Mr. Sargent, the newly-appointed second minister, was in the pulpit—a little, earnest bachelor, who emphasised every sentence with a continual tremor of the voice. " Brethren," he said, after the second hymn—and his tones vibrated with a singular effect through the half-empty building—" before I proceed to my sermon I have one word to say in reference to the awful event which is doubtless uppermost in the minds of all of you. It is not for us to judge the man who is now gone from us, ushered into the dread presence of his Maker with the crime of self-murder upon his soul. I say it is not for us to judge him. The ways of the Almighty are past finding out. Therefore at such a moment we may fitly humble ourselves before the Throne, and while prostrate there let us intercede for the poor young man who is left behind, bereft, and full of grief and shame. We will engage in silent prayer." He lifted his hand, and closed his eyes, and the congregation leaned forward against the fronts of the pews. The appealing face of Willie presented itself vividly to Anna.

"Who is it?" Agnes asked, in a whisper of apalling distinctness. Anna frowned angrily, and gave no reply.

While the last hymn was being sung, Anna signed to Agnes that she wished to leave the chapel. Everyone would be aware that she was among Price's creditors, and she feared that, if she stayed till the end of the service some chatterer might draw her into a distressing conversation. The sisters went out, and Agnes's burning curiosity was at length relieved.

"Mr. Price has hanged himself," Anna said to her father when they reached home.

The miser looked through the window for a moment. "I am na' surprised," he said. "Suicide's i' that blood. Titus's uncle 'Lijah tried to kill himself twice afore he died o' gravel. Us'n have to do summat wi' Edward Street at last."

She wanted to ask Ephraim if he had been demanding more rent lately, but she could not find courage to do so.

Agnes had to go to Sunday School alone that afternoon. Without saying anything to her father, Anna decided to stay at home. She spent the time in her bedroom, idle, preoccupied; and did not come downstairs till half-past three. Ephraim had gone out. Agnes presently returned, and then Henry came in with Mr. Tellwright. They were conversing amicably, and Anna knew that her engagement was finally and satisfactorily settled. During tea no reference was made to it, nor to the suicide. Mynors' demeanour was quiet but cheerful. He had perfectly recovered from the morning's agitation, and gave Ephraim and Agnes a vivacious account of the attractions of Port Erin. Anna noticed the amusement in his eye when Agnes, reddening, said to him: " Will you have some more bread-and-butter, Henry? " It seemed to be tacitly understood afterwards that Agnes and her father would attend chapel, while Anna and Henry kept house. No one was ingenious enough to detect an impropriety in the arrangement. For some obscure reason, immediately upon the departure of the chapel-goers, Anna went into the kitchen, rattled some plates, stroked her hair mechanically, and then stole back again to the parlour. It was a chilly evening, and instead of walking up and down the strip of garden the betrothed lovers sat together under the window. Anna wondered whether or not she was happy. The presence of Mynors was, at any rate, marvellously soothing.

" Did your father say anything about the Price affair? " he began, yielding at once to the powerful hypnotism of the subject which fascinated the whole town that night, and which Anna could bear neither to discuss nor to ignore.

" Not much," she said, and repeated to him her father's remark.

Mynors told her all he knew; how Willie had discovered

his father with his toes actually touching the floor, leaning slightly forward, quite dead; how he had then cut the rope and fetched Mynors, who went with him to the police-station; how they had tied up the head of the corpse, and then waited till night to wheel the body on a hand-cart from Edward Street to the mortuary chamber at the police-station; how the police had telephoned to the coroner, and settled at once that the inquest should be held on Monday, in the court-room at the town-hall; and how quiet, self-contained, and dignified Willie had been, surprising everyone by this new-found manliness. It all seemed hideously real to Anna, as Henry added detail to detail.

" I think I ought to tell you," she said very calmly, when he had finished the recital, " that I—I'm dreadfully upset over it. I can't help thinking that I—that father and I, I mean—are somehow partly responsible for this."

" For Price's death? How? "

" We have been so hard on him for his rent lately, you know."

" My dearest girl! What next? " He took her hand in his. " I assure you the idea is absurd. You've only got it because you're so sensitive and high-strung. I undertake to say Price was stuck fast everywhere—everywhere—hadn't a chance."

" Me high-strung! " she exclaimed. He kissed her lovingly. But, beneath the feeling of reassurance, which by superior force he had imposed on her, there lay a feeling that she was treated like a frightened child who must be tranquillised in the night. Nevertheless, she was grateful for his kindness, and when she went to bed she obtained relief from the returning obsession of the suicide by making anew her vows to him.

As a theatrical effect the death of Titus Price could scarcely have been surpassed. The town was profoundly moved by the spectacle of this abject, yet heroic, surrender of all those pretences by means of which society contrives to tolerate itself. Here was a man whom no one respected, but everyone pretended to respect—who knew that he was respected by none, but pretended that he was respected by all; whose whole career was made up of dissimulations: religious, moral, and social. If any man could have been trusted to continue the decent sham to the end, and so preserve the general self-esteem, surely it was this man. But no! Suddenly abandoning all imposture, he transgresses openly, brazenly; and, snatching a bit of hemp cries: "Behold me; this is real human nature. this is the truth; the rest was lies. I lied; you lied. I confess it, and you shall confess it." Such a thunderclap shakes the very base of the microcosm. The young folk in particular could with difficulty believe their ears. It seemed incredible to them that Titus Price, the Methodist, the Sunday-school superintendent, the loud champion of the highest virtues, should commit the sin of all sins—murder. They were dazed. The remembrance of his insincerity did nothing to mitigate the blow. In their view it was perhaps even worse that he had played false to his own falsity. The elders were a little less disturbed. The event was not unique in their experience. They had lived longer and felt these seismic shocks before. They could go back into the past and find other cases where a swift impulse had shattered the edifice of a lifetime. They knew that the history of families and of communities is crowded with disillusion. They had discovered that character is changeless, irrepressible, incurable. They were aware of the astonishing fact, which takes at least thirty years to learn, that a Sunday-school superintendent is a man. And the suicide of Titus Price, when they had realised it, served but to confirm their most secret and honest estimate of humanity, that estimate which they never confided to a soul. The young folk thought the Methodist Society shamed and branded by the tragic incident, and imagined that years must elapse before it could again hold up its head in the town. The old folk were wiser, foreseeing with certainty that in only a few days this all-engrossing phenomenon would lose its significance, and be as though it had never been.

Even in two days, time had already begun its work, for by Tuesday morning the interest of the affair—on Sunday at the highest pitch—had waned so much that the thought of the inquest was capable of reviving it. Although everyone knew that the case presented no unusual features, and that the coroner's inquiry would be nothing more than a formal ceremony, the almost greedy curiosity of Methodist circles lifted it to the level of a *cause célèbre*. The court was filled with irreproachable respectability when the coroner drove into the town, and each animated face said to its fellow: " So you're here, are you? " Late comers of the official world—councillors, guardians of the poor, members of the school board, and one or two of their ladies—were forced to intrigue for room with the police and the town-hall keeper, and, having succeeded, sank into their narrow seats with a sigh of expectancy and triumph. Late comers with less influence had to retire, and by a kind of sinister fascination were kept wandering about the corridor before they could decide to go home. The market-place was occupied by hundreds of loafers, who seemed to find a mystic satisfaction in beholding the coroner's dogcart and the exterior of the building which now held the corpse.

It was by accident that Anna was in the town. She knew that the inquest was to occur that morning, but had not dreamed of attending it. When, however, she saw the stir of excitement in the market-place, and the police guarding the entrances of the town-hall, she walked directly across the road, past the two officers at the east door, and into the dark main corridor of the building, which was dotted with small groups idly conversing. She was conscious of two things: a vehement curiosity, and the existence somewhere in the precincts of a dead body, unsightly, monstrous, calm, silent, careless—the insensible origin of all this simmering ferment, which disgusted her even while she shared in it. At a small door, half hidden by a curtain, she was startled to see Mynors.

" You here ! " he exclaimed, as if painfully surprised, and shook hands with a preoccupied air. " They are examining Willie. I came outside while he was in the witness-box."

" Is the inquest going on in there? " she asked, pointing

to the door.  Each appeared to be concealing a certain resentment against the other; but this appearance was due only to nervous agitation.

A policeman down the corridor called: " Mr. Mynors, a moment."  Henry hurried away, answering Anna's question as he went: " Yes, in there.  That's the witnesses' and jurors' door; but please don't go in.  I don't like you to, and it is sure to upset you."

She opened the door and went in.  None said nay, and she found a few inches of standing-room behind the jury-box.  A terrible stench nauseated her; the chamber was crammed, and not a window open.  There was silence in the court—no one seemed to be doing anything; but at last she perceived that the coroner, enthroned on the bench of justice, was writing, in a book with blue leaves.  In the witness-box stood William Price, dressed in black, with kid gloves, not lounging in an ungainly attitude, as might have been expected, but perfectly erect; he kept his eyes fixed on the coroner's head.  Sarah Vodrey, Price's aged house-keeper, sat on a chair near the witness-box, weeping into a black-bordered handkerchief; at intervals she raised her small, wrinkled, red face, with its glistening, inflamed eyes, and then buried it again in the handkerchief.  The members of the jury, whom Anna could see only in profile, shuffled to and fro on their long, pew-like seats—they were mostly workingmen, shabbily clothed; but the foreman was Mr. Leal, the provision dealer, a freemason, and a sidesman at the parish church.  The general public sat intent and vacuous; their minds gaped, if not their mouths; occasionally

one whispered inaudibly to another; the jury, conscious of
an official status, exchanged remarks in a whisper courageously loud. Several tall policemen, helmet in hand,
stood in various corners of the room, and the coroner's officer sat near the witness-box to administer the oath. At
length the coroner lifted his head. He was rather a young
man, with a large, unintelligent face; he wore eyeglasses,
and his chin was covered with a short, wavy beard. His
manner showed that, while secretly proud of his supreme
position in that assemblage, he was deliberately trying to
make it appear that this exercise of judicial authority was
nothing to him, that in truth these eternal inquiries, which
interested others so deeply, were to him a weariness con-
scientiously endured.

"Now, Mr. Price," the coroner said blandly, and it was
plain that he was being ceremoniously polite to an inferior,
in obedience to the rules of good form, "I must ask you
some more questions. They may be inconvenient, even
painful; but I am here simply as the instrument of the law,
and I must do my duty. And these gentlemen here," he
waved a hand in the direction of the jury, "must be told
the whole facts of the case. We know, of course, that the
deceased committed suicide—that has been proved beyond
doubt; but as I say, we have the right to know more." He
paused, well satisfied with the sound of his voice, and evidently thinking that he had said something very weighty
and impressive.

"What do you want to know?" Willie Price demanded,
his broad Five Towns speech contrasting with the Kensing-

tonian accents of the coroner. The latter, who came originally from Manchester, was irritated by the brusque interruption; but he controlled his annoyance, at the same time glancing at the public, as if to signify to them that he had learnt not to take too seriously the unintentional rudeness characteristic of their district.

" You say it was probably business troubles that caused your late father to commit the rash act? "

" Yes."

" You are sure there was nothing else? "

" What else could there be? "

" Your late father was a widower? "

" Yes."

" Now as to these business troubles—what were they? "

" We were being pressed by creditors."

" Were you a partner with your late father? "

" Yes."

" Oh! You were a partner with him! "

The jury seemed surprised, and the coroner wrote again: " What was your share in the business? "

" I don't know."

" You don't know? Surely that is rather singular? "

" My father took me in Co. not long since. We signed a deed, but I forget what was in it. My place was principally on the bank, not in the office."

" And so you were being pressed by creditors? "

" Yes. And we were behind with the rent."

" Was the landlord pressing you, too? "

Anna lowered her eyes, fearful lest every head had turned towards her.

" Not then ; he had been—she, I mean."

" The landlord is a lady? " Here the coroner faintly smiled. " Then, as regards the landlord, the pressure was less than it had been? "

" Yes; we had paid some rent, and settled some other claims."

" Does it not seem strange——? " the coroner began, with a suave air of suggesting an idea.

" If you must know," Willie surprisingly burst out, " I believe it was the failure of a firm in London that owed us money that caused father to hang himself."

" Ah ! " exclaimed the coroner. " When did you hear of that failure? "

" By second post on Friday. Eleven in the morning."

" I think we have heard enough, Mr. Coroner," said Leal, standing up in the jury-box. " We have decided on our verdict."

" Thank you, Mr. Price," said the coroner, dismissing Willie. He added, in a tone of icy severity to the foreman : " I had concluded my examination of the witness." Then he wrote further in his book.

" Now, gentlemen of the jury," the coroner resumed, having first cleared his throat, " I think you will agree with me that this is a peculiarly painful case. Yet at the same time——"

Anna hastened from the court as impulsively as she had

entered it. She could think of nothing but the quiet, silent, pitiful corpse; and all this vapid mouthing exasperated her beyond sufferance.

On the Thursday afternoon, Anna was sitting alone in the house, with the Persian cat and a pile of stockings on her knee, darning. Agnes had with sorrow returned to school; Ephraim was out. The bell sounded violently, and Anna, thinking that perhaps for some reason her father had chosen to enter by the front door, ran to open it. The visitor was Willie Price; he wore the new black suit which had figured in the coroner's court. She invited him to the parlour and they both sat down, tongue-tied. Now that she had learnt from his evidence given at the inquest that Ephraim had not been pressing for rent during her absence in the Isle of Man, she felt less like a criminal before Willie than she would have felt without that assurance. But at the best she was nervous, self-conscious, and shamed. She supposed that he had called to make some arrangement with reference to the tenure of the works, or, more probably, to announce a bankruptcy and stoppage.

"Well, Miss Tellwright," Willie began, "I've buried him. He's gone."

The simple and profound grief, and the restrained bitterness against all the world, which were expressed in these words—the sole epitaph of Titus Price—nearly made Anna cry. She would have cried, if the cat had not opportunely jumped on her knee again; she controlled herself by dint of stroking it. She sympathised with him more intensely in that first moment of his loneliness than she had ever sympathised with anyone, even Agnes. She wished passionately to shield, shelter, and comfort him, to do something, however small, to diminish his sorrow and humiliation; and this despite his size, his ungainliness, his coarse features, his rough voice, his lack of all the conventional refinements. A single look from his guileless and timid eyes atoned for every shortcoming. Yet she could scarcely open her mouth. She knew not what to say. She had no phrases to soften the frightful blow which Providence had dealt him.

" I'm very sorry," she said. " You must be relieved it's all over."

If she could have been Mrs. Sutton for half an hour! But she was Anna, and her feelings could only find outlet in her eyes. Happily young Price was of those meek ones who know by instinct the language of the eyes.

" You've come up about the works, I suppose? " she went on.

" Yes," he said. " Is your father in? I want to see him very particular."

" He isn't in now," she replied: " but he will be back by four o'clock."

" That's an hour. You don't know where he is? " She shook her head. " Well," he continued, " I must tell you, then. I've come up to do it, and do it I must. I can't come up again; neither can I wait. You remember that bill of exchange as we gave you some weeks back toward rent? "

" Yes," she said. There was a pause. He stood up,

and moved to the mantelpiece. Her gaze followed him intently, but she had no idea what he was about to say.

"It's forged, Miss Tellwright." He sat down again, and seemed calmer, braver, ready to meet any conceivable set of consequences.

"Forged!" she repeated, not immediately grasping the significance of the avowal.

"Mr. Sutton's name is forged on it. So I came to tell your father; but you'll do as well. I feel as if I should like to tell you all about it," he said, smiling sadly. "Mr. Sutton had really given us a bill for thirty pounds, but we'd paid that away when Mr. Tellwright sent word down—you remember—that he should put bailiffs in if he didn't have twenty-five pounds next day. We were just turning the corner then, father said to me. There was a goodish sum due to us from a London firm in a month's time, and if we could only hold out till then, father said he could see daylight for us. But he knew as there'd be no getting round Mr. Tellwright. So he had the idea of using Mr. Sutton's name—just temporary like. He sent me to the post-office to buy a bill stamp, and he wrote out the bill all but the name. 'You take this up to Tellwright's,' he says, 'and ask 'em to take and hold it, and we'll redeem it, and that 'll be all right. No harm done there, Will!' he says. Then he tries Sutton's name on the back of an envelope. It's an easy signature, as you know; but he couldn't do it. 'Here, Will,' he says, 'my old hand shakes; you have a go,' and he gives me a letter of Sutton's to copy from. I did it easy

enough after a try or two. 'That 'll be all right, Will,'
he says, and I put my hat on and brought the bill up here.
That's the truth, Miss Tellwright. It was the smash
of that London firm that finished my poor old father
off.''

Her one feeling was the sense of being herself a culprit.
After all, it was her father's action, more than anything else, that had led to the suicide, and he was her
agent.

" Oh, Mr. Price," she said foolishly, " whatever shall you
do? "

" There's nothing to be done," he replied. " It was bound
to be. It's our luck. We'd no thought but what we should
bring you thirty pound in cash and get that bit of paper
back, and rip it up, and no one the worse. But we were
always unlucky, me and him. All you've got to do is just
to tell your father, and say I'm ready to go to the police-
station when he gives the word. It's a bad business, but
I'm ready for it."

" Can't we do something? " she naïvely inquired, with a
vision of a trial and sentence, and years of prison.

" Your father keeps the bill, doesn't he? Not you? "

" I could ask him to destroy it."

" He wouldn't," said Willie. " You'll excuse me saying
that, Miss Tellwright, but he wouldn't."

He rose as if to go, bitterly. As for Anna, she knew well
that her father would never permit the bill to be destroyed.
But at any cost she meant to comfort him then, to ease his
lot, to send him away less grievous than he came.

" Listen ! " she said, standing up, and abandoning the
cat, " I will see what can be done. Yes. Something *shall*
be done—something or other. I will come and see you
at the works to-morrow afternoon. You may rely on
me."

She saw hope brighten his eyes at the earnestness and
resolution of her tone, and she felt richly rewarded. He
never said another word, but gripped her hand with such
force that she flinched in pain. When he had gone, she
perceived clearly the dire dilemma ; but cared nothing, in the
first bliss of having reassured him.

During tea it occurred to her that as soon as Agnes had
gone to bed she would put the situation plainly before her
father, and, for the first and last time in life, assert herself.
She would tell him that the affair was, after all, entirely
her own, she would firmly demand possession of the bill of
exchange, and she would insist on it being destroyed. She
would point out to the old man that, her promise having
been given to Willie Price, no other course than this was
possible. In planning this night-surprise on her father's
obstinacy, she found argument after argument auspicious
of its success. The formidable tyrant was at last to meet
his equal, in force, in resolution, and in pugnacity. The
swiftness of her onrush would sweep him, for once, off his
feet. At whatever cost, she was bound to win, even though
victory resulted in eternal enmity between father and
daughter. She saw herself towering over him, morally,
with blazing eye and scornful nostril. And, thus meditat-
ing on the grandeur of her adventure, she fed her courage

with indignation. By the act of death, Titus Price had put her father forever in the wrong. His corpse accused the miser, and Anna, incapable now of seeing aught save the pathos of suicide, acquiesced in the accusation with all the strength of her remorse. She did not reason—she felt; reason was shrivelled up in the fire of emotion. She almost trembled with the urgency of her desire to protect from further shame the figure of Willie Price, so frank, simple, innocent, and big; and to protect also the lifeless and dishonoured body of his parent. She reviewed the whole circumstances again and again, each time finding less excuse for her father's implacable and fatal cruelty.

So her thoughts ran until the appointed hour of Agnes's bedtime. It was always necessary to remind Agnes of that hour; left to herself, the child would have stayed up till the very Day of Judgment. The clock struck, but Anna kept silence. To utter the word " bedtime " to Agnes was to open the attack on her father, and she felt as the conductor of an opera feels before setting in motion a complicated activity which may end in either triumph or an unspeakable fiasco. The child was reading; Anna looked and looked at her, and at length her lips were set for the phrase, " Now, Agnes," when, suddenly, the old man forestalled her:

" Is that wench going for sit here all night? " he asked of Anna menacingly.

Agnes shut her book and crept away.

This accident was the ruin of Anna's scheme. Her father, always the favourite of circumstance, had by chance

struck the first blow; ignorant of the battle that awaited
him, he had unwittingly won it by putting her in the wrong,
as Titus Price had put him in the wrong.   She knew in a
flash that her enterprise was hopeless; she knew that her
father's position in regard to her was impregnable, that no
moral force, no consciousness of right, would avail to over-
throw that authority which she had herself made absolute
by a life-long submission.   She knew that face to face with
her father she was, and would always be, a coward.   And
now, instead of finding arguments for success, she found
arguments for failure.   She divined all the retorts that he
would fling at her.   What about Mr. Sutton—in a sense the
victim of this fraud?   It was not merely a matter of thirty
pounds.   A man's name had been used.   Was he, Ephraim
Tellwright, and she, his daughter, to connive at a felony?
The felony was done, and could not be undone.   Were they
to render themselves liable, even in theory, to a criminal
prosecution?   If Titus Price had killed himself, what of
that?   If Willie Price was threatened with ruin, what of
that?   Them as made the bed must lie on it.   At the best,
and apart from any forgery, the Prices had swindled their
creditors; even in dying, old Price had been guilty of a
commercial swindle.   And was the fact that father and son
between them had committed a direct and flagrant crime to
serve as an excuse for sympathising with the survivor?   Why
was Anna so anxious to shield the forger?   What claim had
he?   A forger was a forger, and that was the end
of it.

She went to bed without opening her mouth.   Irresolute,

shamed, and despairing, she tried to pray for guidance, but she could bring no sincerity of appeal into this prayer; it seemed an empty form. Where, indeed, was her religion? She was obliged to acknowledge that the fervour of her aspirations had been steadily cooling for weeks. She was not a whit more a true Christian now than she had been before the Revival; it appeared that she was incapable of real religion, possibly one of those souls foreordained to damnation.

This admission added to the general sense of futility, and increased her misery. She lay awake for hours, confronting her deliberate promise to Willie Price. *Something shall be done. Rely on me.* He was relying on her, then. But on whom could she rely? To whom could she turn? It is significant that the idea of confiding in Henry Mynors did not present itself for a single moment as practical. Mynors had been kind to Willie in his trouble, but Anna almost resented this kindness on account of the condescending superiority which she thought she detected therein. It was as though she had overheard Mynors saying to himself: " Here is this poor, crushed worm. It is my duty as a Christian to pity and succour him. I will do so. I am a righteous man." The thought of anyone stooping to Willie was hateful to her. She felt equal with him, as a mother feels equal with her child when it cries and she soothes it. And she felt, in another way, that he was equal with her, as she thought of his sturdy and simple confession, and of the loyal love in his voice when he spoke of his father. She liked him for hurting her hand, and for refusing to snatch at the slender chance of her father's clemency. She could never reveal Willie's sin, if it was a sin, to Henry Mynors—that symbol of correctness and of success. She had fraternised with sinners, like Christ; and, with amazing injustice, she was capable of deeming Mynors a Pharisee because she could not find fault with him, because he lived and loved so impeccably and so triumphantly. There was only one person from whom she could have asked advice and help, and that wise and consoling heart was far away in the Isle of Man.

"Why won't father give up the bill?" she demanded, half-aloud, in sullen wrath. She could not frame the answer in words, but nevertheless she knew it and felt it. Such an act of grace would have been impossible to her father's nature—that was all.

Suddenly the expression of her face changed from utter disgust into a bitter and proud smile. Without thinking further, without daring to think, she rose out of bed and, night-gowned and barefooted, crept with infinite precaution downstairs. The oilcloth on the stairs froze her feet; a cold grey light, issuing through the glass square over the front door, showed that dawn was beginning. The door of the front-parlour was shut; she opened it gently, and went within. Every object in the room was faintly visible, the bureau, the chair, the files of papers, the pictures, the books on the mantelshelf, and the safe in the corner. The bureau, she knew, was never locked; fear of their father had always kept its privacy inviolate from Anna and Agnes, without the aid of a key. As Anna stood in front of it, a shaking figure with hair hanging loose, she dimly remembered having one day seen a blue paper among white in the pigeon-holes. But if the bill was not there she vowed that she would steal her father's keys while he slept, and force the safe. She opened the bureau, and at once saw the edge of a blue paper corresponding with her recollection. She pulled it forth and scanned it. " Three months after date pay to our order . . . Accepted payable, *William Sutton.*"

So here was the forgery, here the two words for which Willie Price might have gone to prison! What a trifle! She tore the flimsy document to bits, and crumpled the bits into a little ball. How should she dispose of the ball? After a moment's reflection she went into the kitchen, stretched on tiptoe to reach the match-box from the high mantelpiece, struck a match, and burnt the ball in the grate. Then, with a restrained and sinister laugh, she ran softly upstairs.

" What's the matter, Anna? " Agnes was sitting up in bed, wide awake.

" Nothing; go to sleep, and don't bother," Anna angrily whispered.

Had she closed the lid of the bureau? She was compelled to return in order to make sure. Yes, it was closed. When at length she lay in bed, breathless, her heart violently beating, her feet like icicles, she realised what she had done. She had saved Willie Price, but she had ruined herself with her father. She knew well that he would never forgive her.

On the following afternoon she planned to hurry to Edward Street and back while Ephraim and Agnes were both out of the house. But for some reason her father sat persistently after dinner, conning a sale catalogue. At a quarter to three he had not moved. She decided to go at any risks. She put on her hat and jacket, and opened the front door. He heard her.

" Anna! " he called sharply. She obeyed the summons in terror. " Art going out? "

" Yes, father."

" Where to? "

" Down town to buy some things."

" Seems thou'rt always buying."

That was all; he let her free. In an unworthy attempt to appease her conscience she did in fact go first into the town; she bought some wool; the trick was despicable. Then she hastened to Edward Street. The decrepit works seemed to have undergone no change. She had expected the business would be suspended, and Willie Price alone on the bank; but manufacture was proceeding as usual. She went direct to the office, fancying, as she climbed the stairs, that every window of all the workshops was full of eyes to discern her purpose. Without knocking, she pushed against the unlatched door and entered. Willie was lolling in his father's chair, gloomy, meditative, apparently idle. He was coatless, and wore a dirty apron; a battered hat was at the back of his head, and his great hands, which lay on the desk in front of him, were soiled. He sprang up, flushing red, and she shut the door; they were alone together.

" I'm all in my dirt," he murmured apologetically. Simple and silly creature, to imagine that she cared for his dirt!

" It's all right," she said; " you needn't worry any more. It's all right." They were glorious words for her, and her face shone.

" What do you mean? " he asked gruffly.

" Why," she smiled, full of happiness, " I got that paper and burnt it! "

He looked at her exactly as if he had not understood. " Does your father know? "

She still smiled at him happily. " No; but I shall tell him this afternoon. It's all right. I've burnt it."

He sank down in the chair, and, laying his head on the desk, burst into sobbing tears. She stood over him, and put a hand on the sleeve of his shirt. At that touch he sobbed more violently.

" Mr. Price, what is it? " She asked the question in a calm, soothing tone.

He glanced up at her, his face wet, yet apparently not shamed by the tears. She could not meet his gaze without herself crying, and so she turned her head. " I was only thinking," he stammered, " only thinking—what an angel you are."

Only the meek, the timid, the silent, can, in moments of deep feeling, use this language of hyperbole without seeming ridiculous.

He was her great child, and she knew that he worshipped

her.    Oh, ineffable power, that out of misfortune canst
create divine happiness!

Later, he remarked in his ordinary tone: " I was expecting your father here this afternoon about the lease.    There
is to be a deed of arrangement with the creditors."

" My father! " she exclaimed, and she bade him good-
bye.

As she passed under the archway she heard a familiar
voice: " I reckon I shall find young Mester Price in th'
office? "    Ephraim, who had wandered into the packing-
house, turned and saw her through the doorway; a second's
delay, and she would have escaped.    She stood waiting the
storm, and then they walked out into the road together.

" Anna, what art doing here? "

She did not know what to say.

" What art doing here? " he repeated coldly.

" Father, I—was just going back home."

He hesitated an instant.    " I'll go with thee," he said.
They walked to Manor Terrace in silence.    They had tea
in silence; except that Agnes, with dreadful inopportune-
ness, continually worried her father for a definite promise
that she might leave school at Christmas.    The idea was
preposterous; but Agnes, fired by her recent success as a
housekeeper, clung to it.    Ignorant of her imminent danger,
and misinterpreting the signs of his face, she at last pushed
her insistence too far.

" Get to bed, this minute," he said, in a voice suddenly
terrible.    She perceived her error then, but it was too late.
Looking wistfully at Anna, the child fled.

" I was told this morning, miss," Ephraim began, as soon as Agnes was gone, " that young Price had bin seen coming to this house 'ere yesterday afternoon. I thought as it was strange as thoud'st said nowt about it to thy feyther; but I never suspected as a daughter o' mine was up to any tricks. There was a hang-dog look on thy face this afternoon when I asked where thou wast going, but I didna' think thou wast lying to me."

" I wasn't," she began, and stopped.

" Thou wast! Now, what is it? What's this carrying-on between thee and Will Price? I'll have it out of thee."

" There is no carrying-on, father."

" Then why hast thou gotten secrets? Why dost go sneaking about to see him—sneaking, creeping, like any brazen moll? "

The miser was wounded in the one spot where there remained to him any sentiment capable of being wounded: his faith in the irreproachable, absolute chastity, in thought and deed, of his womankind.

" Willie Price came in here yesterday," Anna began, white and calm, " to see you. But you weren't in. So he saw me. He told me that bill of exchange, that blue paper, for thirty pounds, was forged. He said he had forged Mr. Sutton's name on it." She stopped, expecting the thunder.

" Get on with thy tale," said Ephraim, breathing loudly.

" He said he was ready to go to prison as soon as you

gave the word. But I told him, ' No such thing!' I said it must be settled quietly. I told him to leave it to me. He was driven to the forgery, and I thought——"

" Dost mean to say," the miser shouted, " as that blasted scoundrel came here and told thee he'd forged a bill, and thou told him to leave it to thee to settle? " Without waiting for an answer, he jumped up and strode to the door, evidently with the intention of examining the forged document for himself.

" It isn't there—it isn't there!" Anna called to him wildly.

" What isna' there? "

" The paper. I may as well tell you, father. I got up early this morning and burnt it."

The man was staggered at this audacious and astounding impiety.

" It was mine, really," she continued; " and I thought——"

" Thou thought!"

Agnes, upstairs, heard that passionate and consuming roar. " Shame on thee, Anna Tellwright! Shame on thee for a shameless hussy! A daughter o' mine, and just promised to another man! Thou'rt an accomplice in forgery. Thou sees the scamp on the sly! Thou——" He paused, and then added, with furious scorn: " Shalt speak o' this to Henry Mynors? "

" I will tell him if you like," she said proudly.

" Look thee here!" he hissed, " if thou breathes a word o' this to Henry Mynors, or any other man, I'll cut thy tongue out. A daughter o' mine! If thou breathes a word——"

" I shall not, father."

It was finished; grey with frightful anger, Ephraim left the room.

## XII: AT THE PRIORY

SHE was not to be pardoned: the offence was too monstrous, daring, and final. At the same time, the unappeasable ire of the old man tended to weaken his power over her. All her life she had been terrorised by the fear of a wrath which had never reached the superlative degree until that day. Now that she had seen and felt the limit of his anger, she became aware that she could endure it; the curse was heavy, and perhaps more irksome than heavy, but she survived; she continued to breathe, eat, drink, and sleep; her father's power stopped short of annihilation. Here, too, was a satisfaction: that things could not be worse. And still greater comfort lay in the fact that she had not only accomplished the deliverance of Willie Price, but had secured absolute secrecy concerning the episode.

The next day was Saturday, when, after breakfast, it was Ephraim's custom to give Anna the weekly sovereign for housekeeping.

" Here, Agnes," he said, turning in his armchair to face the child, and drawing a sovereign from his waistcoatpocket, " take charge o' this, and mind ye make it go as far as ye can." His tone conveyed a subsidiary message: " I am terribly angry, but I am not angry with you. However, behave yourself."

The child mechanically took the coin, scared by this proof of an unprecedented domestic convulsion. Anna, with a tightening of the lips, rose and went into the kitchen. Agnes followed, after a discreet interval, and in silence gave up the sovereign.

" What is it all about, Anna? " she ventured to ask that night.

" Never mind," said Anna curtly.

The question had needed some courage, for, at certain times, Agnes would as easily have trifled with her father as with Anna. From that moment, with the passive fatalism characteristic of her years, Agnes' spirits began to rise again to the normal level. She accepted the new situation, and fitted herself into it with a child's adaptability. If Anna naturally felt a slight resentment against this too impartial and apparently callous attitude on the part of the child, she never showed it.

Nearly a week later Anna received a postcard from Beatrice announcing her complete recovery, and the immediate return of her parents and herself to Bursley. That same afternoon a cab encumbered with much luggage passed up the street as Anna was fixing clean curtains in her father's bedroom. Beatrice, on the look-out, waved a hand and smiled, and Anna responded to the signals. She was glad now that the Suttons had come back, though for several days she had almost forgotten their existence. On the Saturday afternoon, Mynors called. Anna was in the kitchen; she heard him scuffling with Agnes in the lobby, and then talking to her father. Three times she had seen him since her disgrace, and each time the secret bitterness of her soul, despite conscientious effort to repress it, had marred the meeting—it had been plain, indeed, that she was profoundly disturbed; he had affected at first not to observe the change in her, and she, anticipating his questions, hinted briefly that the trouble was with her father, and had no reference to himself, and that she preferred not to discuss it at all; reassured, and too young in courtship yet to presume on a lover's rights, he respected her wish, and endeavoured by every art to restore her to equanimity. This time, as she went to greet him in the parlour, she resolved that he should see no more of the shadow. He noticed instantly the difference in her face.

" I've come to take you into Suttons' for tea—and for the evening," he said eagerly. " You must come. They are very anxious to see you. I've told your father," he added. Ephraim had vanished into his office.

" What did he say, Henry? " she asked timidly.

" He said you must please yourself, of course. Come along, love. Mustn't she, Agnes? "

Agnes concurred, and said that she would get her father's tea, and his supper too.

" You will come," he urged. She nodded, smiling thoughtfully, and he kissed her, for the first time in front of Agnes, who was filled with pride at this proof of their confidence in her.

" I'm ready, Henry," Anna said, a quarter of an hour later, and they went across to Suttons'.

" Anna, tell me all about it," Beatrice burst out when she and Anna had fled to her bedroom. " I'm so glad. Do you love him really—truly? He's dreadfully fond of you.

He told me so this morning; we had quite a long chat in the market. I think you're both very lucky, you know." She kissed Anna effusively for the third time. Anna looked at her, smiling but silent.

" Well? " Beatrice said.

" What do you want me to say? "

" Oh! You are the funniest girl, Anna, I ever met. ' What do you want me to say,' indeed! " Beatrice added in a different tone: " Don't imagine this affair was the least bit of a surprise to us. It wasn't. The fact is, Henry had—oh! well, never mind. Do you know, mother and dad used to think there was something between Henry and me. But there wasn't, you know—not really. I tell you that, so that you won't be able to say you were kept in the dark. When shall you be married, Anna? "

" I haven't the least idea," Anna replied, and began to question Beatrice about her convalescence.

" I'm perfectly well," Beatrice said. " It's always the same. If I catch anything I catch it bad and get it over quickly."

" Now, how long are you two chatterboxes going to stay here? " It was Mrs. Sutton who came into the room. " Bee, you've got those sewing-meeting letters to write. Eh, Anna, but I'm glad of this. You'll make him a good wife. You two 'll just suit each other."

Anna could not but be impressed by this unaffected joy of her friends in the engagement. Her spirits rose, and once more she saw visions of future happiness. At tea, Alderman Sutton added his felicitations to the rest, with

that flattering air of intimate sympathy and comprehension
which some middle-aged men can adopt towards young
girls. The tea, made specially magnificent in honour of the
betrothal, was such a meal as could only have been com-
passed in Staffordshire or Yorkshire—a high tea of the
last richness and excellence, exquisitely gracious to the
palate, but ruthless in its demands on the stomach. At
one end of the table, which glittered with silver, glass, and
Longshaw china, was a fowl which had been boiled for four
hours; at the other, a hot pork-pie, islanded in liquor, which
might have satisfied a regiment. Between these two dishes
were all the delicacies which differentiate high tea from
tea, and on the quality of which the success of the meal
really depends; hot pikelets, hot crumpets, hot toast, sar-
dines with tomatoes, raisin-bread, currant-bread, seed-cake,
lettuce, home-made marmalade and home-made jams. The
repast occupied over an hour, and even then not a quarter
of the food was consumed. Surrounded by all that good
fare and good will, with the Alderman on her left, Henry
on her right, and a bright fire in front of her, Anna quickly
caught the gaiety of the others. She forgot everything
but the gladness of reunion, the joy of the moment, the
luxurious comfort of the house. Conversation was busy
with the doings of the Suttons at Port Erin after Anna and
Henry had left. A listener would have caught fragments
like this: "You know such-and-such a point. . . . No,
not there, over the hill. Well, we hired a carriage
and drove. . . . The weather was simply. . . . Tom
Kelly said he'd never. . . . And that little guard

on the railway came all the way down to the steamer.
. . . Did you see anything in the 'Signal' about
the actress being drowned? Oh! It was awfully sad.
We saw the corpse just after. . . . Beatrice, will you
hush? "

" Wasn't it terrible about Titus Price? " Beatrice exclaimed.

" Eh, my ! " sighed Mrs. Sutton, glancing at Anna.
" You can never tell what's going to happen next. I'm
always afraid to go away for fear of something happen-
ing."

A silence followed. When tea was finished Beatrice was
taken away by her mother to write the letters concerning
the immediate resumption of sewing meetings, and for a
little time Anna was left in the drawing-room alone with the
two men, who began to talk about the affairs of the Prices.
It appeared that Mr. Sutton had been asked to become
trustee for the creditors under a deed of arrangement, and
that he had hopes of being able to sell the business as a
going concern. In the meantime it would need careful man-
agement.

" Will Willie Price manage it? " Anna inquired. The
question seemed to divert Henry and the Alderman, to afford them a contemptuous and somewhat inimical amusement at the expense of Willie.

" No," said the Alderman quietly, but emphatically.

" Master William is fairly good on the works," said
Henry ; " but in the office, I imagine, he is worse than useless."

Grieved and confused, Anna bent down and moved a hassock in order to hide her face. The attitude of these men to Willie Price, that victim of circumstances and of his own simplicity, wounded Anna inexpressibly. She perceived that they could see in him only a defaulting debtor, that his misfortune made no appeal to their charity. She wondered that men so warm-hearted and kind in some relations could be so hard in others.

"I had a talk with your father at the creditors' meeting yesterday," said the Alderman. " *You* won't lose much. Of course you've got a preferential claim for six months' rent."

He said this reassuringly, as though it would give satisfaction. Anna did not know what a preferential claim might be, nor was she aware of any creditors' meeting. She wished ardently that she might lose as much as possible— hundreds of pounds. She was relieved when Beatrice swept in, her mother following.

"Now, your worship," said Beatrice to her father, "seven stamps for these letters, please." Anna glanced up inquiringly on hearing the form of address. "You don't mean to say you didn't know that father is going to be mayor this year?" Beatrice asked, as if shocked at this ignorance of affairs. "Yes, it was all settled rather late, wasn't it, dad? And the mayor-elect pretends not to care much, but actually he is filled with pride, isn't he, dad? As for the mayoress——?"

"Eh, Bee!" Mrs. Sutton stopped her, smiling; "you'll tumble over that tongue of yours some day."

" Mother said I wasn't to mention it," said Beatrice, " lest you should think we were putting on airs."

" Nay, not I ! " Mrs. Sutton protested. " I said no such thing. Anna knows us too well for that. But I'm not so set up with this mayor business as some people will think I am."

" Or as Beatrice is," Mynors added.

At half-past eight, and again at nine, Anna said that she must go home ; but the Suttons, now frankly absorbed in the topic of the mayoralty, their secret preoccupation, would not spoil the confidential talk which had ensued by letting the lovers depart. It was nearly half-past nine before Anna and Henry stood on the pavement outside, and Beatrice, after facetious farewells, had shut the door.

" Let us just walk round by the Manor Farm," Henry pleaded. " It won't take more than a quarter of an hour or so."

She agreed dutifully. The footpath ran at right angles to Trafalgar Road, past a colliery whose engine-fires glowed in the dark, moonless, autumn night, and then across a field. They stood on a knoll near the old farmstead, that extraordinary and pathetic survival of a vanished agriculture. Immediately in front of them stretched acres of burning ironstone—a vast tremulous carpet of flame woven in red, purple, and strange greens. Beyond were the skeleton-like silhouettes of pit-heads, and the solid forms of furnace and chimney-shaft. In the distance a canal reflected the gigantic illuminations of Cauldon Bar Ironworks. It was a scene mysterious and romantic enough to kindle the raptures of love, but Anna felt cold, melancholy, and apprehensive of vague sorrows. " Why am I so? " she asked herself, and tried in vain to shake off the mood.

" What will Willie Price do if the business is sold? " she questioned Mynors suddenly.

" Surely," he said to soothe her, " you aren't still worrying about that misfortune. I wish you had never gone near the inquest; the thing seems to have got on your mind."

" Oh, no! " she protested, with an air of cheerfulness. " But I was just wondering."

" Well, Willie will have to do the best he can. Get a place somewhere, I suppose. It won't be much, at the best."

Had he guessed what perhaps hung on that answer, Mynors might have given it in a tone less callous and perfunctory. Could he have seen the tightening of her lips, he might even afterwards have repaired his error by some voluntary assurance that Willie Price should be watched over with a benevolent eye and protected with a strong arm. But how was he to know that in misprizing Willie Price before her, he was misprizing the child to its mother? He had done something for Willie Price, and considered that he had done enough. His thoughts, moreover, were on other matters.

" Do you remember that day we went up to the park? " he murmured fondly; " that Sunday? I have never told you that that evening I came out of chapel after the first hymn, when I noticed you weren't there, and walked up past your house. I couldn't help it. Something drew me. I nearly called in to see you. Then I thought I had better not."

" I saw you," she said calmly. His warmth made her feel sad. " I saw you stop at the gate."

" You did? But you weren't at the window? "

" I saw you through the glass of the front door." Her voice grew fainter, more reluctant.

" Then you were watching? " In the dark he seized her with such violence, and kissed her so vehemently, that she was startled out of herself.

" Oh, Henry! " she exclaimed.

" Call me Harry," he entreated, his arm still round her waist; " I want you to call me Harry. No one else does or ever has done, and no one shall, now."

" Harry," she said deliberately, bracing her mind to a positive determination. She must please him, and she said it again: " Harry; yes, it has a nice sound."

Ephraim sat reading the " Signal " in the parlour when she arrived home at five minutes to ten. Imbued then with ideas of duty, submission, and systematic kindliness, she had an impulse to attempt a reconciliation with her father.

" Good-night, father," she said; " I hope I've not kept you up."

He was deaf.

She went to bed resigned; sad, but not gloomy. It was not for nothing that during all her life she had been accustomed to infelicity. Experience had taught her this:

to be the mistress of herself. She knew that she could face any fact—even the fact of her dispassionate frigidity under Mynors' caresses. It was on the firm, almost rapturous resolve to succour Willie Price, if need were, that she fell asleep.

The engagement, which had hitherto been kept private, became the theme of universal gossip immediately upon the return of the Suttons from the Isle of Man. Two words let fall by Beatrice in the St. Luke's covered market on Saturday morning had increased and multiplied till the whole town echoed with the news. Anna's private fortune rose as high as a quarter of a million. As for Henry Mynors, it was said that Henry Mynors knew what he was about. After all, he was like the rest. Money, money! Of course it was inconceivable that a fine, prosperous figure of a man, such as Mynors, would have made up to *her*, if she had not been simply rolling in money. Well, there was one thing to be said for young Mynors, he would put money to good use; you might rely he would not hoard it up same as it had been hoarded up. However, the more saved, the more for young Mynors, so *he* needn't grumble. It was to be hoped he would make her dress herself a bit better—though indeed it hadn't been her fault she went about so shabby; the old skinflint would never allow her a penny of her own. So tongues wagged.

The first Sunday was a tiresome ordeal for Anna, both at school and at chapel. "Well, I never!" seemed to be written like a note of exclamation on every brow; the monotony of the congratulations fatigued her as much as her

involuntary efforts to grasp what each speaker had left un-
said of innuendo, malice, envy, or sycophany. Even the
people in the shops, during the next few days, could not
serve her without direct and curious reference to her private
affairs. The general opinion that she was a cold and blood-
less creature was strengthened by her attitude at this period.
But the apathy which she displayed was neither affected
nor due to an excessive diffidence. As she seemed, so she
felt. She often wondered what would have happened to her
if that vague " something " between Henry and Beatrice,
to which Beatrice had confessed, had ever taken definite
shape.

" Hancock came back from Lancashire last night," said
Mynors, when he arrived at Manor Terrace on the next
Saturday afternoon. Ephraim was in the room, and Henry,
evidently joyous and triumphant, addressed both him and
Anna.

" Is Hancock the commercial traveller? " Anna asked.
She knew that Hancock was the commercial traveller, but
she experienced a nervous compulsion to make idle remarks
in order to hide the breach of intercourse between her father
and herself.

" Yes," said Mynors; " he's had a magnificent journey."

" How much? " asked the miser.

Henry named the amount of orders taken in a fortnight's
journey.

" Humph! " the miser ejaculated. " That's better than
a bat in the eye with a burnt stick." From him, this was

the superlative of praise. " You're making good money at, that rate? "

" We are," said Mynors.

" That reminds me," Ephraim remarked gruffly. " When dost think o' getting wed? I'm not much for long engagements, and so I tell ye." He threw a cold glance sideways at Anna. The idea penetrated her heart like a stab: " He wants to get me out of the house ! "

" Well," said Mynors, surprised at the question and the tone, and, looking at Anna as if for an explanation: " I had scarcely thought of that. What does Anna say? "

" I don't know," she murmured ; and then, more bravely, in a louder voice, and with a smile: " The sooner the better." She thought, in her bitter and painful resentment: " If he wants me to go, go I will."

Henry tactfully passed on to another phase of the subject: " I met Mr. Sutton yesterday, and he was telling me of Price's house up at Toft End. It belonged to Mr. Price, but of course it was mortgaged up to the hilt. The mortgagees have taken possession, and Mr. Sutton said it would be to let cheap at Christmas. Of course Willie and old Sarah Vodrey, the housekeeper, will clear out. I was thinking it might do for us. It's not a bad sort of house, or, rather, it won't be when it's repaired."

" What will they ask for it? " Ephraim inquired.

" Twenty-five or twenty-eight. It's a nice large house —four bedrooms, and a very good garden."

" Four bedrooms ! the miser exclaimed. " What dost

want wi' four bedrooms? You'd have for keep a servant."

"Naturally we should keep a servant," Mynors said, with calm politeness.

"You could get one o' them new houses up by th' park for fifteen pounds as would do you well enough"; the miser protested against these dreams of extravagance.

"I don't care for that part of the town," said Mynors. "It's too new for my taste."

After tea, when Henry and Anna went out for the Saturday evening stroll, Mynors suddenly suggested: "Why not go up and look through that house of Price's?"

"Won't it seem like turning them out if we happen to take it?" she asked.

"Turning them out! Willie is bound to leave it. What use is it to him? Besides, it's in the hands of the mortgagees now. Why shouldn't we take it just as well as anyone else, if it suits us?"

Anna had no reply, and she surrendered herself placidly enough to his will; nevertheless she could not entirely banish a misgiving that Willie Price was again to be victimised. Infinitely more disturbing than this illogical sensation, however, was the instinctive and sure knowledge, revealed in a flash, that her father wished to be rid of her. So implacable, then, was his animosity against her! Never, never had she been so deeply hurt. The wound, in fact, was so severe that at first she felt only a numbness that reduced everything to unimportance, robbing her of volition. She walked up to Toft End as if walking in her sleep.

Price's house, sometimes called Priory House, in accordance with a legend that a priory had once occupied the site, stood in the middle of the mean and struggling suburb of Toft End, which was flung up the hillside like a ragged scarf. Built of red brick, towards the end of the eighteenth century, double-fronted, with small, evenly disposed windows, and a chimney stack at either side, it looked westward over the town smoke towards a horizon of hills. It had a long, narrow garden, which ran parallel with the road. Behind it, adjoining, was a small, disused potworks, already advanced in decay. On the north side, and enclosed by a brick wall which surrounded also the garden, was a small orchard of sterile and withered fruit-trees. In parts the wall had crumbled under the assaults of generations of boys, and from the orchard, through the gaps, could be seen an expanse of grey-green field, with a few abandoned pit-shafts scattered over it. These shafts, imperfectly protected by ruinous masonry, presented an appearance strangely sinister and forlorn, raising visions in the mind of dark and mysterious depths peopled with miserable ghosts of those who had toiled there in the days when to be a miner was to be a slave. The whole place, house and garden, looked ashamed and sad, with a shabby mournfulness acquired gradually from its inmates during many years. But, nevertheless, the house was substantial, and the air on that height fresh and pure.

Mynors rang in vain at the front door, and then they walked round the house to the orchard, and discovered Sarah Vodrey taking in clothes from a line—a diminutive and

wasted figure, with scanty, grey hair, a tiny face permanently soured, and bony hands contorted by rheumatism.

"My rheumatism's that bad," she said in response to
greetings, "I can scarce move about, and this house is a
regular barracks to keep clean. No; Willie's not in. He's
at th' works, as usual—Saturday like any other day. I'm
by myself here all day and every day. But I reckon us'n
be flitting soon, and me lived here eight-and-twenty year!
Praise God, there's a mansion up there for me at last. And
not sorry shall I be when He calls."

"It must be very lonely for you, Miss Vodrey," said Mynors. He knew exactly how to speak to this dame who
lived her life like a fly between two panes of glass, and who
could find room in her head for only three ideas, namely:
that God and herself were on terms of intimacy; that she
was, and had always been, indispensable to the Price family;
and that her social status was far above that of a servant.
"It's a pity you never married," Mynors added.

"Me marry! What would *they* ha' done without me?
No, I'm none for marriage and never was. I'd be shamed
to be like some o' them spinsters down at chapel, always
hanging round chapel-yard on the off-chance of a service,
to catch that there young Mr. Sargent, the new minister.
It's a sign of a hard winter, Miss Terrick, when the hay
runs after the horse, that's what I say."

"Miss Tellwright and myself are in search of a house,"
Mynors gently interrupted the flow, and gave her a peculiar
glance which she appreciated. "We heard you and Willie

were going to leave here, and so we came up just to look over the place, if it's quite convenient to you."

" Eh, I understand ye," she said ; " come in. But ye mun tak' things as ye find 'em, Miss Terrick."

Dismal and unkempt, the interior of the house matched the exterior. The carpets were threadbare, the discoloured wall-papers hung loose on the walls, the ceilings were almost black, the paint had nearly been rubbed away from the woodwork; the exhausted furniture looked as though it would fall to pieces in despair if compelled to face the threatened ordeal of an auction-sale. But to Anna the rooms were surprisingly large, and there seemed so many of them! It was as if she were exploring an immense abode, like a castle, with odd chambers continually showing them-selves in unexpected places. The upper story was even less inviting than the ground-floor—barer, more chill, utterly comfortless.

" This is the best bedroom," said Miss Vodrey. " And a rare big room, too! It's not used now. *He* slept here. Willie sleeps at back."

" A very nice room," Mynors agreed blandly, and meas-ured it, as he had done all the others, with a two-foot, enter-ing the figures in his pocketbook.

Anna's eye wandered uneasily across the room, with its dismantled bed and decrepit mahogany suite.

" I'm glad he hanged himself at the works, and not here," she thought. Then she looked out at the window. " What a splendid view! " she remarked to Mynors.

She saw that he had taken a fancy to the house. The

sagacious fellow esteemed it, not as it was, but as it would be, repapered, repainted, refurnished, the outer walls pointed, the garden stocked; everything cleansed, brightened, renewed. And there was indeed much to be said for his fancy. The house was large, with plenty of ground; the boundary wall secured that privacy which young husbands and young wives instinctively demand; the outlook was unlimited, the air the purest in the Five Towns. And the rent was low, because the great majority of those who could afford such a house would never deign to exist in a quarter so poverty-stricken and unfashionable.

After leaving the house they continued their walk up the hill, and then turned off to the left on the high-road from Hanbridge to Moorthorne. The venerable, but not dignified town lay below them, a huddled medley of brown brick under a thick black cloud of smoke. The gold angel of the town-hall gleamed in the evening light, and the dark, squat tower of the parish church, sole relic of the past, stood out grim and obdurate amid the featureless buildings which surrounded it. To the north and east miles of moorland, defaced by collieries and murky hamlets, ran to the horizon. Across the great field at their feet a figure slouched along, past the abandoned pit-shafts. They both recognised the man.

" There's Willie Price going home! " said Mynors.

" He looks tired," she said. She was relieved that they had not met him at the house.

" I say," Mynors began earnestly, after a pause, " why shouldn't we get married soon, since the old gentleman seems rather to expect it? He's been rather awkward lately, hasn't he?"

This was the only reference made by Mynors to her father's temper. She nodded. "How soon?" she asked.

"Well, I was just thinking. Suppose, for the sake of argument, this house turns out all right. I couldn't get it thoroughly done up much before the middle of January—couldn't begin till these people had moved. Suppose we said early in February?"

"Yes!"

"Could you be ready by that time?"

"Oh, yes!" she answered, "I could be ready."

"Well, why shouldn't we fix February, then?"

"There's the question of Agnes," she said.

"Yes; and there will always be the question of Agnes. Your father will have to get a housekeeper. You and I will be able to see after little Agnes, never fear." So, with tenderness in his voice, he reassured her on that point.

"Why not February?" she reflected. "Why not to-morrow, as father wants me out of the house?"

It was agreed.

"I've taken the Priory, subject to your approval," Henry said, less than a fortnight later. From that time he invariably referred to the place as the Priory.

It was on the very night after this eager announcement that the approaching tragedy came one step nearer. Beatrice, in a modest evening-dress, with a white cloak—excited, hurried, and important—ran in to speak to Anna. The carriage was waiting outside. She and her father and mother had to attend a very important dinner at the mayor's house at Hillport, in connection with Mr. Sutton's impending mayoralty. Old Sarah Vodrey had just sent down a girl to say that she was unwell, and would be grateful if Mrs. Sutton or Beatrice would visit her. It was a most unreasonable time for such a summons, but Sarah was a fidgety old crotchet, and knew how frightfully good-natured Mrs. Sutton was. Would Anna mind going up to Toft End? And would Anna come out to the carriage and personally assure Mrs. Sutton that old Sarah should be attended to? If not, Beatrice was afraid her mother would take it into her head to do something stupid.

"It's very good of you, Anna," said Mrs. Sutton, when Anna went outside with Beatrice. "But I think I'd better go myself. The poor old thing may feel slighted if I don't, and Beatrice can well take my place at this affair at Hillport, which I've no mind for." She was already half out of the carriage.

"Nothing of the kind," said Anna firmly, pushing her back. "I shall be delighted to go and do what I can."

"That's right, Anna," said the Alderman from the darkness of the carriage, where his shirt-front gleamed; "Bee said you'd go, and we're much obliged to ye."

"I expect it will be nothing," said Beatrice, as the vehicle drove off; "Sarah has served mother this trick before now."

As Anna opened the garden-gate of the Priory she discerned a figure amid the rank bushes, which had been allowed to grow till they almost met across the narrow path leading to the front door of the house. It was a thick and mysterious night—such a night as death chooses; and Anna jumped in vague terror at the apparition.

"Who's there?" said a voice sharply.

"It's me," said Anna. "Miss Vodrey sent down to ask Mrs. Sutton to come up and see her, but Mrs. Sutton had an engagement, so I came instead."

The figure moved forward; it was Willie Price. He peered into her face, and she could see the mortal pallor of his cheeks.

"Oh!" he exclaimed, "it's Miss Tellwright, is it? Will ye come in, Miss Tellwright?"

She followed him with beating heart, alarmed, apprehensive. The front door stood wide open, and at the far end of the gloomy passage a faint light shone from the open door of the kitchen. "This way," he said. In the large, bare, stone-floored kitchen Sarah Vodrey sat limp and with closed eyes in an old rocking-chair close to the fireless range. The window, which gave on to the street, was open; through that window Sarah, in her extremity, had called the child who ran down to Mrs. Sutton's. On the deal table were a dirty cup and saucer, a tea-pot, bread, butter, and a lighted candle—sole illumination of the chamber.

" I come home, and I find this," he said.

Daunted for a moment by the scene of misery, Anna could say nothing.

" I find this," he repeated, as if accusing God of spitefulness; and he lifted the candle to show the apparently insensible form of the woman. Sarah's wrinkled and seamed face had the flush of fever, and the features were drawn into the expression of a terrible anxiety; her hands hung loose; she breathed like a dog after a run.

" I wanted her to have the doctor yesterday," he said, " but she wouldn't. Ever since you and Mr. Mynors called she's been cleaning the house down. She said you'd happen be coming again soon, and the place wasn't fit to be seen. No use me arguing with her."

" You had better run for a doctor," Anna said.

" I was just going off when you came. She's been complaining more of her rheumatism, and pain in her hips, lately."

" Go now; fetch Mr. Macpherson, and call at our house and say I shall stay here all night. Wait a moment." Seeing that he was exhausted from lack of food, she cut a thick piece of bread-and-butter. " Eat this as you go," she said.

" I can't eat; it 'll choke me."

" Let it choke you," she said. " You've got to swallow it."

Child of a hundred sorrows, he must be treated as a child. As soon as Willie was gone she took off her hat and jacket, and lit a lamp; there was no gas in the kitchen.

" What's that light? " the old woman asked peevishly, rousing herself, and sitting up. " I doubt I'll be late with Willie's tea. Eh, Miss Terrick, what's amiss? "

" You're not quite well, Miss Vodrey," Anna answered. " If you'll show me your room, I'll see you into bed." Without giving her a moment for hesitation, Anna seized the feeble creature under the arms, and so, coaxing, supporting, carrying, got her to bed. At length she lay on the narrow mattress, panting, exhausted. It was Sarah's final effort.

Anna lit fires in the kitchen and in the bedroom, and when Willie returned with Dr. Macpherson, water was boiling and tea made.

" You'd better get a woman in," said the doctor curtly, in the kitchen, when he had finished his examination of Sarah. " Some neighbour for to-night, and I'll send a nurse up from the cottage-hospital early to-morrow morning. Not that it will be the least use. She must have been dying for the last two days at least. She's got pericarditis and pleurisy. She's breathing I don't know how many to the minute, and her temperature is just about as high as it can be. It all follows from rheumatism, and then taking cold. Gross carelessness and neglect all through! I've no patience with such work." He turned angrily to Willie. " I don't know what on earth you were thinking of, Mr. Price, not to send for me earlier."

Willie, abashed and guilty, found nothing to say. His eye had the meek wistfulness of Holman Hunt's " Scapegoat."

"Mr. Price wanted her to have the doctor," said Anna, defending him with warmth; "but she wouldn't. He is out at the works all day till late at night. How was he to know how she was? She could walk about."

The tall doctor glanced at Anna in surprise, and at once modified his tone. "Yes," he said, "that's the curious thing. It passes me how she managed to get about. But there is no knowing what an obstinate woman won't force herself to do. I'll send the medicine up to-night, and come along myself with the nurse early to-morrow. Meantime, keep carefully to my instructions."

That night remains forever fixed in Anna's memory: the grim rooms, echoing and shadowy; the countless journeys up and down dark stairs and passages; Willie sitting always immovable in the kitchen, idle because there was nothing for him to do; Sarah incessantly panting on the truckle-bed; the hired woman from up the street, buxom, kindly, useful, but fatuous in the endless monotony of her commiserations.

Towards morning, Sarah Vodrey gave sign of a desire to talk.

"I've fought the fight," she murmured to Anna, who alone was in the bedroom with her. "I've fought the fight; I've kept the faith. In that box there ye'll see a purse. There's seventeen pound six in it. That will pay for the funeral, and Willie must have what's over. There would ha' been more for the lad, but *he* never paid me no wages this two years past. I never troubled him."

"Don't tell Willie that," Anna said impetuously.

" Eh, bless ye, no! " said the dying drudge, and then seemed to doze.

Anna went to the kitchen, and sent the woman upstairs.

" How is she? " asked Willie, without stirring. Anna shook her head. " Neither her nor me will be here much longer, I'm thinking," he said, smiling wearily.

" What? " she exclaimed, startled.

" Mr. Sutton has arranged to sell our business as a go-ing-concern—some people at Turnhill are buying it. I shall go to Australia; there's no room for me here. The creditors have promised to allow me twenty-five pounds, and I can get an assisted passage. Bursley 'll know me no more. But—but—I shall always remember you and what you've done."

She longed to kneel at his feet, and to comfort him, and to cry: " It is I who have ruined you—driven your father to cheating his servant, to crime, to suicide; driven you to forgery, and turned you out of your house which your old servant killed herself in making clean for me. I have wronged you, and I love you like a mother because I have wronged you and because I saved you from prison."

But she said nothing except: " Some of us will miss you."

The next day Sarah Vodrey died—she who had never lived save in the fetters of slavery and fanaticism. After fifty years of ceaseless labour, she had gained the affection of one person, and enough money to pay for her own fu-neral. Willie Price took a cheap lodging with the woman who had been called in on the night of Sarah's collapse. Before Christmas he was to sail for Melbourne. The

Priory, deserted, gave up its rickety furniture to a van from Hanbridge, where, in an auction-room, the frail sticks lost their identity in a medley of other sticks, and ceased to be. Then the bricklayer, the plasterer, the painter, and the paper-hanger, came to the Priory, and whistled and sang in it.

## XIII: THE BAZAAR

THE Wesleyan Bazaar, the greatest undertaking of its kind ever known in Bursley, gradually became a cloud which filled the entire social horizon. Mrs. Sutton, organiser of the Sunday-school stall, pressed all her friends into the service, and for a fortnight after the death of Sarah Vodrey, Anna and even Agnes gave much of their spare time to the work, which was carried on under pressure increasing daily as the final moments approached. This was well for Anna, in that it diverted her thoughts by keeping her energies fully engaged. One morning, however, it occurred to Mrs. Sutton to reflect that Anna, at such a period of life, should be otherwise employed. Anna had called at the Suttons' to deliver some finished garments.

" My dear," she said, " I am very much obliged to you for all this industry. But I've been thinking that, as you are to be married in February, you ought to be preparing your things."

" My things ! " Anna repeated idly ; and then she remembered Mynors' phrase, on the hill, " Can you be ready by that time ? "

" Yes," said Mrs. Sutton ; " but possibly you've been getting forward with them on the quiet."

" Tell me," said Anna, with an air of interest ; " I've meant to ask you before : Is it the bride's place to provide all the house-linen, and that sort of thing ? "

" It was in my day ; but those things alter so.  The bride took all the house-linen to her husband, and as many clothes for herself as would last a year; that was the rule.  We used to stitch everything at home in those days—everything; and we had what we called a ' bottom drawer ' to store them in.  As soon as a girl had passed her fifteenth birthday, she began to sew for the ' bottom drawer.' But all those things change so, I dare say it's different now."

" How much will it cost to buy everything, do you think? " Anna asked.

Just then Beatrice entered the room.

" Beatrice, Anna is enquiring how much it will cost to buy her trousseau, and the house-linen.  What do you say? "

" Oh ! " Beatrice replied, without any hesitation, " a couple of hundred at least."

Mrs. Sutton, reading Anna's face, smiled reassuringly. " Nonsense, Bee !  I dare say you could do it on a hundred with care, Anna."

" Why should Anna want to do it with care? " Beatrice asked curtly.

Anna went straight across the road to her father, and asked him for a hundred pounds of her own money.  She had not spoken to him, save under necessity, since the evening spent at the Suttons'.

" What's afoot now? " he questioned savagely.

" I must buy things for the wedding—clothes and things, father,"

" Ay! clothes! clothes! What clothes dost want? A few pounds would cover them."

" There'll be all the linen for the house."

" Linen for——— It's none thy place for buy that."

" Yes, father, it is."

" I say it isna'," he shouted.

" But I've asked Mrs. Sutton, and she says it is."

" What business an' ye for go blabbing thy affairs all over Bursley? I say it isna' thy place for buy the linen, and let that be sufficient. Go and get dinner. It's nigh on twelve now."

That evening, when Agnes had gone to bed, she resumed the struggle.

" Father, I must have that hundred pounds. I really must. I mean it."

" *Thou means it!* What? "

" I mean I must have a hundred pounds."

" I'd advise thee to tak' care o' thy tongue, my lass. *Thou means it!* "

" But you needn't give it me all at once," she pursued.

He gazed at her, glowering.

" I shanna' give it thee. It's Henry's place for buy th' house-linen."

" Father, it isn't." Her voice broke, but only for an instant. " I'm asking you for my own money. You seem to want to make me miserable just before my wedding."

" I wish to God thou'dst never seen Henry Mynors. It's given thee pride and made thee undutiful."

" I'm only asking you for my own money."

Her calm insistence maddened him. Jumping up from his chair, he stamped out of the room, and she heard him strike a match in his office. Presently he returned, and threw angrily on to the table in front of her a cheque-book and pass-book. The deposit-book she had always kept herself for convenience of paying into the bank.

" Here," he said scornfully, " tak' thy traps and ne'er speak to me again. I wash my hands of ye. Tak' 'em and do what ye'n a mind. Chuck thy money into th' cut* for aught I care."

The next evening Henry came up. She observed that his face had a grave look, but intent on her own difficulties she did not remark on it, and proceeded at once to what she had resolved to do. It was a cold night in November, yet the miser, wrathfully sullen, chose to sit in his office without a fire. Agnes was working sums in the kitchen.

" Henry," Anna began, " I've had a difficulty with father, and I must tell you."

" Not about the wedding, I hope," he said.

" It was about money. Of course, Henry, I can't get married without a lot of money."

" Why not? " he inquired.

" I've my own things to get," she said, " and I've all the house-linen to buy."

" Oh! You buy the house-linen, do you? " She saw that he was relieved by that information.

" Of course. Well, I told father I must have a hundred pounds, and he wouldn't give it me. And when I stuck to him he got angry—you know he can't bear to see money

* *Cut:* canal.

spent—and at last he got a little savage and gave me my bank-books, and said he'd have nothing more to do with my money."

Henry's face broke into a laugh, and Anna was obliged to smile. "Capital!" he said. "Couldn't be better."

"I want you to tell me how much I've got in the bank," she said. "I only know I'm always paying in odd cheques."

He examined the three books. "A very tidy bit," he said; "something over two hundred and fifty pounds. So you can draw cheques at your ease."

"Draw me a cheque for twenty pounds," she said; and then, while he wrote: "Henry, after we're married, I shall want you to take charge of all this."

"Yes, of course; I will do that, dear. But your money will be yours. There ought to be a settlement on you. Still, if your father says nothing, it is not for me to say anything."

"Father will say nothing—now," she said. "You've never shown any interest in it, Henry; but as we're talking of money, I may as well tell you that father says I'm worth fifty thousand pounds."

The man of business was astonished and enraptured beyond measure. His countenance shone with delight.

"Surely not!" he protested formally.

"That's what father told me, and he made me read a list of shares, and so on."

"We will go slow, to begin with," said Mynors solemnly. He had not expected more than fifteen or twenty thousand pounds, and even this sum had dazzled his imagination. He was glad that he had only taken the house at Toft End on a yearly tenancy. He now saw himself the dominant figure in all the Five Towns.

Later in the evening he disclosed, perfunctorily, the matter which had been a serious weight on his mind when he entered the house, but which this revelation of vast wealth had diminished to a trifle. Titus Price had been the treasurer of the building fund which the bazaar was designed to assist. Mynors had assumed the position of the dead man, and that day, in going through the accounts, he had discovered that a sum of fifty pounds was missing.

"It's a dreadful thing for Willie, if it gets about," he said; "a tale of that sort would follow him to Australia."

"Oh, Henry, it is!" she exclaimed, sorrow-stricken; "but we mustn't let it get about. Let us pay the money ourselves. You must enter it in the books and say nothing."

"That is impossible," he said firmly. "I can't alter the accounts. At least I can't alter the bank-book and the vouchers. The auditor would detect it in a minute. Besides, I should not be doing my duty if I kept a thing like this from the superintendent-minister. He, at any rate, must know, and perhaps the stewards."

"But you can urge them to say nothing. Tell them that you will make it good. I will write a cheque at once."

"I had meant to find the fifty myself," he said. It was a peddling sum to him now.

"Let me pay half, then," she asked.

" If you like," he urged, smiling faintly at her eagerness.
" The thing is bound to be kept quiet—it would create such
a frightful scandal.  Poor old chap ! " he added  carelessly,
" I suppose he was hard run, and meant to put it back—as
they all do mean."

But it was useless for Mynors to affect depression of
spirits, or mournful sympathy with the errors of a dead
sinner.  The fifty thousand danced a jig in his brain that
night.

Anna was absorbed in contemplating the misfortune of
Willie Price.  She prayed wildly that he might never learn
the full depth of his father's fall.  The miserable robbery
of Sarah's wages was buried for evermore, and this new
delinquency, which all would regard as flagrant sacrilege,
must be buried also.  A soul less loyal than Anna's might
have feared that Willie, a self-convicted forger, had been a
party to the embezzlement ; but Anna knew that it could not
be so.

It was characteristic of Mynors' cautious prudence that,
the first intoxication having passed, he made no further
reference of any kind to Anna's fortune.  The arrangements for their married life were planned on a scale which
ignored the fifty thousand pounds.  For both their sakes he
wished to avoid all friction with the miser, at any rate until
his status as Anna's husband would enable him to enforce
her rights, if that should be necessary, with dignity and
effectiveness.  He did not precisely anticipate trouble, but
the fact had not escaped him that Ephraim still held the
whole of Anna's securities.  He was in no hurry to enlarge

his borders. He knew that there were twenty-four hours in every day, three hundred and sixty-five days in every year, and thirty good years of life still left to him; and, therefore, that there would be ample time, after the wedding, for the execution of his purposes in regard to that fifty thousand pounds. Meanwhile, he told Anna that he had set aside two hundred pounds for the purchase of furniture for the Priory—a modest sum; but he judged it sufficient. His method was to buy a piece at a time, always second-hand, but always good. The bargain-hunt was up, and Anna soon yielded to its mild satisfactions. In the matter of her trousseau and the house-linen, Anna, having obtained the needed money—at so dear a cost—found yet another obstacle in the imminent bazaar, which occupied Mrs. Sutton and Beatrice so completely that they could not contrive any opportunity to assist her in shopping. It was decided between them that every article should be bought ready-made and seamed, and that the first week of the New Year, if indeed Mrs. Sutton survived the bazaar, should be entirely and absolutely devoted to Anna's business.

At nights, when she had leisure to think, Anna was astonished, how, during the day, she had forgotten her preoccupations in the activities precedent to the bazaar, or in choosing furniture with Mynors. But she never slept without thinking of Willie Price, and hoping that no further disaster might overtake him. The incident of the embezzled fifty pounds had been closed, and she had given a cheque for twenty-five pounds to Mynors. He had acquainted the minister with the facts, and Mr. Banks had decided that the two circuit stewards must be informed. Beyond these the scandalous secret was not to go. But Anna wondered whether a secret shared by five persons could long remain a secret.

The bazaar was a triumphant and unparalleled success, and, of the seven stalls, the Sunday-school stall stood first each night in the nightly returns. The scene in the town-hall, on the fourth and final night, a Saturday, was as delirious and gay as a carnival. Four hundred and twenty pounds had been raised up to tea-time, and it was the impassioned desire of everyone to achieve five hundred. The price of admission had been reduced to threepence, in order that the artisan might enter and spend his wages in an excellent cause.

The seven stalls, ranged round the room like so many bowers of beauty, draped and frilled and floriated, and still laden with countless articles of use and ornament, were continually reinforced with purchasers by emissaries canvassing the crowd which filled the middle of the paper-strewn floor. The horse was not only taken to the water, but compelled to drink; and many a man who, outside, would have laughed at the risk of being robbed, was robbed openly, shamelessly, under the gaze of ministers and class-leaders. Bouquets were sold at a shilling each, and at the refreshment stall a glass of milk cost sixpence. The noise rivalled that of a fair; there was no quiet anywhere, save in the farthest recess of each stall, where the lady in supreme charge of it, like a spider in the middle of its web, watched customers and cash-box with equal cupidity.

Mrs. Sutton, at seven o'clock, had not returned from tea, and Anna and Beatrice, who managed the Sunday-school stall in her absence, feared that she had at last succumbed under the strain. But shortly afterwards she hurried back breathless to her place.

" See that, Anna? It will be reckoned in our returns," she said, exhibiting a piece of paper. It was Ephraim's check for the twenty-five pounds promised months ago, but on a condition which had not been fulfilled.

" She has the secret of persuading him," thought Anna. " Why have I never found it? "

Then Agnes, in a new white frock, came up with three shillings, proceeds of bouquets.

" But you must take that to the flower-stall, my pet," said Mrs. Sutton.

" Can't I give it to you? " the child pleaded. " I want your stall to be the best."

Mynors arrived next, with something concealed in tissue-paper. He removed the paper, and showed, in a frame of crimson plush, a common white plate decorated with a simple band and line, and a monogram in the centre—" A. T." Anna blushed, recognising the plate which she had painted that afternoon in July at Mynors' works.

" Can you sell this? " Mynors asked Mrs. Sutton.

" I'll try to," said Mrs. Sutton doubtfully—not in the secret. " What's it meant for? "

" Try to sell it to me," said Mynors.

" Well," she laughed, " what will you give? "

" A couple of sovereigns."

"Make it guineas."

He paid the money, and requested Anna to keep the plate for him.

At nine o'clock it was announced that, though raffling was forbidden, the bazaar would be enlivened by an auction. A licensed auctioneer was brought, and the sale commenced. The auctioneer, however, failed to attune himself to the wild spirit of the hour, and his professional efforts would have resulted in a fiasco had not Mynors, perceiving the danger, leaped to the platform and masterfully assumed the hammer. Mynors surpassed himself in the kind of wit that amuses an excited crowd, and the auction soon monopolised the attention of the room; it was always afterwards remembered as the crowning success of the bazaar. The incredible man took ten pounds in twenty minutes. During this episode Anna, who had been left alone in the stall, first noticed Willie Price in the room. His ship sailed on the Monday, but steerage passengers had to be aboard on Sunday, and he was saying good-bye to a few acquaintances. He seemed quite cheerful, as he walked about with his hands in his pockets, chatting with this one and that; it was the false and hysterical gaiety that precedes a final separation. As soon as he saw Anna he came towards her.

"Well, good-bye, Miss Tellwright," he said jauntily. "I leave for Liverpool to-morrow morning. Wish me luck."

Nothing more; no word, no accent, to recall the terrible but sublime past.

"I do," she answered. They shook hands. Others approaching, he drifted away. Her glance followed him like a beneficent influence.

For three days she had carried in her pocket an envelope containing a banknote for a hundred pounds, intending by some device to force it on him as a parting gift. Now the last chance was lost, and she had not even attempted this difficult feat of charity. Such futility, she reflected, self-scorning, was of a piece with her life. " He hasn't really gone. He hasn't really gone," she kept repeating, and yet knew well that he had gone.

" Do you know what they are saying, Anna? " said Beatrice, when, after eleven o'clock, the bazaar was closed to the public, and the stall-holders and their assistants were preparing to depart, their movements hastened by the stern aspect of the town-hall keeper.

" No. What? " said Anna; and in the same moment guessed.

" They say that old Titus Price embezzled fifty pounds from the building fund, and Henry made it up, privately, so that there shouldn't be a scandal. Just fancy! Do you believe it? "

The secret was abroad. She looked round the room, and saw it in every face.

" Who says? " Anna demanded fiercely.

" It's all over the place. Miss Dickinson told me."

" You will be glad to know, ladies," Mynors' voice sang out from the platform, " that the total proceeds, so far as we can calculate them now, exceed five hundred and twenty-five pounds."

There was clapping of hands, which died out suddenly.

"Now, Agnes," Anna called, "come along, quick; you're as white as a sheet. Good-night, Mrs. Sutton; good-night, Bee."

Mynors was still occupied on the platform.

The town-hall keeper extinguished some of the lights. The bazaar was over.

## XIV: END OF A SIMPLE SOUL

THE next morning, at half-past seven, Anna was standing in the garden-doorway of the Priory. The sun had just risen, the air was cold; roof and pavement were damp; rain had fallen, and more was to fall. A door opened higher up the street, and Willie Price came out, carrying a small bag. He turned to speak to some person within the house, and then stepped forward. As he passed Anna she sprang forth.

" Oh! " she cried, " I had just come up here to see if the workmen had locked up properly. We have some of our new furniture in the house, you know." She was as red as the sun over Hillport.

He glanced at her. " Have *you* heard? " he asked simply.

" About what? " she whispered.

" About my poor old father."

" Yes. I was hoping—hoping you would never know."

By a common impulse they went into the garden of the Priory, and he shut the door.

" Never know? " he repeated. " Oh! they took care to tell me."

A silence followed.

" Is that your luggage? " she inquired. He lifted up the handbag, and nodded.

" All of it? "

" Yes," he said. " I'm only an emigrant."

" I've got a note here for you," she said. " I should have posted it to the steamer; but now you can take it yourself. I want you not to read it till you get to Melbourne."

" Very well," he said, and crumpled the proffered envelope into his pocket. He was not thinking of the note at all. Presently he asked: " Why didn't you tell me about my father? If I had to hear it, I'd sooner have heard it from you."

" You must try to forget it," she urged him. " You are not your father."

" I wish I had never been born," he said. " I wish I'd gone to prison."

Now was the moment when, if ever, the mother's influence should be exerted.

" Be a man," she said softly. " I did the best I could for you. I shall always think of you, in Australia, getting on."

She put a hand on his shoulder. " Yes," she said again, passionately: " I shall always remember you—always."

The hand with which he touched her arm shook like an old man's hand. As their eyes met in an intense and painful gaze, to her, at least, it was revealed that they were lovers. What he had learnt in that instant can only be guessed from his next action. . . .

Anna ran out of the garden into the street, and so home,

never looking behind to see if he pursued his way to the station.

Some may argue that Anna, knowing she loved another man, ought not to have married Mynors. But she did not reason thus; such a notion never even occurred to her. She had promised to marry Mynors and she married him. Nothing else was possible. She who had never failed in duty did not fail then. She who had always submitted and bowed the head, submitted and bowed the head then. She had sucked in with her mother's milk the profound truth that a woman's life is always a renunciation, greater or less. Hers by chance was greater. Facing the future calmly and genially, she took oath with herself to be a good wife to the man whom, with all his excellences, she had never loved. Her thoughts often dwelt lovingly on Willie Price, whom she deemed to be pursuing in Australia an honourable and successful career, quickened at the outset by her hundred pounds. This vision of him was her stay. But neither she nor anyone in the Five Towns or elsewhere ever heard of Willie Price again. And well might none hear! The abandoned pitshaft does not deliver up its secret. And so —the Bank of England is the richer by a hundred pounds unclaimed, and the world the poorer by a simple and meek soul stung to revolt only in its last hour.

**THE END**